CAUGHT IN THE HAIRS OF THE MOB

In a city full of gangsters and crooked cops, Joe Boyle just wanted to live as much of a normal life as possible. But one day his life was turned upside down when he was paid to deliver a message to a well-known thug—a thug with a reputation for dope smuggling and murder! Before long Joe found himself battered and bruised and caught up in the middle of a drug war between different mobsters, all of whom were searching for an elusive, unknown arch nemesis known simply as "the invisible man." Only a passionate dame, an aging old man, and a no-nonsense cop stood between Joe Boyle and the mark on his life. One thing was certain, the mob believed Joe had info they needed—and they would stop at nothing to get it from him. So Joe Boyle had to play the dangerous game of always having to be one quick step ahead of the mob.

FOR A COMPLETE SECOND NOVEL, TURN TO PAGE 91

POLICE LINEUP:

JOE BOYLE
One day he was just a young man pushing a cart for metal scraps—the next day he was wanted by everyone!

HELEN TROY
This sultry blonde had a body that would stop a truck and the brains to go along with it—a deadly combination.

BUCKY EDWARDS
Known as the old man who had his finger on the pulse of everything that was going on around town.

MARK RENZO
He was a low down dirty rat of a gangster—with a twisted mind for killing.

JOHNNY
Renzo's top lieutenant was a monstrous-looking thug with the most evil of intentions.

PHIL CARBOY
He wasn't afraid to get tough and nasty, perhaps even pump a bullet into someone—and he had the reputation to prove it.

CAPTAIN GEROT
This tough cop had been in the police game for a long time and hated every low life gangster in his town.

SERGEANT GONZALES
This veteran policeman was the epitome of the tough detective. But just being a cop wasn't good enough for him.

EVERYBODY'S WATCHING ME

By
MICKEY SPILLANE

ARMCHAIR FICTION
PO Box 4369, Medford, Oregon 97504

The original text of this novel was first published by Flying Eagle Productions, Inc.

Armchair Edition, Copyright 2016 by Gregory J. Luce
All Rights Reserved

For more information about Armchair Books and products, visit our website at…

www.armchairfiction.com

Or email us at…

armchairfiction@yahoo.com

CHAPTER ONE

I HANDED the guy the note and shivered a little bit because the guy was as big as they come, and even though he had a belly you couldn't get your arms around, you wouldn't want to be the one who figured you could sink your fist in it. The belly was as hard as the rest of him, but not quite as hard as his face.

Then I knew how hard the back of his hand was because he smashed it across my jaw and I could taste the blood where my teeth bit into my cheek.

Maybe the guy holding my arm knew I couldn't talk because he said, "A guy give him a fin to bring it, boss. He said that."

"Who, kid?"

I spit the blood out easy so it dribbled down my chin instead of going on the floor.

"Gee, Mr. Renzo…"

His hand made a dull, soggy crack on my skin. The buzz got louder in my ears and there was a jagged, pounding pain in my skull.

"Maybe you didn't hear me the first time, kid. I said who."

The hand let go my arm and I slumped to the floor. I didn't want to, but I had to. There were no legs under me anymore. My eyes were open, conscious of only the movement of ponderous things that got closer. Things that moved quickly and seemed to dent my side without causing any feeling at all.

That other voice said, "He's out, boss. He ain't saying a thing."

"I'll make him talk."

"Won't help none. So a guy gives him a fin to bring the note. He's not going into a song and dance with it. To the kid a fin's a lot of dough. He watches the fin and not the guy."

EVERYBODY'S WATCHING ME

*Illustrations by
Ray Houlihan*

"You're getting too damn bright," Renzo said.

"That's what you pay me for being, boss."

"Then act bright. You think a guy hands a note like this to some kid? Any kid at all? You think a kid's gonna bull in here to deliver it when he can chuck it down a drain and take off with the fin?"

"So the kid's got morals."

"So the kid knows the guy or the guy knows him. He ain't letting no kid get away with his fin." The feet moved away from me, propped themselves against the dark blur of the desk. "You read this thing?" Renzo asked in a hoarse voice.

"No."

"Listen then. 'Cooley is dead. Now, my fine fat louse, I'm going to spill your guts all over your own floor.' " Renzo's voice droned to a stop. He sucked hard on the cigar and said, "It's signed, Vetter."

You could hear the unspoken words in the silence. That hush that comes when the name was mentioned and the other's half-whispered, "So they were buddies, boss?"

"Who cares? If that crumb shows his face around here, I'll break his lousy back. Vetter, Vetter, Vetter. Everyplace you go that crumb's name you hear."

"Boss, look. You don't want to tangle with that guy. He's killed plenty of guys. He's…"

"He's different from me? You think he's a hard guy?"

"You ask around, boss. They'll tell you. That guy don't give a damn for nobody. He'll kill you for looking at him."

"Maybe in his own back yard he will. Not here, Johnny, not here. This is my city and my back yard. Here things go my way and Vetter'll get what Cooley got." He sucked on the cigar again and I began to smell the smoke. "Guys who pull a fastie on me get killed. Now Cooley don't work my tables for no more smart plays. Pretty soon the cops can take Vetter off their list because he won't be around no more either."

"You going to take him, boss?" Johnny said.

"What do you think?"

"Anything you say, boss. I'll pass the word around. Somebody'll know what he looks like and'll finger him." He paused, then said, "What about the kid?"

"He's our finger, Johnny."

"Him?"

"You ain't so bright as I thought. You should get your ears to the ground more. You should hear things about Vetter. He pays off for favors. The errand was worth a fin, but he's gonna look in to make sure the letter got here. Then he spots the kid for his busted up face. First time he makes contact we got him. You know what, Johnny? To Vetter I'm gonna to do things slow. When they find him the cops get all excited but they don't do nothing. They're glad to see Vetter dead. But other places the word gets around, see? Anybody can bump Vetter gets to be pretty big and nobody pulls any more smart ones. You get it?"

"Sure, boss. I get it. You're going to do it yourself?"

"Just me, kid, just me. Like Helen says, I got a passion to do something myself and I just got to do it. Vetter's for me. He better be plenty big, plenty fast and ready to start shooting the second we meet up."

It was like when Pop used to say he'd do something and we knew he'd do it sure. You look at him with your face showing the awe a kid gets when he knows fear and respect at the same time and that's how Johnny must have been looking at Renzo. I knew it because it was in his voice too when he said, "You'll do it, boss. You'll own this town lock, stock and gun butt yet."

"I own it now, Johnny. Don't forget it. Now wake the kid up."

This time I had feeling and it hurt. The hand that slapped the full vision back to my eyes started the blood running in my mouth again and I could feel my lungs choking on a sob.

"What was he like, kid?" The hand came down again and this time Renzo took a step forward. His fingers grabbed my coat and jerked me off the floor.

"You got asked a question. What was he like?"

"He was...big," I said. The damn slob choked me again and I wanted to break something over his head.

"How big?"

"Like you. Bigger'n six. Heavy."

Renzo's mouth twisted into a sneer and he grinned at me. "More. What was his face like?"

"I don't know. It was dark. I couldn't see him good."

He threw me. Right across the room he threw me and my back smashed the wall and twisted and I could feel the tears rolling down my face from the pain.

"You don't lie to Renzo, kid. If you was older and bigger I'd break you up into little pieces until you talked. It ain't worth a fin. Now you start telling me what I want to hear and maybe I'll slip you something."

"I…I don't know. Honest, I…if I saw him again it'd be different." The pain caught me again and I had to gag back my voice.

"You'd know him again?"

"Yes."

Johnny said, "What's your name, kid?"

"Joe…Boyle."

"Where do you live?" It was Renzo this time.

"Gidney Street," I told him. "Number three."

"You work?"

"Gordon's. I…push."

"What'd he say?" Renzo's voice had a nasty tone to it.

"Gordon's a junkie," Johnny said for me. "Has a place on River Street. The kid pushes a cart for him collecting metal scraps."

"Check on it," Renzo said, "then stick with him. You know what to do."

"He won't get away, boss. He'll be around whenever we want him. You think Vetter will do what you say?"

"Don't things always happen like I say? Now get him out of here. Go over him again so he'll know we mean what we say. That was a lousy fin he worked for."

CHAPTER TWO

After things hurt so much they begin to stop hurting completely. I could feel the way I went through the air, knew my foot hit the railing and could taste the cinders that ground in my mouth. I lay there like I was pressed out, waiting for the pain to come swelling back, making sounds I didn't want to make. My stomach wanted to break loose but couldn't find the strength and I just lay there cursing guys like Renzo who could do anything they wanted and get away with it.

Then the darkness came, went away briefly, and came back again. When it lost itself in the dawn of agony there were hands brushing the dirt from my face and the smell of flowers from the softness that was a woman who held me and said, "You poor kid, you poor kid."

My eyes opened and looked at her. It was like something you dream about because she was the kind of woman you always stare at, knowing you can't have. She was beautiful, with yellow hair that tumbled down her neck like a torch that lit up her whole body. Her name was Helen Troy and I wanted to say, "Hello, Helen," but couldn't get the words out of my mouth.

Know her? Sure, everybody knew her. She was Renzo's feature attraction at his Hideaway Club and her picture was all over town. But I never thought I'd get to have my head in her lap.

There were feet coming up the path that turned into one of the men from the stop at the gate and Helen said, "Give me a hand, Finney. Something happened to the kid? Did he do this to you?"

The guy she called Finney stood there with his hands on his hips shaking his head. "Something'll happen to you if you don't leave him be. The boss gives orders."

She tightened up all over, her fingers biting into my shoulder. It hurt but I didn't care a bit. "Renzo? The pig!" She spat it out with a hiss. She turned her head slowly and looked at me. "Did he do this, kid?"

I nodded. It was all I could do. "Finney," she said, "go get my car. I'm taking the kid to a doctor."

"Helen, I'm telling you…"

"Suppose I told the cops…no, not the cops, the feds in this town that you have holes in your arms?"

I thought Finney was going to smack her. He reached down with his hand back but he stopped. When a dame looks at you that way you don't do anything except what she tells you to.

"I'll get the car," he said.

She got me on my feet and I had to lean on her to stay there. She was just as big as I was. Stronger at the moment. Faces as bad off as mine weren't new to her, so she smiled and I tried to smile back and we started off down the path.

CHAPTER THREE

We said it was a fight and the doctor did what he had to do. He laid on the tape and told me to rest a week then come back. I saw my face in his mirror, shuddered and turned away. No matter what I did I hurt all over and when I thought of Renzo all I could think of was that I hoped somebody would kill him. I hoped they'd kill him while I watched and I hoped it would take a long, long time for him to die.

Helen got me out to the car, closed the door after me, and slid in behind the wheel. I told her where I lived and she drove up to the house. The garbage cans had been spilled all over the sidewalk and it stank.

She looked at me curiously.

"Here?"

"That's right," I told her. "Thanks for everything."

Then she saw the sign on the door. It read, *Rooms*. "Your family live here too?"

"I don't have a family. It's a rooming house."

For a second I saw her teeth, white and even, as she pulled her mouth tight. "I can't leave you here. Somebody has to look after you."

"Lady, if…"

"Ease off, kid. What did you say your name was?"

"Joe."

"Okay, Joe. Let me do things my way. I'm not much good for anything but every once in a while I come in handy for something decent."

"Gee, lady…"

"Helen."

"Well, you're the nicest person I've ever known."

I said she was beautiful. She had the beauty of the flashiest tramp you could find. That kind of beauty. She was like the dames in the big shows who are always tall and sleepy looking and who you'd always look at but wouldn't marry or take home to your folks. That's the kind of beauty she had. But for a long couple of seconds she seemed to grow a new kind of beauty that was entirely different and she smiled at me.

"Joe..." and her voice was warm and husky, "that's the nicest thing said in the nicest way I've heard in a very long time."

My mouth still hurt too much to smile back so I did it with my eyes. Then something happened to her face. It got all strange and curious, a little bit puzzled and she leaned forward and I could smell the flowers again as that impossible something happened when she barely touched her mouth to mine before drawing back with that searching movement of her eyes.

"You're a funny kid, Joe."

She shoved the car into gear and let it roll away from the curb. I tried to sit upright, my hand on the door latch. "Look, I got to get out."

"I can't leave you here."

"Then where..."

"You're going back to my place. Damn it, Renzo did this to you and I feel partly responsible."

"That's all right. You only work for him. You're not responsible."

"It doesn't matter. You can't stay there."

"You're going to get in trouble, Helen."

She turned and flashed me a smile. "I'm always in trouble."

"Not with him."

"I can handle that guy."

She must have felt the shudder that went through me.

"You'd be surprised how I can handle that fat slob," she said. Then added in an undertone I wasn't supposed to hear, "Sometimes."

It was a place that belonged to her like flowers belong in a rock garden. It was the top floor of an apartment hotel where the wheels all stayed in the best part of town with a private lawn twelve stories up where you could look out over the city and watch the light wink back at you.

She made me take all my clothes off and while I soaked in a warm bath full of suds she scrounged up a decent suit that was a size too big, but still the cleanest thing I had worn in a long while. I put it on and came out in the living room feeling good and sat down in the big chair while she brought in tea.

Helen of Troy, I thought. So this is what she looked like. Somebody it would take a million bucks and a million years to get close to…and here I was with nothing and no time at all.

"Feel better, Joe?"

"A little."

"Want to talk? You don't have to if you don't want to."

"There's not much to say. He worked me over."

"How old are you, Joe?"

I didn't want to go too high. "Twenty-one," I said.

There it was again, that same curious expression. I was glad of the bandages across my face so she couldn't be sure if I was lying or not.

I said, "How old are you?" and grinned at her.

"Almost thirty, Joe. That's pretty old, isn't it?"

"Not so old."

She sipped at the tea in her hand. "How did you happen to cross Renzo?"

It hurt to think about it. "Tonight," I said, "it had just gotten dark. A guy asked me if I'd run a message to somebody for five bucks and I said I would. It was for Mr. Renzo and he told me to take it to the Hideaway Club.

"At first the guy at the gate wouldn't let me in, then he called down that other one, Johnny. He took me in, all right."

"Yes?"

"Renzo started giving it to me."

"Remember what the message said?"

Remember? I'd never forget it. I'd hope from now until I died that the guy who wrote it did everything he said he'd do.

"Somebody called Vetter said he'd kill Renzo," I told her.

Her smile was distant, hard. "He'll have to be a pretty tough guy," she said. What she said next was almost under her breath and she was staring into the night when she said it, "A guy like that I could go for."

"What?"

"Nothing, Joe." The hardness left her smile until she was a soft thing. "What else happened?"

Inside my chest my heart beat so fast it felt like it was going to smash my ribs loose. "I...heard them say...I would have to finger the man for them."

"You?"

I nodded, my hand feeling the soreness across my jaw.

She stood up slowly, the way a cat would. She was all mad and tense but you couldn't tell unless you saw her eyes. They were the same eyes that made the Finney guy jump. "Vetter," she said. "I've heard the name before."

"The note said something about a guy named Cooley who's dead."

I was watching her back and I saw the shock of the name make the muscles across her shoulders dance in the light. The tightness went down her body until she stood there stiff-legged, the flowing curves of her chest the only things that moved at all.

"Vetter," she said. "He was Cooley's friend."

"You knew Cooley?"

Her shoulders relaxed and she picked a cigarette out of a box and lit it. She turned around, smiling, the beauty I had seen in the car there again.

"Yes," Helen said softly. "I knew Cooley."

"Gee."

She wasn't talking to me anymore. She was speaking to somebody who wasn't there and each word stabbed her deeper until her eyes were wet. "I knew Cooley very well. He was…nice. He was a big man, broad in the shoulders with hands that could squeeze a woman…" She paused and took a slow pull on the cigarette. "His voice could make you laugh or cry. Sometimes both. He was an engineer with a quick mind. He figured how he could make money from Renzo's tables and did it. He even laughed at Renzo and told him crooked wheels could be taken by anybody who knew how."

The tears started in the corners of her eyes but didn't fall. They stayed there, held back by pride maybe.

"We met one night. I had never met anyone like him before. It was wonderful, but we were never meant for each other. It was one of those things. Cooley was engaged to a girl in town, a very prominent girl."

The smoke of the cigarette in her hand swirled up and blurred her face.

"But I loved him," she said. With a sudden flick of her fingers she snapped the butt on the rug and ground it out with her shoe. "I hope he kills him! I hope he kills him!"

Her eyes drew a line up the floor until they were on mine. They were clear again, steady, curious for another moment, then steady again. I said, "You don't…like Renzo very much?"

"How well do you know people, Joe?"

I didn't say anything.

"You know them too, don't you? You don't live in the nice section of town. You know the dirt and how people are underneath. In a way you're lucky. You know it now, not when you're too old. Look at me, Joe. You've seen women like me before? I'm not much good. I look like a million but I'm not worth a cent. A lot of names fit me and they belong. I didn't get that way because I wanted to. He did it. Renzo. I was doing fine until I met him.

"Sure, some young kids might think I'm on top, but they never get to peek behind the curtain. They never see what I'm forced into and the kind of people I have to know because others don't want to know me. If they do they don't want anybody to know about it."

"Don't say those things, Helen."

"Kid, in ten years I've met two decent people. Cooley was the first." She grinned and the hate left her face. "You're the other one. You don't give a hang what I'm like, do you?"

"I never met anybody like you before."

"Tell me more." Her grin got bigger.

"Well, you're beautiful. I mean real beautiful. And nice. You sure are built..."

"Good enough," she said and let the laugh come out. It was a deep, happy laugh and sounded just right for her. "Finish your tea."

I had almost forgotten about it. I drained it down, the heat of it biting into the cuts along my cheek. "Helen...I ought to go home. If Mr. Renzo finds out about this, he's going to burn up."

"He won't touch me, Joe." I let out a grunt.

"You either. There's a bed in there. Crawl in to it. You've had enough talk for the night."

CHAPTER FOUR

I woke up before she did. My back hurt too much to sleep and the blood pounded in my head too hard to keep it on the pillow. The clock beside the bed said it was seven-twenty and I kicked off the covers and dragged my clothes on.

The telephone was in the living room and I took it off the cradle quietly. When I dialed the number I waited, said hello as softly as I could and asked for Nick.

He came on in a minute with a coarse, "Yeah?"

"This is Joe, Nick."

"Hey, where are you, boy? I been scrounging all over the dump for you. Gordon'll kick your tail if you don't get down here. Two other guys didn't show..."

"Shut up and listen. I'm in a spot."

"You ain't kidding..." Gordon said.

"Not that, jerk. You see anybody around the house this morning?"

I could almost hear him think. Finally he said, "Car parked across the street. Think there was a guy in it." Then, "Yeah, yeah, wait up. Somebody was giving the old lady some lip this morning. Guess I was still half-asleep. Heard your name mentioned."

"Brother!"

"What's up, pal?"

"I can't tell you now. You tell Gordon I'm sick or something, okay?"

"Nuts. I'll tell him you're in the clink. He's tired of that sick business. You ain't been there long enough to get sick yet."

"Tell him what you please. Just tell him. I'll call you tonight." I slipped the phone back and turned around. I hadn't been as quiet as I thought I'd been. Helen was standing there in the doorway of her bedroom, a lovely golden girl, a bright morning flower wrapped in a black stem like a bud ready to pop.

"What is it, Joe?"

There wasn't any use hiding things from her. "Somebody's watching the house. They were looking for me this morning."

"Scared, Joe?"

"Darn right I'm scared! I don't want to get laid out in some swamp with my neck broken. That guy Renzo is nuts. He'll do anything when he gets mad."

"I know," Helen said quietly. Her hand made an unconscious movement across her mouth. "Come on, let's get some breakfast."

CHAPTER FIVE

We found out who Vetter was that morning. At least Helen found out. She didn't cut corners or make sly inquiries. She did an impossible thing and drove me into town, parked the car and took a cab to a big brownstone building that didn't look a bit different from any other building like it in the country. Across the door it said, *Precinct No. 4* and the cop at the desk said the captain would be more than pleased to see us.

The captain was more than pleased, all right. It started his day off right when she came in and he almost offered me a cigar. The nameplate said his name was Gerot and if I had to pick a cop out to talk to, I'd pick him. He was in his late thirties with a build like a wrestler and I'd hate to be in the guy's shoes who tried to bribe him.

It took him a minute to settle down. A gorgeous blonde in a dark green gabardine suit blossoming with curves didn't walk in every day. And when he did settle down, it was to look at me and say, "What can I do for you?" but looking like he already knew what happened.

Helen surprised him. "I'd like to know something about a man," she said. "His name is Vetter."

The scowl started in the middle of his forehead and spread to his hairline.

"Why?"

She surprised him again. "Because he promised to kill Mark Renzo."

You could watch his face change, see it grow intense, sharpen, notice the beginning of a caustic smile twitch at his lips. "Lady, do you know what you're talking about?"

"I think so."

"You think?"

"Look at me," she said. Captain Gerot's eyes met hers, narrowed and stayed that way. "What do you see, Captain?"

"Somebody's who's been around. You know the answers, don't you?"

"All of them, Captain. The questions, too."

I was forgotten. I was something that didn't matter and I was happy about it.

Helen said, "What do you think about Renzo, Captain?"

"He stinks. He operates outside city limits where the police have no jurisdiction and he has the county police sewed up. I think he has some of my men sewed up too. I can't be sure but

I wish I were. He's got a record in two states, he's clean here. I'd like to pin a few jobs on that guy. There's no evidence, yet he pulled them. I know this…if I start investigating I'm going to have some wheels on my neck."

Helen nodded. "I could add more. It really doesn't matter. You know what happened to Jack Cooley?"

Gerot's face looked mean. "I know I've had the papers and the state attorney climb me for it."

"I don't mean that."

The captain dropped his face in his hands resignedly, wiped his eyes and looked up again. "His car was found with bullet holes in it. The quantity of blood in the car indicated that nobody could have spilled that much and kept on living. We never found the body."

"You know why he died?"

"Who knows? I can guess from what I heard. He crossed Renzo, some said. I even picked up some info that said he was in the narcotics racket. He had plenty of cash and no place to show where it came from."

"Even so, Captain, if it was murder, and Renzo's behind it, you'd like it to be paid for."

The light blue of Gerot's eyes softened dangerously. "One way or another…if you must know."

"It could happen. Who is Vetter?"

He leaned back in his chair and folded his hands behind his neck. "I could show you reams of copy written about that guy. I could show you transcripts of statements we've taken down and copies that the police in other cities have sent out. I could show you all that but I can't pull out a picture and I can't drop in a print number on the guy. The people who got to know him and who finally saw him all seem to be dead."

My voice didn't sound right. "Dead?"

Gerot's hands came down and flattened on the desk. "The guy's a killer. He's wanted every place I could think of. Word has it that he's the one who bumped Tony Briggs in Chicago. When Birdie Cullen was going to sing to the grand jury, somebody was paid fifty thousand to cool him off and Vetter collected from the syndicate. Vetter was paid another ten to knock off the guy who paid him the first time so somebody could move into his spot."

"So far he's only a name, Captain?"

"Not quite. We have a few details on him but we can't give them out. That much you understand, of course."

"Of course. But I'm still interested."

"He's tough. He seems to know things and do things nobody else would touch. He's a professional gunman in the worst sense of the word and he'll sell that gun as long as the price is right."

Helen crossed her legs with a motion that brought her whole body into play. "Supposing, Captain, that this Vetter was a friend of Jack Cooley? Supposing he got mad at the thought of his friend being killed and wanted to do something about it?"

Gerot said, "Go on."

"What would you do, Captain?"

The smile went up one side of his face. "Most likely nothing." He sat back again. "Nothing at all...until it happened."

"Two birds with one stone, Captain? Let Vetter get Renzo...and you get Vetter?"

"The papers would like that," he mused.

"No doubt." Helen seemed to uncoil from the chair. I stood up too and that's when I found out just how shrewd the captain was. He didn't bother to look at Helen at all. His blue eyes were all on me and being very, very sleepy.

"Where do you come in, kid?" he asked me.

Helen said it for me. "Vetter gave him a warning note to hand to Renzo."

Gerot smiled silently and you could see that he had the whole picture in his mind. He had our faces, he knew who she was and all about her, he was thinking of me and wanted to know all about me. He would. He was that kind of cop. You could tell.

We stood on the steps of the building and the cops coming in gave her the kind of look every man on the street gave her. Appreciative. It made me feel good just to be with her. I said, "He's a smart cop."

"They're all smart. Some are just smarter than others." A look of impatience crossed her face. "He said something…"

"Reams of copy?" I suggested.

I was easy for her to smile at. She didn't have to look up or down. Just a turn of her head. "Bright boy."

She took my hand and this time I led the way. I took her to the street I knew. It was off the main drag and the people on it had a look in their eyes you don't see uptown. It was a place where the dames walked at night and followed you into bars if they thought you had an extra buck to pass out.

They're little joints, most of them. They don't have neon lights and padded stools, but when a guy talks he says something and doesn't play games. There's excitement there and always that feeling that something is going to happen.

One of those places was called *The Clipper* and the boys from the *news* made it their hangout. Cagey boys with the big think under their hats. Fast boys with a buck and always ready to pay off on something hot. Guys who took you like you were and didn't ask too many questions.

My kind of people.

CHAPTER SIX

Bucky Edwards was at his usual stool getting a little bit potted because it was his day off. I got the big stare and the exaggerated wink when he saw the blonde, which meant I'd finally made good about dragging one in with me. I didn't feel like bragging, though. I brought Helen over, went to introduce her, but Bucky said, "Hi, Helen. Never thought I'd see you out in the daylight," before I could pass on her name.

"Okay, so you caught a show at the Hideaway," I said, "We have something to ask you."

"Come on, Joe. Let the lady ask me alone."

"Layoff. We want to know about Vetter."

The long eyebrows settled down low. He looked at me, then Helen, then back at me again. "You're making big sounds, boy."

I didn't want anyone else in on it. I leaned forward and said, "He's in town, Bucky. He's after Renzo." He let out a long whistle. "Who else knows about it?"

"Gerot. Renzo. Us."

"There's going to be trouble, sure."

Helen said, "Only for Renzo."

Bucky's head made a slow negative. "You don't know. The rackets boys'll flip their lids at this. If Vetter moves in here there's going to be some mighty big trouble."

My face started working under the bandages. "Renzo's top dog, isn't he?"

Bucky's tongue made a swipe at his lips. "One of 'em. There's a few more. They're not going to like Renzo pulling in trouble like Vetter." For the first time Bucky seemed to really look at us hard. "Vetter is poison. He'll cut into everything and they'll payoff. Sure as shooting, if he sticks around they'll be piling the cabbage in his lap."

"Then everybody'll be after Vetter," I said.

Bucky's face furrowed in a frown. "Uh-uh. I wasn't thinking that." He polished off his drink and set the empty on the bar. "If Vetter's here after Renzo they'll do better nailing Renzo's hide to the wall. Maybe they can stop it before it starts."

It was trouble, all right. The kind I wasn't feeling too bad about.

Bucky stared into his empty glass and said. "They'll bury Renzo or he'll come out of it bigger than ever."

The bartender came down and filled his glass again. I shook my head when he wanted to know what we'd have. "Good story," Bucky said, "if it happens." Then he threw the drink down and Bucky was all finished. His eyes got frosty and he sat there grinning at himself in the mirror with his mind saying things to itself. I knew him too well to say anything else so I nudged Helen and we walked out.

Some days go fast and this was one of them. She was nice to be with and nice to talk to. I wasn't important enough to hide anything from so for one day she opened her life up and fed me pieces of it. She seemed to grow younger as the day wore on and when we reached her apartment the sun was gilding her hair with golden reddish streaks and I was gone, all gone. For one day I was king and there wasn't any trouble. The laughter poured out of us and people stopped to look and laugh back. It was a day to remember when all the days are done with and you're on your last.

I was tired, dead tired. I didn't try to refuse when she told me to come up and I didn't want to. She let me open the door for her and I followed her inside. She had almost started for the kitchen to cook up the bacon and eggs we had talked about when she stopped by the arch leading to the living room.

The voice from the chair said, "Come on in, sugar pie. You too, kid."

And there was Johnny, a nasty smile on his mouth, leering at us.

"How did you get in here?"

He laughed at her. "I do tricks with locks, remember?" His head moved with a short jerk. "Get in here!" There was a flat, nasal tone in his voice.

I moved in beside Helen. My hands kept opening and closing at my side and my breath was coming a little fast in my throat.

"You like kids now, Helen?"

"Shut up, you louse," she said.

His lips peeled back showing his teeth. "The mother type. Old fashioned type, you know." He leered again like it was funny. My chest started to hurt from the breathing. "Too big for a bottle, so…"

I grabbed the lamp and let it fly and if the cord hadn't caught in the wall it would have taken his head off. I was all set to go into him but all he had to do to stop me was bring his hand up. The rod was one of those Banker's Specials that were deadly as hell at close range and Johnny looked too much like he wanted to use it for me to move.

He said, "The boss don't like your little arrangement, Helen. It didn't take him long to catch on.

Come over here, kid."

I took a half step.

"Closer."

I moved closer.

"Now listen carefully, kid. You go home, see. Go home and do what you feel like doing, but stay home and away from this place. You do that and you'll pick up a few bucks from Mr. Renzo. Now after you had it so nice here, you might not want to go home, so just in case you don't, I'm going to show you what's going to happen to you."

I heard Helen's breath suck in with a harsh gasp and my own sounded the same way. You could see what Johnny was setting himself to do and he was letting me know all about it and there wasn't a thing I could do. The gun was pointing right at my belly even while he jammed his elbows into the arms of the chair to get the leverage for the kick that was going to maim me the rest of my life. His shoe was hard and pointed, a deadly weight that swung like a gentle pendulum.

I saw it coming and thought there might be a chance even yet but I didn't have to take it. From the side of the room Helen said, "Don't move, Johnny. I've got a gun in my hand."

And she had.

The ugly grimace on Johnny's face turned into a snarl when he knew how stupid he'd been in taking his eyes off her to enjoy what he was doing to me.

"Make him drop it, Helen."

"You heard the kid, Johnny."

Johnny dropped the gun. It lay there on the floor and I hooked it with my toe. I picked it up, punched the shells out of the chambers, and tossed them under the sofa. The gun followed them.

"Come here, Helen," I said.

I felt her come up behind me and reached around for the .25 automatic in her hand. For a second Johnny's face turned pale and when it did I grinned at him.

Then I threw the .25 under the sofa too.

They look funny when you do things like that. Their little brains don't get it right away and it stuns them or something. I let him get right in the middle of that surprised look before I slammed my fist into his face and felt his teeth rip loose under my knuckles.

Helen went down on her knees for the gun and I yelled for her to let it along; then Johnny was on me. At least he thought he was on me. I had his arm over my shoulder, laid him into a hip roll, and tumbled him easy. I didn't want too much noise.

I walked up. I took my time. He started to get up and I chopped down on his neck and watched his head bob. I got him twice more in the same place and Johnny simply fell back. His eyes were seeing, his brain thinking and feeling but he couldn't move. While he lay there, I chopped twice again and Johnny's face became blotched and swollen while his eyes screamed in agony.

I put him in a cab downstairs. I told the driver he was drunk and fell and gave him a ten spot from Johnny's own wallet with instructions to take him out to the Hideaway and deliver he to Mr. Renzo. The driver was very sympathetic and took him away.

Then I went back for Helen. She was sitting on the couch waiting for me, the strangeness back in her eyes. She said, "When he finished with you, he would have started on me."

"I know."

"Joe, you did pretty good for a kid."

"I was brought up tough."

"I've seen Johnny take some pretty big guys. He's awfully strong."

"You know what I do for a living, Helen? I push a junk car, loaded with iron. There's competition and pretty soon you learn things. Those iron loaders are strong gees too. If they can tumble you, they lift your pay."

"You had a gun, Joe," she reminded me.

And her eyes mellowed into a strange softness that sent chills right through me. They were eyes that called me closer and I couldn't say no to them. I stood there looking at her, wondering what she saw under the bandages.

"Renzo's going after us for that," I said.

"That's right, Joe."

"We'll have to get out of here. You, anyway."

"Later we'll think about it."

"Now, damn it."

Her face seemed to laugh at me. A curious laugh. A strange laugh. A bewildered laugh. There was a sparkling dance to her eyes she kept half-veiled and her mouth parted just a little bit. Her tongue touched the tip of her teeth, withdrew, and she said, "Now is for something else, Joe. Now is for a woman going back a long time who sees somebody she could have loved then."

I looked at her and held my breath. She was so completely beautiful I ached and I didn't want to make a fool of myself. Not yet.

"Now is for you to kiss me, Joe," she said.

I tasted her.

CHAPTER SEVEN

I waited until midnight before I left. I looked in her room and saw her bathed in moonlight, her features softly relaxed into the faintest trace of a smile, a soft, golden halo around her head.

They should take your picture like you are now, Helen, I thought. It wouldn't need a retoucher and there would never be a man who saw it who would forget it. You're beautiful, baby. You're lovely as a woman could ever be and you don't know it. You've had it so rough you can't think of anything else and thinking of it puts the lines in your face and that chiseled granite in your eyes. But you've been around and so have I. There have been dozens of dames I've thought things about but not things like I'm thinking now. You don't care what or who a guy is; you just give him part of yourself as a favor and ask for nothing back.

Sorry, Helen, you have to take something back. Or at least keep what you have. For you I'll let Renzo push me around. For you I'll let him make me finger a guy. Maybe at the end I'll have a chance to make a break. Maybe not. At least it's for you and you'll know that much. If I stay around, Renzo'll squeeze you and do it so hard you'll never be the same. I'll leave, beautiful. I'm not much. You're not much either. It was a wonderful day.

I put the note I'd written her by the lamp on the night table where she couldn't miss it. I leaned over and blew a kiss into her hair, then turned and got out of there.

Nobody had to tell me to be careful. I made sure nobody saw me leave the building and double-checked on it when I got to the corner. The trip over the back fences wasn't easy, but it was quiet and dark and if anybody so much as breathed near me I would have heard it. Then when I stood in the shadows of the store at the intersection I was glad I had made the trip the hard way. Buried between the parked cars along the curb was a police cruiser. There were no markings. Just a trunk aerial and the red glow of a cigarette behind the wheel.

Captain Gerot wasn't taking any chances. It made me feel a little better. Upstairs there Helen could go on sleeping and always be sure of waking up. I waited a few minutes longer then drifted back into the shadows toward the rooming house.

That's where they were waiting for me. I knew it a long time before I got there because I had seen them wait for other guys before. Things like that you don't miss when you live around the factories and near the waterfronts. Things like that you watch and remember so that when it happens to you, it's no surprise and you figure things out beforehand.

They saw me and as long as I kept on going in the right direction they didn't say anything. I knew they were where I couldn't see them and even if I made a break for it, it wouldn't do me any good at all.

You get a funny feeling after a while. Like a rabbit walking between rows of guns wondering which one is going to go off. Hoping that if one does you don't get to see it or feel it. Your stomach seems to get all loose inside you and your heart makes too much noise against your ribs. You try not to, but you sweat and the little muscles in your hands and thighs start to jump and twitch and all the while there's no sound at all, just a deep, startling silence with a voice that's there just the same. A statue, laughing with its mouth open. No sound, but you can hear the voice. You keep walking, and the breathing keeps time with your footsteps, sometimes trying to get ahead of them. You find yourself chewing on your lips because you already know the horrible impact of a fist against your flesh and the uncontrollable spasms that come after a pointed shoe bites into the muscle and bone of your side.

So much so that when you're almost there and a hand grabs your arm you don't do anything except look at the face above it and wait until it says, "Where you been, kid?"

I felt the hand tighten with a gentle pressure, pulling me in close. "Layoff me. I'm minding my own…"

"I said something, sonny."

"So I was out. What's it to you?"

His expression said he didn't give a hang at all. "Somebody wants to know. Feel like taking a little ride?"

"You asking?"

"I'm telling." The hand tightened again. "The car's over there, bud. Let's go get in it, huh?"

For a second I wondered if I could take him or not and knew I couldn't. He was too big and too relaxed. He'd known trouble all his life, from little guys to big guys and he didn't fool easily. You can tell after you've seen a lot of them. They knew that someday they'd wind up holding their hands over a bullet hole or screaming through the bars of a cell, but until then they were trouble and too big to buck.

I got in the car and sat next to the guy in the back seat. I kept my mouth shut and my eyes open and when we started to head the wrong way, I looked at the guy next to me, "Where we going?"

He grinned on one side of his face and looked out the window again.

"Come on, come on, quit messing around! Where we going?"

"Shut up."

"Nuts, brother. If I'm getting knocked off, I'm doing a lot of yelling first, starting right now. Where…"

"Shut up. You ain't getting knocked off." He rolled the window down, flipped the dead cigar butt out, and cranked it back up again. He said it too easily not to mean it and the jumps in my hands quieted down a little.

No, they weren't going to bump me. Not with all the trouble they went to in finding me. You don't put a couple dozen men on a mug like me if all you wanted was a simple kill. One hopped-up punk would do that for a week's supply of snow.

We went back through town, turned west into the suburbs, and kept right on going to where the suburbs turned into estates and when we came to the right one the car turned into a surfaced driveway that wound past a dozen flashy heaps parked bumper to bumper and stopped in front of the fieldstone mansion.

The guy beside me got out first. He jerked his head at me and stayed at my back when I got out too. The driver grinned, but it was the kind of face a dog makes when he sees you with a chunk of meat in your fist.

A flunky met us at the door. He didn't look comfortable in his monkey suit and his face had scar tissue it took a lot of leather-covered punches to produce. He waved us in, shut the door, and led the way down the hall to a room cloudy with smoke, rumbling with the voices of a dozen men.

When we came in the rumble stopped and I could feel the eyes crawl over me. The guy who drove the car looked across the room at the one in the tux and said, "Here he is, boss," and gave me a gentle push into the middle of the room.

"Hi, kid." He finished pouring out of the decanter, stopped it, and picked up his glass. He wasn't an inch bigger than me, but he had the walk of a cat and the eyes of something dead. He got up close to me, faked a smile, and held out the glass. "In case the boys had you worried."

"I'm not worried."

He shrugged and sipped the top off the drink himself. "Sit down, kid. You're among friends here." He looked over my shoulder. "Haul a chair up, Rocco."

All over the room the others settled down and shifted into position. A chair seat hit the back of my legs and I sat. When I looked around everybody was sitting, which was the way the little guy wanted it. He didn't like to have to look up to anybody.

He made it real casual. He introduced the boys when they didn't have to be introduced because they were always in the papers and the kind of guys people point out when they go by in their cars. You heard their names mentioned even in the junk business and among the punks in the streets. These were the big boys. Top dogs. Fat fingers. Big rings. The little guy was biggest of all. He was Phil Carboy and he ran the West Side the way he wanted it run.

When everything quieted down just right, Carboy leaned on the back of a chair and said, "In case you're wondering why you're here, kid, I'm going to tell you."

"I got my own ideas," I said.

"Fine. That's just fine. Let's check your ideas with mine, okay? Now we hear a lot of things around here. Things like that note you delivered to Renzo and who gave it to you and what Renzo did to you." He finished his drink and smiled. "Like what you did to Johnny, too. That's all straight now, isn't it?"

"So far."

"Swell. Tell you what I want now. I want to give you a job. How'd you like to make a cool hundred a week, kid?"

"Peanuts."

Somebody grunted. Carboy smiled again, a little thinner. "The kid's in the know," he said. "That's what I like. Okay, kid. We'll make it five hundred per for a month. If it don't run a month you get it anyway. That's better than having Renzo slap you around, right?"

"Anything's better than that." My voice started getting chalky.

Carboy held out his hand and said, "Rocco..." Another hand slid a sheaf of bills into his. He counted it out, reached two thousand, and tossed it into my lap. "Yours, kid."

"For what?"

His lips were a narrow gash between his cheekbones. "For a guy named Vetter. The guy who gave you a note. Describe him."

"Tall," I said. "Big shoulders. I didn't see his face. Deep voice that sounded tough. He had on a trench coat and a hat."

"That's not enough."

"A funny way of standing," I told him. "I saw Sling Herman when I was a kid before the cops got him. He stood like that. Always ready to go for something in his pocket, the cops said."

"You saw more than that, kid."

The room was too quiet now. They were all hanging on, waiting for the word. They were sitting there without smoking, beady little eyes waiting for the finger to swing until it stopped and I was the one who could stop it.

My throat squeezed out the words. I went back into the night to remember a guy and drag up the little things that would bring him into the light. I said, "I'd know him again. He was a guy to be scared of. When he talks you get a cold feeling and you know what he's like." My tongue ran over my lips and I lifted my eyes up to Carboy. "I wouldn't want to mess with a guy like that. Nobody's ever going to be tougher."

"You'll know him again. You're sure?"

"I'm sure." I looked around the room at the faces. Anyone of them a guy who could say a word and have me dead the next day. "He's tougher than any of you."

Carboy grinned and let his tiny white teeth show through. "Nobody's that tough, kid."

"He'll kill me," I said. "Maybe you too. I don't like this."

"You don't have to like it. You just do it. In a way you're lucky. I'm paying you cash. If I wanted I could just tell you and you'd do it. You know that?"

I nodded.

"Tonight starts it. From now on you'll have somebody close by, see? In one pocket you'll carry a white handkerchief. If you gotta blow, use it. In the other one there'll be a red wiper. When you see him blow into that."

"That's all?"

"Just duck about then, kid," Phil Carboy said softly, "and maybe you'll get to spend that two grand. Try to use it for runout money and you won't get past the bus station." He stared into his glass, looked up at Rocco expectantly, and held it out for a refill. "Kid, let me tell you something. I'm an old hand in this racket. I can tell what a guy or a dame is like from a block away. You've been around. I can tell that. I'm giving you a break because you're the type who knows the score and will play on the right side. I don't have to warn you about anything, do I?"

"No. I got the pitch."

"Any questions?"

"Just one," I said. "Renzo wants me to finger Vetter too. He isn't putting out any two grand for it. He just wants it, see? Suppose he catches up with me? What then?"

Carboy shouldn't've hesitated. He shouldn't have let that momentary look come into his eyes because it told me everything I wanted to know. Renzo was bigger than the whole pack of them and they got the jumps just thinking about it. All by himself he held a fifty-one percent interest and they were moving slowly when they bucked him. The little guy threw down the fresh drink with a quick motion of his hand and brought the smile back again. In that second he had done a lot of thinking and spilled the answer straight out. "We'll take care of Mark Renzo," he said. "Rocco, you and Lou take the kid home."

So I went out to the car and we drove back to the slums again. In the rear the reflections from the headlights of another car showed and the killers in it would be waiting for me to show the red handkerchief Carboy had handed me. I didn't know them and unless I was on the ball every minute, I'd never get to know them. But they'd always be there, shadows that had no substance until the red showed, then the ground would get sticky with an even brighter red and maybe some of it would be mine.

CHAPTER EIGHT

They let me out two blocks away. The other car didn't show at all and I didn't look for it. My feet made hollow sounds on the sidewalk, going faster and faster until I was running up the steps of the house and when I was inside I slammed the door and leaned against it, trying hard to stop the pain in my chest.

Three-fifteen, the clock said. It ticked monotonously in the stillness, trailing me upstairs to my room. I eased inside, shut the door and locked it, standing there in the darkness until my eyes could see things. Outside a truck clashed its gears as it pulled up the hill and off in the distance a horn sounded.

I listened to them; familiar face tightening as a not-so-familiar sound echoed behind them. It was a soft thing, a whisper that came at regular intervals in a choked-up way. Then I knew it was a sob coming from the other room and I went back to the hall and knocked on Nick's door.

His feet hit the floor, stayed there, and I could hear his breathing coming hard. "It's Joe—open up."

I heard the wheeze his breath made as he let it out. The bedsprings creaked, he fell once getting to the door and the bolt snapped back. I looked at the purple blotches on his face and the open cuts over his eyes and grabbed him before he fell again. "Nick! What happened to you?"

"I'm...okay." He steadied himself on me and I led him back to the bed. "You got...some friends, pal."

"Cut it out. What happened? Who ran you through? Damn it, who did it?"

Nick managed to show a smile. It wasn't much and it hurt, but he made it. "You...in pretty big trouble, Joe."

"Pretty big."

"I didn't say nothing. They were here...asking questions. They didn't...believe what I told them, I guess. They sure laced me."

"The miserable slobs! You recognize them?"

His smile got twisted and he nodded his head. "Sure, Joe...I know 'em. The fat one sat in the car while they did it." His mouth clamped together hard. "It hurt...brother, it hurt!"

"Look," I said, "We're..."

"Nothing doing. I got enough. I don't want no more. Maybe they figured it's enough. That Renzo feller...he got hard boys around. See what they did, Joe? One...used a gun on me. You shoulda stood with Gordon, Joe. What the hell got into you to mess with them guys?"

"It wasn't me, Nick. Something came up. We can square it. I'll nail that fat slob if it's the last thing I do."

"It'll be the last thing. They had a message for you, pal. You're to stick around, see? You get seen with any other big boys in this town...and that's all. You know?"

"I know. Renzo told me that himself. He didn't have to go through you."

"Joe..."

"Yeah?"

"He said for you to take a good look...at me. I'm an example. A little one. He says to do what he told you."

"He knows what he can do."

"Joe...for me. Layoff, huh? I don't feel so good. Now I can't work for a while." I patted his arm, fished a hundred buck bill out of my pocket and squeezed it into his hand. "Don't worry about it," I told him.

He looked at the bill unbelievingly, then at me.

"Dough can't pay for this, Joe. Kind of...stay away from me...for a while anyway, okay?" He smiled again, lamely this time. "Thanks for the C anyway. We been pretty good buddies, huh?"

"Sure, Nick."

"Later we'll be again. Let me knock off now. You take it easy." His hands came up to his face and covered it. I could hear the sobs starting again and cursed the whole damn system up and down and Renzo in particular. I swore at the filth men like to wade in and the things they do to other men. When I was done I got up off the bed and walked to the door.

Behind me Nick said, "Joey..."

"Right here."

"Something's crazy in this town. Stories are going around...there's going to be a lot of trouble. Everybody is after...you. You'll...be careful?"

"Sure." I opened the door, shut it softly, and went back to my room. I stripped off my clothes and lay down in the bed, my mind turning over fast until I had it straightened out, then I closed my eyes and fell asleep.

CHAPTER NINE

My landlady waited until a quarter to twelve before she gave it the business on my door. She didn't do it like she usually did it. No jarring smashes against the panels, just a light tapping that grew louder until I said, "Yeah?"

"Mrs. Stacey, Joe. You think you should get up? A man is downstairs to see you."

"What kind of a man?"

This time the knob twisted slowly and the door opened a crack. Her voice was a harsh whisper that sounded nervous. "He's got on old clothes and a city water truck is parked outside. He didn't come to look at my water."

I grinned at that one. "I'll be right down," I said. I splashed water over my face, shaved it close, and worked the adhesive off the bridge of my nose. It was swollen on one side, the blue running down to my mouth. One eye was smudged with purple.

Before I pulled on my jacket I stuffed the wad of dough into the lining through the tear in the sleeve, then I took a look in Nick's room. There were traces of blood on his pillow and the place was pretty upset, but Nick had managed to get out somehow for a day's work.

The guy in the chair sitting by the window was short and wiry looking. There was dirt under his fingernails and a stubble on his chin. He had a couple of small wrenches in a leather holster on his belt that bulged his coat out but the stuff was pure camouflage. There was a gun further back and I saw the same thing Mrs. Stacey saw. The guy was pure copper with badges for eyes.

He looked at me, nodded and said, "Joe Boyle?"

"Suppose I said no?" I sat down opposite him with a grin that said I knew all about it and though I knew he got it nothing registered at all.

"Captain Gerot tells me you'll cooperate. That true?"

There was a laugh in his eyes, an attitude of being deliberately polite when he didn't have to be. "Why?" I asked him. "Everybody seems to think I'm pretty hot stuff all of a sudden."

"You are, junior, you are. You're the only guy who can put his finger on a million-dollar baby that we want bad. So you'll cooperate."

"Like a good citizen?" I made it sound the same as he did. "How much rides on Vetter and how much do I get?"

The sarcasm in his eyes turned to a nasty sneer. "Thousands ride, junior...and you don't get any. You just cooperate. Too many cops have worked too damn long on Vetter to let a crummy kid cut into the cake. Now I'll tell you why you'll cooperate. There's a dame, see? Helen Troy. There's ways of slapping that tomato with a fat conviction for various reasons and unless you want to see her slapped, you'll cooperate. Catch now?"

I called him something that fitted him right down to his shoes. He didn't lose a bit of that grin at all. "Catch something else," he said. "Get smart and I'll make your other playmates look like school kids. I like tough guys. I have fun working 'em over because that's what they understand. What there is to know I know. Take last night for instance. The boys paid you off for a finger job. Mark Renzo pays but in his own way. Now I'm setting up a deal. Hell, you don't have to take it…you can do what you please. Three people are dickering for what you know. I'm the only one who can hit where it really hurts.

"Think it over, Joey boy. Think hard but do it fast. I'll be waiting for a call from you and wherever you are, I'll know about it. I get impatient sometimes, so let's hear from you soon. Maybe if you take too long I'll prod you a little bit." He got up, stretched, and wiped his eyes like he was tired. "Just ask for Detective Sergeant Gonzales," he said. "That's me."

The cop patted the tools on his belt and stood by the door. I said, "It's stinking to be a little man, isn't it? You got to keep making up for it."

There was pure, cold hate in his eyes for an answer. He gave me a long look that a snake would give a rabbit when he isn't too hungry yet. A look that said wait a little while, brother. Wait until I'm real hungry.

I watched the car pull away, then sat there at the window looking at the street. I had to wait almost an hour before I spotted the first, then picked up the second one ten minutes later. If there were more I didn't see them. I went back to the kitchen and took a look through the curtains at the blank behinds of the warehouses across the alley. Mrs. Stacey didn't say anything. She sat there with her coffee, making clicking noises with her false teeth.

I said, "Somebody washed the windows upstairs in the wholesale house."

"A man. Early this morning."

"They haven't been washed since I've been here."

"Not for two years."

I turned around and she was looking at me as if something had scared her to death. *"How much are they paying you?" I said.*

She couldn't keep that greedy look out of her face even with all the phony indignation she tried to put on. Her mouth opened to say something when the phone rang and gave her the chance to cover up. She came back a few seconds later and said, "It's for you. Some man."

Then she stood there by the door where she always stood whenever somebody was on the phone. I said, "Joe Boyle speaking," and that was all. I let the other one speak his few words and when he was done I hung up.

I felt it starting to burn in me. A nasty feeling that makes you want to slam something. Nobody asked me...they just told me and I was supposed to jump. I was the low man on the totem pole, a lousy kid who happened to fit into things...just the right size to get pushed around.

Vetter, I kept saying to myself. They were all scared to death of Vetter. The guy had something they couldn't touch. He was tough. He was smart. He was moving in for a kill and if ever one was needed it was needed now. They were all after him and no matter how many people who didn't belong there stood in the way their bullets would go right through them to reach Vetter. Yeah, they wanted him bad. So bad they'd kill each other to make sure he died too.

CHAPTER TEN

I pulled my jacket on and got outside. I went up the corner, grabbed a downtown bus, and sat there without bothering to look around. At Third and Main I hopped off, ducked into a cafeteria, and had a combination lunch. I let Mrs. Stacey get her calls in, gave them time to keep me well under cover, then flagged down a roving cab and gave the driver Helen's address. On the way over I looked out the back window for the second time and the light blue Chevy was still in place, two cars behind and trailing steadily. In a way it didn't bother me if the boys inside were smart enough to check the black Caddie that rode behind it again.

I tapped the cabbie a block away, told him to let me out on the corner and paid him off. There wasn't a parking place along the street so the laddies in the cars were either going to cruise or double park, but it would keep them moving around so I could see what they were like anyway.

When I punched the bell I had to wait a full minute before the lobby door clicked open. I went up the stairs, jolted the apartment door a few times, and walked right into those beautiful eyes that were even prettier than the last time because they were worried first, then relieved when they saw me. She grabbed my arm and gave me that quick grin then pulled me inside and stood with her back to the door.

"Joe, Joe, you little jughead," she laughed. "You had me scared silly. Don't do anything like that again."

"Had to, Helen. I wasn't going to come back but I had to do that too."

Maybe it was the way I said it that made her frown. "You're a funny kid."

"Don't say that."

Something changed in her eyes. "No. Maybe I shouldn't, should I?" She looked at me hard, her eyes soft, but piercing. "I feel funny when I look at you. I don't know why. Sometimes I've thought it was because I had a brother who was always in trouble. Always getting hurt. I used to worry about him too."

"What happened to him?"

"He was killed on the Anzio beachhead."

"Sorry."

She shook her head. "He didn't join the army because he was patriotic. He and another kid held up a joint. The owner was shot. He was dead by the time they found out who did it."

"You've been running all your life too, haven't you?"

The eyes dropped a second. "You could put it that way."

"What ties you here?"

"Guess."

"If you had the dough you'd beat it? Some place where nobody knew you?"

She laughed, a short jerky laugh. It was answer enough. I reached in the jacket, got out the pack of bills and flipped off a couple for myself. I shoved the rest in her hand before she knew what it was. "Get going. Don't even bother to pack. Just move out of here and keep moving."

Her eyes were big and wide with an incredulous sort of wonder, then slightly misty when they came back to mine and she shook her head a little bit and said, "Joe...why? Why?"

"It would sound silly if I said it."

"Say it."

"When I'm all grown up I'll tell you, maybe."

"Now."

I could feel the ache starting in me and my tongue didn't want to move, but I said, "Sometimes even a kid can feel pretty hard about a woman. Sad, isn't it?"

Helen said, "Joe," softly and had my face in her hands and her mouth was a hot torch that played against mine with a crazy kind of fierceness and it was all I could do to keep from grabbing her instead of pushing her away. My hands squeezed her hard, then I yanked the door open and got out of there. Behind me there was a sob and I heard my name said again, softly.

I ran the rest of the way down with my face all screwed up tight.

The blue Chevy was down the street on the other side. It seemed to be empty and I didn't bother to poke around it. All I wanted was for whoever followed me to follow me away from there. So I gave it the full treatment. I made it look great. To them I must have seemed pretty jumpy and on my way to see somebody important. It took a full hour to reach *The Clipper* that way and the only important one around was Bucky Edwards and he wasn't drunk this time.

He nodded, said, "Beer?" and when I shook my head, called down the bar for a tall orange. "Figured you'd be in sooner or later."

"Yeah?"

That wise old face wrinkled a little. "How does it feel to be live bait, kiddo?"

"You got big ears, grandma."

"I get around." He toasted his beer against my orange, put it down and said, "You're in pretty big trouble, Joe. Maybe you don't know it."

"I know it."

"You don't know how big. You haven't been here that long. Those boys put on the big squeeze."

It was my turn to squint. His face was set as if he smelled something he didn't like and there was ice in his eyes. "How much do you know, Bucky?"

His shoulders made a quick shrug. "Phil Carboy didn't post the depot and the bus station for nothing. He's got cars cruising the highways too. Making sure, isn't he?"

He looked at me and I nodded.

"Renzo is kicking loose too. He's pulling the strings tight. The guys on his payroll are getting nervous but they can't do a thing. No, sir, not a thing. Like a war. Everybody's just waiting." The set mouth flashed me a quick grin. "You're the key, boy. If there was a way out I'd tell you to take it."

"Suppose I went to the cops?"

"Gerot?" Bucky shook his head.

"You'd get help as long as he could keep you in a cell. People'd like to see him dead too. He's got an awfully bad habit of being honest. Ask him to show you his scars someday. It wouldn't be so bad if he was just honest, but he's smart and mean as hell too."

I drank half the orange and set it down in the wet circle on the bar. "Funny how things work out. All because of Vetter. And he's here because of Jack Cooley."

"I was wondering when you were gonna get around to it, kid," Bucky said.

"What?"

He didn't look at me. "Who *are* you working for?"

I waited a pretty long time before he turned his head around. I let him look at my face another long time before I said anything. Then: "I was pushing a junk cart, friend. I was doing okay, too. I wasn't working for trouble. Now I'm getting pretty curious. In my own way, I'm not so stupid, but now I want to find out the score. One way or another I'm finding out. So they paid me off but they aren't figuring on me spending much of that cabbage. After it's over I get chopped down and it starts all over again, whatever it is. That's what I'm finding out. Why I'm bait for whatever it is. Who do I see, Bucky? You're in the know. Where do I find out?"

"Cooley could have told you," he said quietly.

"Nuts. He's dead."

"Maybe he can still tell you."

My fingers were tight around the glass. "The business about Cooley getting it because of the deal on Renzo's tables is out?"

"Might be."

"Talk straight unless you're scared silly of those punks too. Don't give me any puzzles if you know something."

Bucky's eyebrows went up, then down slowly over the grin in his eyes. "Talk may be cheap, son," he said, "but life comes pretty expensively." He nodded sagely and said, "I met Cooley in lots of places. Places he shouldn't have been. He was a man looking around. He could have found something."

"Like what?"

"Like why we have gangs in this formerly peaceful city of ours. Why we have paid-for politicians and clambakes with some big faces showing. They're not eating clams...they're talking."

"These places where you kept seeing Cooley…"

"River joints. Maybe he liked fish."

You could tell when Bucky was done talking. I went down to Main, found a show I hadn't seen and went in. There were a lot of things I wanted to think about.

CHAPTER ELEVEN

At eleven-fifteen the feature wound up and I started back outside. In the glass reflection of the lobby door I saw somebody behind me but I didn't look back. There could have been one more in the crowd that was around the entrance outside. Maybe two. Nobody seemed to pay any attention to me and I didn't care if they did or not.

I waited for a Main Street bus, took it down about a half mile, got off at the darkened supermarket, and started up the road. You get the creeps in places like that. It was an area where some optimist had started a factory and ran it until the swamp crept in. When the footings gave and the walls cracked, they moved out, and now the black skeletons of the buildings were all that were left, with gaping holes for eyes and a mouth that seemed to breathe out a fetid swamp odor. But there were still people there. The dozen or so company houses that were propped against the invading swamp showed dull yellow lights, and the garbage smell of unwanted humanity fought the swamp odor. You could hear them, too, knowing that they watched you from the shadows of their porches. You could feel them stirring in their jungle shacks and catch the pungency of the alcohol they brewed out of anything they could find.

There was a low moan of a train from the south side and its single eye picked out the trestle across the bay and followed it. The freight lumbered up, slowed for the curve that ran through the swamps and I heard the bindle stiffs yelling as they hopped off, looking for the single hard-topped road that took them to their quarters for the night.

The circus sign was on the board fence. In the darkness it was nothing but a bleached white square, but when I lit a cigarette I could see the faint orange impressions that used to be pictures of supposedly wild animals. The match went out and I lit another, got the smoke fired up and stood there a minute in the dark.

The voice was low. A soft, quiet voice more inaudible than a whisper. "One is back at the corner. There's another a hundred feet down."

"I know," I said.

"You got nerve."

"Let's not kid me. I got your message. Sorry I had to cut it short, but a pair of paid-for ears were listening in."

"Sorry Renzo gave you a hard time."

"So am I. The others did better by me."

Somebody coughed down the road and I flattened against the boards away from the white sign. It came again, further away this time and I felt better. I said, "What gives?"

"You had a cop at your place this morning."

"I spotted him."

"There's a regular parade behind you." A pause, then, "What did you tell them?"

I dragged in on the smoke, watched it curl up against the fence. "I told them he was big. Tough. I didn't see his face too well. What did you expect me to tell them?"

I had a feeling like he smiled.

"They aren't happy," he said.

I grinned too. "Vetter. They hate the name. It scares them." *I pulled on the butt again.* "It scares me too when I think of it too much."

"You don't have anything to worry about."

"Thanks."

"Keep playing it smart. You know what they're after?"

I nodded, even though he couldn't see me. "Cooley comes into it someplace. It was something he knew."

"Smart lad. I knew you were a smart lad the first time I saw you. Yes, it was Cooley."

"Who was he?" I asked.

Nothing for a moment. I could hear him breathing and his feet moved but that was all. The red light on the tail of the caboose winked at me and I knew it would have to be short.

"An adventurer, son. A romantic adventurer who went where the hunting was profitable and the odds long. He liked long odds. He found how they were slipping narcotics in through a new door and tapped them for a sweet haul. They say four million. It was a paid-for shipment and he got away with it. Now the boys have to make good."

The caboose was almost past now. He said, "I'll call you if I want you."

I flipped the butt away, watching it bounce sparks across the dirt. I went on a little bit further where I could watch the fires from the jungles and when I had enough of it I started back.

At the tree the guy who had been waiting there said, "You weren't thinking of hopping that freight, were you, kid?"

I didn't jump like I was supposed to. I said, "When I want to leave, I'll leave."

"Be sure to tell Mr. Carboy first, huh?"

"I'll tell him," I said.

He stayed there, not following me. I passed the buildings again, then felt better when I saw the single streetlight on the corner of Main. There was nobody there that I could see, but that didn't count. He was around someplace.

CHAPTER TWELVE

I had to wait ten minutes for a bus. It seemed longer than it was. I stayed drenched in the yellow light and thought of the voice behind the fence and what it had to say. When the bus pulled up I got on, stayed there until I reached the lights again and got off. By that time a lot of things were making sense, falling into a recognizable pattern. I walked down the street to an all night drug store, had a drink at the counter, then went back to the phone booth.

I dialed the police number and asked for Gonzales, Sergeant Gonzales. There was a series of clicks as the call was switched and the cop said, "Gonzales speaking."

"This is Joe, copper. Remember me?"

"Don't get too fresh, sonny," he said. His voice had a knife in it.

"Phil Carboy paid me some big money to finger Vetter. He's got men tailing me."

His pencil kept up a steady tapping against the side of the phone. Finally he said, "I was wondering when you'd call it in. You were real lucky, Joe. For a while I thought I was going to have to persuade you a little to cooperate. You were real lucky. Keep me posted."

I heard the click in my ear as he hung up and I spat out the things into the dead phone I felt like telling him to his face. Then I fished out another coin, dropped it in and dialed the same number. This time I asked for Captain Gerot. The guy at the switchboard said he had left about six but that he could probably be reached at his club. He gave me the number and I checked it through. The attendant who answered said he had left about an hour ago but would probably call back to see if there were any messages for him and were there? I told him to get the number so I could put the call through myself and hung up.

It took me a little longer to find Bucky Edwards. He had stewed in his own juices too long and he was almost all gone. I said, "Bucky, I need something bad. I want Jack Cooley's last address. You remember that much?"

He hummed a little bit. "Rooming house. Between Wells and Capitol. It's all white, Joe. Only white house."

"Thanks, Bucky."

"You in trouble, Joe?"

"Not yet."

"You will be. Now you will be."

That was all. He put the phone back so easily I didn't hear it go. Damn, I thought, he knows the score but he won't talk. He's got all the scoop and he clams up.

I had another drink at the counter, picked up a deck of smokes and stood outside while I lit one. The street was quieting down.

Both curbs were lined with parked heaps, dead things that rested until morning when they'd be whipped alive again.

Not all of them, though. I was sure of that. I thought I caught a movement across the street in a doorway. It was hard to tell. I turned north and walked fast until I reached Benson Road, then cut down it to the used car lot.

Now was when they'd have a hard time. Now was when they were playing games in my back yard and if they didn't know every inch of the way somebody was going to get hurt. They weren't kids, these guys. They had played the game themselves and they'd know all the angles. Almost all, anyway. They'd know when I tried to get out of the noose and as soon as they did, they'd quit playing and start working. They wouldn't break their necks sticking to a trail when they could bottle me up.

All I had to do was keep them from knowing for a while.

I crossed the lot, cutting through the parked cars, picked up the alley going back of the houses and stuck to the hedgerows until I was well down it. By that time I had a lead. If I looked back I'd spoil it so I didn't look back. I picked up another block at the fork in the alley, standing deliberately under the lone light at the end, not hurrying, so they could see me. I made it seem as though I were trying to pick out one of the houses in the darkness, and when I made up my mind, went through the gate in the fence.

After that I hurried. I picked up the short cuts, made the street and crossed it between lights. I reached Main again, grabbed a cruising cab in the middle of the block, had him haul me across town to the docks, and got out. It took fifteen minutes longer to reach the white house Bucky told me about. I grinned to myself and wondered if the boys were still watching the place they thought I went into. Maybe it would be a little while before they figured the thing out.

It would be time enough.

The guy who answered the door was all wrapped up in a bathrobe, his hair stringing down his face. He squinted at me, reluctant to be polite, but not naturally tough enough to be anything else but. He said, "If you're looking for a room you'll have to come around in the morning. I'm sorry."

I showed him a bill with two numbers on it.

"Well..."

"I don't want a room."

He looked at the bill again, then a quick flash of terror crossed his face. His eyes rounded open, looked at me hard, then dissolved into curiosity. "*Come...in.*"

The door closed and he stepped around me into a small sitting room and snapped on a shaded desk lamp. His eyes went back down to the bill. I handed it over and watched it disappear into the bathrobe.

"Yes?"

"Jack Cooley."

The words did something to his face. It showed terror again, but not as much as before.

"I really don't..."

"Forget the act. I'm not working for anybody in town. I was a friend of his."

This time he scowled, not believing me.

I said, "Maybe I don't look it, but I was."

"So? What is it you want?" He licked his lips, seemed to tune his ears for some sound from upstairs. "Everybody's been here. Police, newspapers. Those...men from town. They all want something."

"Did Jack leave anything behind?"

"Sure. Clothes, letters, the usual junk. The police have all that."

"Did you get to see any of it?"

"Well...the letters were from dames. Nothing important."

I nodded, fished around for a question a second before I found one. "How about his habits?"

The guy shrugged. "He paid on time. Usually came in late and slept late. No dames in his room."

"That's all?"

He was getting edgy. "What else is there? I didn't go out with the guy. So now I know he spent plenty of nights in Renzo's joint.

I hear talk. You want to know what kind of butts he smoked? Hobbies, maybe? Hell, what is there to tell? He goes out at night. Sometimes he goes fishing. Sometimes…"

"Where?" I interrupted.

"Where, what?"

"Fishing."

"On one of his boats. He borrowed my stuff. He was fishing the day before he got bumped. Sometimes he'd slip me a ticket and I'd get away from the old lady."

"How do the boats operate?"

He shrugged again, pursing his mouth. "They go down the bay to the tip of the inlet, gas up, pick up beer at Gulley's and go about ten miles out. Coming back they stop at Gulley's for more beer and for the guys to dump the fish they don't want. Gulley sells it in town. Everybody is usually drunk and happy." He gave me another thoughtful look. "You writing a book about your friend?" he said sarcastically.

"Could be. Could be. I hate to see him dead."

"If you ask me, he never should've fooled around Renzo. You better go home and save your money from now on, sonny."

"I'll take your advice," I said, "and be handyman around a rooming house."

He gave me a dull stare as stood up and didn't bother to go to the door with me. He still had his hand in his pocket wrapped around the bill I gave him.

CHAPTER THIRTEEN

The street was empty and dark enough to keep me wrapped in a blanket of shadows. I stayed close to the houses, stopping now and then to listen. When I was sure I was by myself I felt better and followed the water smell of the bay.

At River Road a single pump gas station showed lights and the guy inside sat with his feet propped up on the desk. He opened one eye when I walked in, gave me the change I wanted for the phone, then went back to sleep again. I dialed the number of Gerot's club, got the attendant, and told him what I wanted. He gave me another number and I punched it out on the dial. Two persons answered before a voice said, "Gerot speaking."

"Hello, Captain. This is Joe. I was…"

"I remember," he said.

"I called Sergeant Gonzales tonight. Phil Carboy paid me off to finger Vetter. Now I got two parties pushing me."

"Three. Don't forget us."

"I'm not forgetting."

"I hear you've been moving around, Joe. Those parties are excited. Where are you?"

I didn't think he'd bother to trace the call, so I said, "Some joint in town."

His voice sounded light this time. "About Vetter. Tell me."

"Nothing to tell."

"You had a call this morning."

I felt the chills starting to run up my back. They had a tap on my line already. "The voice wasn't familiar and it said some peculiar things."

"I know. I didn't get it. I thought it was part of Renzo's outfit getting wise. They beat up a buddy of mine so I'd know what a real beat up guy looks like. It was all double talk to me."

He was thinking it over. When he was ready he said, "Maybe so, kid. You hear about that dame you were with?"

I could hardly get the words out of my mouth, "Helen? No… What?"

"Somebody shot at her. Twice."

"Did…"

"Not this time. She was able to walk away from it this time."

"Who was it? Who shot at her?"

"That, little chum, is something we'd like to know too. She was waiting for a train out of town. The next time maybe we'll have better luck. There'll be a next time, in case you're interested."

"Yeah, I'm interested…and thanks. You know where she is now?"

"No, but we're looking around. I hope we can find her first."

I put the phone back and tried to get the dry taste out of my mouth. When I thought I could talk again I dialed Helen's apartment, hung on while the phone rang endlessly, then held the receiver fork down until I got my coin back. I had to get Renzo's club number from the book and the gravelly voice that answered rasped that the feature attraction hadn't put in an appearance that night and for something's sake to cut off the chatter and wait until tomorrow because the club was closed.

So I stood there and said things to myself until I was all balled up into a knot. I could see the parade of faces I hated drifting past my mind and all I could think of was how bad I wanted to smash everyone of them as they came by. Helen had tried to run for it. She didn't get far. Now where could she be? Where does a beautiful blonde go who is trying to hide? Who would take her in if they knew the score?

I could feel the sweat starting on my neck, soaking the back of my shirt. All of a sudden I felt washed out and wrung dry. Gone. All the way gone. Like there wasn't anything left of me any more except a big hate for a whole damn city, the mugs who ran it and the people who were afraid of the mugs. And it wasn't just one city either. There would be more of them scattered all over the states. For the people, by the people, Lincoln had said. Yeah. Great.

I turned around and walked out. I didn't even bother to look back and if they were there, let them come. I walked for a half hour, found a cab parked at a corner with the driver sacking it behind the wheel, and woke him up. I gave him the boarding house address and climbed in the back.

He let me off at the corner, collected his dough, and turned around.

Then I heard that voice again and I froze the butt halfway to my mouth and squashed the matches in the palm of my hand.

It said, "Go ahead and light it."

I breathed that first drag out with the words, "You nuts? They're all around this place."

"I know. Now be still and listen. The dame knows the score. They tried for her..."

We heard the feet at the same time. They were light as a cat, fast. Then he came out of the darkness and all I could see was the glint of the knife in his hand and the yell that was ill my throat choked off when his fingers bit into my flesh. I had time to see that same hardened face that had looked into mine not so long ago, catch an expressionless grin from the hard boy, then the other shadows opened and the side of a palm smashed down against his neck. He pitched forward with his head at a queer, stiff angle, his mouth wrenched open and I knew it was only a reflex that kept it that way because the hard boy was dead. You could hear the knife chatter across the sidewalk and the sound of the body hitting, a sound that really wasn't much yet was a thunderous crash that split the night wide open.

The shadows the hand had reached out from seemed to open and close again, and for a short second I was alone. Just a short second. I heard the whisper that was said too loud. The snick of a gun somewhere, then I closed in against the building and ran for it.

At the third house I faded into the alley and listened. Back there I could hear them talking, then a car started up down the street. I cut around behind the houses, found the fences and stuck with them until I was at my place, then snaked into the cellar door.

When I got upstairs I slipped into the hall and reached for the phone. I asked for the police and got them. All I said was that somebody was being killed and gave the address. Then I grinned at the darkness, hung up without giving my name and went upstairs to my room. From way across town a siren wailed a lonely note, coming closer little by little. It was a pleasant sound at that. It would give my friend from the shadows plenty of warning too. He was quite a guy. Strong. Whoever owned the dead man was going to walk easy with Vetter after this.

CHAPTER FOURTEEN

I walked into my room, closed the door, and was reaching for the bolt when the chair moved in the corner. Then she said, "Hello, Joe," and the air in my lungs hissed out slowly between my teeth.

I said, "Helen." I don't know which one of us moved. I like to think it was her. But suddenly she was there in my arms with her face buried in my shoulder, stifled sobs pouring out of her body while I tried to tell her that it was all right. Her body was pressed against me, a fire that seemed to dance as she trembled, fighting to stay close to me.

"Helen, Helen, take it easy. Nothing will hurt you now. You're okay." I lifted her head away and smoothed back her hair. "Listen, you're all right here."

Her mouth was too close. Her eyes were too wet and my mind was thinking things that didn't belong there. My arms closed tighter and I found her mouth, warm and soft, a salty sweetness that clung desperately and talked to me soundlessly. But it stopped the trembling and when she pulled away she smiled and said my name softly.

"How'd you get here, Helen?"

Her smile tightened. "I was brought up in a place like this a long time ago. There are always ways. I found one."

"I heard what happened. Who was it?"

She tightened under my hands. "I don't know. I was waiting for a train when it happened. I just ran after that. When I got out on the street, it happened again."

"No cops?"

She shook her head. "Too fast. I kept running."

"They know it was you?"

"I was recognized in the station. Two men there had caught my show and said hello. You know how. They could have said something."

I could feel my eyes starting to squint. "Don't be so damn calm about it."

The tight smile twisted up at the corner. It was like she was reading my mind. She seemed to soften a moment and I felt her fingers brush my face. "I told you I wasn't like other girls, Joe. Not like the kind of girl you should know. Let's say it's all something I've seen before. After a bit you get used to it."

"Helen..."

"I'm sorry, Joe."

I shook my head slowly. "No...I'm the one who's sorry. People like you should never get like that. Not you."

"Thanks." She looked at me, something strange in her eyes that I could see even in the half light of the room. And this time it happened slowly, the way it should be. The fire was close again, and real this time, very real. Fire that could have burned deeply if the siren hadn't closed in and stopped outside.

I pushed her away and went to the window. The beams of the flashlights traced paths up the sidewalk. The two cops were cursing the cranks in the neighborhood until one stopped, grunted something, and picked up a sliver of steel that lay by the curb. But there was nothing else. Then they got back in the cruiser and drove off.

Helen said, "What was it?"

"There was a dead man out there. Tomorrow there'll be some fun."

"Joe!"

"Don't worry about it. At least we know how we stand. It was one of their boys. He made a pass at me on the street and got taken."

"You do it?"

I shook my head. "Not me. A guy. A real big guy with hands that can kill."

"*Vetter.*" She said it breathlessly.

I shrugged.

Her voice was a whisper. "I hope he kills them all. Everyone." Her hand touched my arm. "Somebody tried to kill

Renzo earlier. They got one of his boys." Her teeth bit into her lip. "There were two of them so it wasn't Vetter. You know what that means?"

I nodded. "War. They want Renzo dead to get Vetter out of town. They don't want him around or he'll move into their racket sure."

"He already has." I looked at her sharply and she nodded. "I saw one of the boys in the band. Renzo's special car was hijacked as it was leaving the city. Renzo claimed they got nothing but he's pretty upset. I heard other things too. The whole town's tight."

"Where do you come in, Helen?"

"What?" Her voice seemed taut.

"You. Let's say you and Cooley. What string are you pulling?" Her hand left my arm and hung down at her side. If I'd slapped her she would have had the same expression on her face. I said, "I'm sorry. I didn't mean it like that. You liked Jack Cooley pretty well, didn't you?"

"Yes." She said it quietly.

"You told me what he was like once. What was he really like?"

The hurt flashed in her face again. "Like them," she said. "Gay, charming, but like them. He wanted the same things. He just went after them differently, that's all."

"The guy I saw tonight said you know things."

Her breath caught a little bit. "I didn't know before, Joe."

"Tell me."

"When I packed to leave…then I found out. Jack…left certain things with me. One was an envelope. There were cancelled checks in it for thousands of dollars made out to Renzo. The one who wrote the checks is a racketeer in New York. There was a note pad too with dates and amounts that Renzo paid Cooley."

"Blackmail."

"I think so. What was more important was what was in the box he left with me, Heroin."

I swung around slowly, "Where is it?"

"Down a sewer. I've seen what the stuff can do to a person."

"Much of it?"

"Maybe a quarter pound."

"We could have had him," I said. "We could have had him and you dumped the stuff!"

Her hand touched me again. "No…there wasn't that much of it. Don't you see, it's bigger than that. What Jack had was only a sample. Some place there's more of it, much more."

"Yeah," I said. I was beginning to see things now. They were starting to straighten themselves out and it made a pattern. The only trouble was that the pattern was so simple it didn't begin to look real.

"Tomorrow we start," I said. "We work by night. Roll into the sack and get some sleep. If I can keep the landlady out of here we'll be okay. You sure nobody saw you come in?"

"Nobody saw me."

"Good. Then they'll only be looking for me."

"Where will you sleep?"

I grinned at her. "In the chair."

I heard the bed creak as she eased back on it, then I slid into the chair. After a long time she said, "Who are you, Joe?"

I grunted something and closed my eyes. I wished I knew myself sometimes.

CHAPTER FIFTEEN

I woke up just past noon. Helen was still asleep, restlessly tossing in some dream. The sheet had slipped down to her waist, and every time she moved, her body rippled with sinuous grace. I stood looking at her for a long time, my eyes devouring her, every muscle in my body wanting her. There were other things to do, and I cursed those other things and set out to do them.

When I knew the landlady was gone I made a trip downstairs to her icebox and lifted enough for a quick meal. I had to wake Helen up to eat, then sat back with an old magazine to let the rest of the day pass by. At seven we made the first move. It was a nice simple little thing that put the whole neighborhood in an uproar for a half hour but gave us a chance to get out without being spotted.

All I did was call the fire department and tell them there was a gas leak in one of the tenements. They did the rest. Besides holding everybody back from the area they evacuated a whole row of houses, including us and while they were trying to run down the false alarm we grabbed a cab and got out.

Helen asked, "Where to?"

"A place called Gulley's. It's a stop for the fishing boats. You know it?"

"I know it." She leaned back against the cushions. "It's a tough place to be. Jack took me out there a couple of times."

"He did? Why?"

"Oh, we ate, then he met some friends of his. We were there when the place was raided. Gulley was selling liquor after closing hours. Good thing Jack had a friend on the force."

"Who was that?"

"Some detective with a Mexican name."

"Gonzales," I said.

She looked at me. "That's right." She frowned slightly. "I didn't like him at all."

That was a new angle. One that didn't fit in. Jack with a friend on the force. I handed Helen a cigarette, lit it, and sat back with mine.

CHAPTER SIXTEEN

It took a good hour to reach the place and at first glance it didn't seem worth the ride. From the highway the road weaved out onto a sand spit and in the shadows you could see the parked cars and occasionally couples in them. Here and there along the road the lights of the car picked up the glint of beer cans and empty bottles. I gave the cabbie an extra five and told him to wait and when we went down the gravel path, he pulled it under the trees and switched off his lights.

Gulley's was a huge shack built on the sand with a porch extending out over the water. There wasn't a speck of paint on the weather-racked framework and over the whole place the smell of fish hung like a blanket. It looked like a creep joint until you turned the corner and got a peek at the nice modern dock setup he had and the new addition on the side that probably made the place the yacht club's slumming section. If it didn't have anything else it had atmosphere. We were right on the tip of the peninsula that jutted out from the mainland and like the sign said, it was the last chance for the boats to fill up with the bottled stuff before heading out to deep water.

I told Helen to stick in the shadows of the hedgerow that ran around the place while I took a look around, and though she didn't like it, she melted back into the brush. I could see a couple of figures on the porch, but they were talking too low for me to hear what was going on. Behind the bar that ran across the main room inside, a flat-faced fat guy leaned over reading the paper with his ears pinned inside a headset. Twice he reached back, frowning, and fiddled with a radio under the counter. When the phone rang he scowled again, slipped off the headset and said, "Gulley speaking. Yeah. Okay. So long."

When he went back to his paper I crouched down under the rows of windows and eased around the side. The sand was a thick carpet that silenced all noise and the gentle lapping of the water against the docks covered any other racket I could make. I was glad to have it that way too. There were guys spotted around the place that you couldn't see until you looked hard and they were just lounging. Two were by the building and the other two at the foot of the docks, edgy birds who lit occasional cigarettes and shifted around as they smoked them. One of them said something and a pair of them swung around to watch the twin beams of a car coming up the highway. I looked too, saw them turn in a long arc then cut straight for the shack.

One of the boys started walking my way, his feet squeaking in the dry sand. I dropped back around the corner of the building, watched while he pulled a bottle out from under the brush, then started back the way I had come.

The car door slammed. A pair of voices mixed in an argument and another one cut them off. When I heard it I could feel my lips peel back and I knew that if I had a knife in my fist and Mark Renzo passed by me in the dark, whatever he'd had for supper would spill all over the ground. There was another voice, swearing at something. Johnny. Nice, gentle Johnny who was going to cripple me for life.

I wasn't worrying about Helen because she wouldn't be sticking her neck out. I was hoping hard that my cabbie wasn't reading any paper by his dome light and when I heard the boys reach the porch and go in, I let my breath out hardly realizing that my chest hurt from holding it in so long.

You could hear their hellos from inside, muffled sounds that were barely audible. I had maybe a minute to do what I had to do and didn't waste any time doing it. I scuttled back under the window that was at one end of the bar, had time to see Gulley shaking hands with Renzo over by the door, watched him close and lock it, and while they were still far enough away not to notice the movement, slid the window up an inch and flattened against the wall.

They did what I expected they'd do. I heard Gulley invite them to the bar for a drink and set out the glasses. Renzo said, "Good stuff."

"Only the best. You know that."

Johnny said, "Sure. You treat your best customers right."

Bottle and glasses clinked again for another round. Then the headset that was under the bar started clicking. I took a quick look, watched Gulley pick it up, slap one earpiece against his head, and jot something down on a pad.

Renzo said, "She getting in without trouble?"

Gulley set the headset down and leaned across the bar. He looked soft, but he'd been around a long time and not even Renzo was playing any games with him. "Look," he said, "you got your end of the racket. Keep out of mine. You know?"

"Getting tough, Gulley?"

I could almost hear Gulley smile. "Yeah. Yeah, in case you want to know. You damn well better blow off to them city lads, not me."

"Ease off," Renzo told him. He didn't sound rough any more. "Heard a load was due in tonight."

"You hear too damn much."

"It didn't come easy. I put out a bundle for the information. You know why?" Gulley didn't say anything. Renzo said, "I'll tell you why. I need that stuff. You know why?"

"Tough. Too bad. You know. What you want is already paid for and is being delivered. You ought to get your head out of your whosis."

"Gulley..." Johnny said really quiet. "We ain't kidding. We need that stuff. The big boys are getting jumpy. They think we pulled a fast one. They don't like it. They don't like it so bad maybe they'll send a crew down here to straighten everything out, and you may get straightened too."

Inside Gulley's feet were nervous on the floorboards. He passed in front of me once, his hands busy wiping glasses. "You guys are nuts. Carboy paid for this load. So I should stand in the middle?"

"Maybe it's better than standing in front of us," Johnny said.

"You got rocks. Phil's out of the local stuff now. He's got a pretty big outfit."

"Just peanuts, Gulley, just peanuts."

"Not any more. He's moving in since you dumped the big deal."

Gulley's feet stopped moving. His voice had a whisper in it. "So you were big once. Now I see you sliding. The big boys are going for bargains and they don't like who can't deliver, especially when it's been paid for. That was one big load. It was special. So you dumped it. Phil's smart enough to pick it up from there and now he may be top dog. I'm not in the middle. Not without an answer to Phil and he'll need a good one."

"Vetter's in town, Gulley!" Renzo almost spat the word out. "You know how he is? He ain't a gang you bust up. He's got a nasty habit of killing people. Like always, he's moving in. So we pay you for the stuff and deliver what we lost. We make it look good and you tell Phil it was Vetter. He'll believe that."

I could hear Gulley breathing hard. "Jerks, you guys," he said. There was a hiss in his words. "I should string it on Vetter. Man, you're plain nuts. I seen that guy operate before. Who the hell you think edged into that Frisco deal? Who got Morgan in El Paso while he was packing a half a million in cash and another half in powder? So a chowderhead hauls him in to cream some local fish and the guy walks away with the town. *Who the hell is that guy?"*

Johnny's laugh was bitter. Sharp. Gulley had said it all and it was like a knife sticking in and being twisted. "I'd like to meet him. Seems like he was a buddy of Jack Cooley. You remember Jack Cooley, Gulley? You were in on that. Cooley got off with your kick too. Maybe Vetter would like to know about that."

"Shut up."

"Not yet. We got business."

Gulley seemed out of breath. "Business be damned. I ain't tangling with Vetter."

"Scared?"

"Damn right, and so are you. So's everybody else."

"Okay," Johnny said. "So for one guy or a couple he's trouble. In a big town he can make his play and move fast. Thing is with enough guys in a burg like this he can get nailed."

"And how many guys get nailed with him? He's no dope. Who you trying to smoke?"

"Nuts, who cares who gets nailed as long as it ain't your own bunch? You think Phil Carboy'll go easy if he thinks Vetter jacked a load out from under him? Like you told us, Phil's an up and coming guy. He's growing. He figures on being the top kick around here and let Vetter give him the business and he goes all out to get the guy. So two birds are killed. Vetter and Carboy. Even if Carboy gets him, his load's gone. He's small peanuts again."

"Where does that get me?" Gulley asked.

"I was coming to that. You make yours. The percentage goes up ten. Good?"

Gulley must have been thinking greedy. He started moving again, his feet coming closer. He said, "You talk big. Where's the cabbage?"

"I got it on me," Renzo said.

"You know what Phil was paying for the junk?"

"The word said two million."

"It'll cost to take care of the boys on the boat."

"Not so much." Renzo's laugh had no humor in it. "They talk and either Carboy'll finish 'em or Vetter will. They stay shut up for free."

"How much for me?" Gulley asked.

"One hundred thousand for swinging the deal, plus the extra percentage. You think it's worth it?"

"I'll go for it," Gulley said.

Nobody spoke for a second, then Gulley said, "I'll phone the boat to pull into the slipside docks. They can unload there. The stuff is packed in beer cans. It won't make a big package so look around for it. They'll likely shove it under one of the benches."

"Who gets the dough?"

"You row out to the last boat mooring. The thing is red with a white stripe around it. Unscrew the top and drop it in."

"Same as the way we used to work it?"

"Right. The boys on the boat won't like going in the harbor and they'll be plenty careful, so don't stick around to lift the dough and the stuff too. That breed on the ship got a lockerful of chatter guns he likes to hand out to his crew."

"It'll get played straight."

"I'm just telling you."

Renzo said, "What do you tell Phil?"

"You kidding? I don't say nothing. All I know is I lose contact with the boat. Next the word goes that Vetter is mixed up in it. I don't say nothing." He paused for a few seconds, his breath whistling in his throat, then, "But don't forget something... You take Carboy for a sucker and maybe even Vetter. Layoff me. I keep myself covered. Anything happens to me and the next day the cops get a letter naming names. Don't ever forget that."

Renzo must have wanted to say something. He didn't. Instead he rasped, "Go get the cash for this guy."

Somebody said, "Sure, boss," and walked across the room. I heard the lock snick open, then the door.

"This better work," Renzo said. He fiddled with his glass. "I'd sure like to know what that punk did with the other stuff."

"He ain't gonna sell it, that's for sure," Johnny told him. "You think maybe Cooley and Vetter were in business together?"

"I'm thinking maybe Cooley was in business with a lot of people. That lousy blonde. When I get her she'll talk plenty. I should've kept my damn eyes open."

"I tried to tell you, boss."

"Shut up," Renzo said. "You just see that she gets found."

I didn't wait to hear any more. I got down in the darkness and headed back to the path. Overhead the sky was starting to lighten as the moon came up, a red circle that did funny things to the night and started the long fingers of shadows drifting out from the scraggly brush. The trees seemed to be ponderous things that reached down with sharp claws, feeling around in the breeze for something to grab. I found the place where I had left Helen, picked up a couple of pebbles, and tossed them back into the brush. I heard her gasp, then whispered her name.

CHAPTER SEVENTEEN

She came forward silently, said, "Joe?" in a hushed tone.
"Yeah. Let's get out of here."
"What happened?"

"Later. I'll start back to the cab to make sure it's clear. If you don't hear anything, follow me. Got it?"

"...Yes." She was hesitant and I couldn't blame her. I got off the gravel path into the sand, took it easy, and tried to search out the shadows. I reached the clearing, stood there until I was sure the place was empty then hopped over to the cab.

I had to shake the driver awake and he came out of it stupidly. "Look, keep your lights off going back until you're on the highway, then keep 'em on low. There's enough moon to see by."

"Hey...I don't want trouble."

"You'll get it unless you do what I tell you."

"Well, okay."

"A dame's coming out in a minute. Soon as she comes start it up and try to keep it quiet."

I didn't have long to wait. I heard her feet on the gravel, walking fast but not hurrying. Then I heard something else that froze me a second. A long, low whistle of appreciation like the kind any blonde'll get from the pool hall boys. I hopped in the cab, held the door open. "Let's go," I said.

As soon as the engine ticked over Helen started to run. I yanked her inside as the car started moving and kept down under the windows. She said, "Somebody..."

"I heard it."

"I didn't see who it was."

"Maybe it'll pass. Enough cars come out here to park."

Her hand was tight in mine, the nails biting into my palm. She was half-turned on the seat, her dress pulled back over the glossy knees of her nylons, her breasts pressed against my arm. She stayed that way until we reached the highway, then little by little eased up until she was sitting back against the cushions. I tapped my forefinger against my lips then pointed to the driver. Helen nodded, smiled, then squeezed my hand again. This time it was different. The squeeze went with the smile.

I paid off the driver at the edge of town. He got more than the meter said, a lot more. It was big enough to keep a man's mouth shut long enough to get him in trouble when he opened it too late. When he was out of sight we walked until we found another cab, told the driver to get us to a small hotel someplace, and after the usual leer and blonde inspection, he muttered the name of a joint and pulled away from the curb.

CHAPTER EIGHTEEN

It was the kind of a place where they don't ask questions and don't believe what you write in the register anyway. I signed *Mr. and Mrs. Valiscivitch,* paid the bill in advance for a week and when the clerk read the name I got a screwy look because the name was too screw balled to be anything but real to him. Maybe he figured his clientele was changing. When we got to the room I said, "You park here for a few days."

"Are you going to tell me anything?"

"Should I?"

"You're strange, Joe. A very strange boy."

"Stop calling me a boy."

Her face got all beautiful again and when she smiled there was a real grin in it. She stood there with her hands on her hips and her feet apart like she was going into some part of her routine and I could feel my body starting to burn at the sight of her. She could do things with herself by just breathing and she did them, the smile and her eyes getting deeper all the time. She saw what was happening to me and said, "You're not such a boy after all." She held out her hand and I took it, pulling her in close. "The first time you were a boy. All bloody, dirt ground into your face. When Renzo tore you apart I could have killed him. Nobody should do that to another one, especially a boy. But then there was Johnny and you seemed to grow up. I'll never forget what you did to him."

"He would have hurt you."

"You're even older now. Or should I say matured? I think you finished growing up last night, Joe, last night…with me. I saw you grow up, and I only hope I haven't hurt you in the process. I never was much good for anybody. That's why I left home, I guess. Everyone I was near seemed to get hurt. Even me."

"You're better than they are, Helen. The breaks were against you, that's all."

"Joe...do you know you're the first one who did anything nice for me without wanting...something?"

"Helen..."

"No, don't say anything. Just take a good look at me. See everything that I am? It shows. I know it shows. I was a lot of things that weren't nice. I'm the kind men want but won't introduce to their families. I'm a beautiful piece of dirt, Joe." Her eyes were wet. I wanted to brush away the wetness but she wouldn't let my hands go. "You see what I'm telling you? You're young...don't brush up against me too close. You'll get dirty and you'll get hurt."

She tried to hide the sob in her throat but couldn't. It came up anyway and I made her let my hands go and when she did I wrapped them around her and held her tight against me. "Helen," I said. "Helen..."

She looked at me, grinned weakly, "We must make a funny pair," she said. "Run for it, Joe. Don't stay around any longer."

When I didn't answer right away her eyes looked at mine. I could see her starting to frown a little bit and the curious bewilderment crept across her face. Her mouth was red and moist, poised as if she were going to ask a question, but had forgotten what it was she wanted to say. I let her look and look and look and when she shook her head in a minute gesture of puzzlement I said, "Helen...I've rubbed against you. No dirt came off. Maybe it's because I'm no better than you think you are."

"Joe..."

"It never happened to me before, kid. When it happens I sure pick a good one for it to happen with." I ran my fingers through her hair. It was nice looking at her like that. Not down, not up, but right into her eyes. "I don't have any family to introduce you to, but if I had, I would. Yellowhead, don't worry about me getting hurt."

Her eyes were wide now as if she had the answer. She wasn't believing what she saw.

"I love you, Helen. It's not the way a boy would love anybody. It's a peculiar kind of thing I never want to change."

"Joe..."

"But it's yours now. You have to decide. Look at me, kid. Then say it."

Those lovely wide eyes grew misty again and the smile came back slowly. It was a warm, radiant smile that told me more than her words. "It can happen to us, can't it? Perhaps it's happened before to somebody else, but it can happen to *us*, can't it? Joe... It seems so...I can't describe it. There's something..."

"Say it out."

"I love you, Joe. Maybe it's better that I should love a little boy. Twenty...twenty-one, you said? Oh, don't let it be wrong, please..." She pressed herself to me with a deep-throated sob and clung there. My fingers rubbed her neck, ran across the width of her shoulders then I pushed her away. I was grinning a little bit now.

"In eighty years it won't make much difference," I said. Then what else I had to say her mouth cut off like a burning torch that tried to seek out the answer and when it was over it didn't seem important enough to mention anyway.

I pushed her away gently. "Now, listen, there isn't much time. I want you to stay here. Don't go out at all and if you want anything, have it sent up. When I come back, I'll knock once. Just once. Keep that door locked and stay out of sight. You got that?"

"Yes, but..."

"Don't worry about me. I won't be long. Just remember to make sure it's me and nobody else." I grinned at her. "You aren't getting away from me anymore, blondie. Now it's the two of us for keeps, together."

"All right, Joe."

I nudged her chin with my fist, held her face up, and kissed it. That curious look was back and she was trying to think of something again. I grinned, winked at her, and got out before she could keep me. I even grinned at the clerk downstairs, but he didn't grin back. He probably thought anybody who'd leave a blonde like that alone was nuts or married and he wasn't used to it.

But it sure felt good. You know how. You feel so good you want to tear something apart or laugh and maybe you're a little crazy, but that's all part of it. That's how I was feeling until I remembered the other things and knew what I had to do.

CHAPTER NINETEEN

I found a gin mill down the street and changed a buck in to a handful of coins. Three of them got my party and I said, "Mr. Carboy?"

"That's right. Who is this?"

"Joe Boyle."

Carboy told somebody to be quiet then, "What do you want, kid?"

I got the pitch as soon as I caught the tone in his voice. "Your boys haven't got me, if that's what you're thinking," I told him.

"Yeah?"

"I didn't take a powder. I was trying to get something done. For once figure somebody else got brains too."

"You weren't supposed to do any thinking, kid."

"Well, if I don't, you lose a boatload of merchandise, friend."

"What?" It was a whisper that barely came through.

"Renzo's ticking you off. He and Gulley are pulling a switch. Your stuff gets delivered to him."

"Knock it off, kid. What do you know?"

"I know the boat's coming into the slipside docks with the load and Renzo will be picking it up. You hold the bag, brother."

"Joe," he said. "You know what happens if you're queering me."

"I know."

"Where'd you pick it up?"

"Let's say I sat in on Renzo's conference with Gulley."

"Okay, boy. I'll stick with it. You better be right. Hold on." He turned away from the phone and shouted muffled orders at someone. There were more muffled shouts in the background then he got back on the line again. "Just one thing more. What about Vetter?"

"Not yet, Mr. Carboy. Not yet."

"You get some of my boys to stick with you. I don't like my plans interfered with. Where are you?"

"In a place called Patty's. A gin mill."

"I know it. Stay there ten minutes. I'll shoot a couple guys down. You got that handkerchief yet?"

"Still in my pocket."

"Good. Keep your eyes open."

He slapped the phone back and left me there. I checked the clock on the wall, went to the bar and had an orange, then when the ten minutes were up, drifted outside. I was half a block away when a car door slapped shut and I heard the steady tread of footsteps across the street.

Now it was set. Now the big blow. The show ought to be good when it happened and I wanted to see it happen. There was a cabstand at the end of the block and I hopped in the one on the end. He nodded when I gave him the address, looked at the bill in my hand, and took off. In back of us the lights of another car prowled through the night, but always looking our way.

CHAPTER TWENTY

You smelt the place before you reached it. On one side the darkened storefronts were like sleeping drunks, little ones and big ones in a jumbled mass, but all smelling the same. There was the fish smell and on top that of wood the salt spray had started to rot. The bay stretched out endlessly on the other side, a few boats here and there marked with running lights, the rest just vague silhouettes against the sky. In the distance the moon turned the train trestle into a giant spidery hand. The white sign, *Slipside,* pointed on the dock area and I told the driver to turn up the street and keep right on going. He picked the bill from my fingers, slowed around the turn, then sped up when I hopped out. In a few seconds the other car came by, made the turn, and lost itself further up the street. When it was gone I stepped out of the shadows and crossed over. Maybe thirty seconds later the car came tearing back up the street again and I ducked back into a doorway. Phil Carboy was going to be pretty sore at those boys of his.

I stood still when I reached the corner again and listened. It was too quiet. You could hear the things that scurried around on the dock. The things were even bold enough to cross the street, and one was dragging something in its mouth. Another, a curious elongated creature whose fur shone silvery in the streetlight, pounced on it and the two fought and squealed until the raider had what it went after.

It happens even with rats, I thought. Who learns from who? Do the rats watch the men or the men watch the rats?

Another one of them ran into the gutter. It was going to cross, then stood on its hind legs in an attitude of attention, its face pointing toward the dock. I never saw it move, but it disappeared, then I heard what it had heard, carefully muffled sounds, then a curse not so muffled.

It came too quick to say it had a starting point. First the quick stab of orange and the sharp thunder of the gun, then the others following and the screams of the slugs whining off across the water. They didn't try to be quiet now. There was a startled shout, a hoarse scream and the yell of somebody who was hit.

Somebody put out the street light and the darkness was a blanket that slid in. I could hear them running across the street, then the moon reached down before sliding behind a cloud again and I saw them, a dozen or so closing in on the dock from both sides.

Out on the water an engine barked into life, and a boat wheeled away down the channel. The car that had been cruising around suddenly dimmed its lights, turned off the street and stopped. I was right there with no place to duck into and feet started running my way. I couldn't go back and there was trouble ahead. The only other thing was to make a break for it across the street and hope nobody spotted me.

I'd pushed it too far. I was being a dope again. One of them yelled and started behind me at a long angle. I didn't stop at the rail. I went over the side into the water, kicked away from the concrete abutment and hoped I'd come up under the pier. I almost made it. I was a foot away from the piling but it wasn't enough. When I looked back the guy was there at the rail with a gun bucking in his hand and the bullets were walking up the water toward me. He must have still had a half load left and only a foot to go when another shot blasted out over my head and the guy grabbed at his face with a scream and fell back to the street. The guy up above said, "Get the son..." and the last word had a whistle to it as something caught him in the belly. He was all doubled up when he hit the water and his tombstone was a tiny trail of bubbles that broke the surface a few seconds before stopping altogether.

I pulled myself further under the dock. From where I was I could hear the voices and now they had quieted down. Out on the street somebody yelled to stand back and, before the words were out, cut loose with a sharp blast of an automatic rifle. It gave the bunch on the street time to close in and those on the dock scurried back further.

Right over my head the planks were warped away and when a voice said, "I found it," I could pick Johnny's voice out of the racket.

"Where?"

"Back ten feet on the pole. Better hop to it before they get wise and cut the wires."

Johnny moved fast and I tried to move with him. By the time I reached the next piling I could hear him dialing the phone. He talked fast, but kept his voice down. "Renzo? Yeah, they bottled us. Somebody pulled the cork out of the deal. Yeah. The hell with that, you call the cops. Let them break it up. Sure, sure. Move it. We can make it to one of the boats. They got Tommy and Dalco. Two of the others were hit but not bad. Yeah, it's Carboy all right. He ain't here himself, but they're his guys. Yeah, I got the stuff. Shake it."

His feet pounded on the planking overhead and I could hear his voice without making out what he said. The next minute the blasting picked up and I knew they were trying for a standoff. Whatever they had for cover up there must have been pretty good because the guys on the street were swearing at it and yelling for somebody to spread out and get them from the sides. The only trouble was that there was no protection on the street and if the moon came out again they'd be nice easy targets.

It was the moan of the siren that stopped it. First one, then another joined in and I heard them running for the cars. A man screamed and yelled for them to take it easy. Something rattled over my head and when I looked up, a frame of black marred the flooring. Something was rolled to the edge, then crammed over. Another followed it. Men. Dead. They bobbed for a minute, then sank slowly. Somebody said, "Damn, I hate to do that. He was okay."

"Shut up and get out there." It was Johnny.

The voice said, "Yeah, come on, you," then they went over the side. I stayed back of the piling and watched them swim for the boats. The sirens were coming closer now. One had a lead as if it knew the way and the others didn't. Johnny didn't come down. I grinned to myself, reached for a cross-brace and swung up on it. From there it was easy to make the trapdoor.

And there was Johnny by the end of the pier squatting down behind a packing case that seemed to be built around some machinery, squatting with that tenseness of a guy about to run. He had a box in his arms about two feet square and when I said, "Hello, chum," he stood up so fast he dropped it, but he would have had to do that anyway the way he was reaching for his rod.

He almost had it when I belted him across the nose. I got him with another sharp hook and heard the breath hiss out of him. It spun him around until the packing case caught him and when I was coming in he let me have it with his foot. I skidded sidewise, took the toe of his shoe on my hip, then had his arm in a lock that brought a scream tearing out of his throat. He was going for the rod again when the arm broke and in a crazy surge of pain he jerked loose, tripped me, and got the gun out with his good hand. I rolled into his feet as it coughed over my head, grabbed his wrist, and turned it into his neck and he pulled the trigger for the last time in trying to get his hand loose. There was just one last, brief horrified expression in his eyes as he looked at me, then they filmed over to start rotting away.

The siren that was screaming turned the corner with its wail dying out. Brakes squealed against the pavement and the car stopped, the red light on its hood snapping shut. The door opened opposite the driver, stayed open as if the one inside was listening. Then a guy crawled out, a little guy with a big gun in his hand. He said, "Johnny?"

Then he ran. Silently, like an Indian. I almost had Johnny's gun back in my hand when he reached me.

"You," Sergeant Gonzales said. He saw the package there, twisted his mouth into a smile and let me see the hole in the end of his gun. I still made one last try for Johnny's gun when the blast went off. I half expected the sickening smash of a bullet, but none came. When I looked up, Gonzales was still there. Something on the packing crate had hooked into his coat and held him up.

I couldn't see into the shadows where the voice came from. But it was a familiar voice. It said, "You ought to be careful, son."

The gun the voice held slithered back into leather.

"Thirty seconds. No more. You might even do the job right, and beat it in his car. He was in on it. The cop...he was working with Cooley. Then Cooley ran out on him too, so he played along with Renzo. Better move, kid."

The other sirens were almost there. I said, "Watch yourself. And thanks."

"Sure, kid. I hate crooked cops worse than crooks."

I ran for the car, hopped in, and pulled the door shut. Behind me something splashed and a two-foot square package floated on the water a moment, then turned over and sunk out of sight. I left the lights off, turned down the first street I reached and headed across town. At the main drag I pulled up, wiped the wheel and gearshift free of prints, and got out.

There was dawn showing in the sky. It would be another hour yet before it was morning. I walked until I reached the junkyard in back of Gordon's office, found the wreck of a car that still had cushions in it, climbed in, and went to sleep.

CHAPTER TWENTY-ONE

Morning, afternoon, then evening. I slept through the first two. The last one was harder. I sat there thinking things, keeping out of sight. My clothes were dry now, but the cigarettes still had a lousy taste. There was a twinge in my stomach and my mouth was dry. I gave it another hour before I moved, then went back over the fence and down the street to a dirty little diner that everybody avoided except the boys who rode the rods into town. I knocked off a plate of bacon and eggs, paid for it with some of the change I had left, picked up a pack of butts and started out. That was when I saw the paper on the table.

It was made quite a story. GANG WAR FLARES ON WATERFRONT, and under it a subhead that said, *Cop, Hoodlum, Slain in Gun Duel.* It was a masterpiece of writing that said nothing, intimated much and brought out the fact that though the place was bullet-sprayed and though evidence of other wounded was found, there were no bodies to account for what had happened. One sentence mentioned the fact that Johnny was connected with Mark Renzo. The press hinted at police inefficiency. There was the usual statement from Captain Gerot.

The thing stunk. Even the press was afraid to talk out. How long would it take to find out Gonzales didn't die by a shot from Johnny's gun? Not very long. And Johnny…a cute little twist like that would usually get a big splash. There wasn't even any curiosity shown about Johnny. I let out a short laugh and threw the paper back again.

They were like rats, all right. They just went the rats one better. They dragged their bodies away with them so there wouldn't be any ties. Nice.

Now find the doctor who patched them up. Find what they were after on the docks. Maybe they figured to heist ten tons or so of machinery. Yeah, try and find it.

No, they wouldn't say anything. Maybe they'd have to hit it a little harder when the big one broke. When the boys came in who paid a few million out for a package that was never delivered. Maybe when the big trouble came and the blood ran again somebody would crawl back out of his hole long enough to put it into print. Or it could be that Bucky Edwards was right. Life was too precious a thing to sell cheaply.

I thought about it, remembering everything he had told me. When I had it all back in my head again I turned toward the place where I knew Bucky would be and walked faster. Halfway there it started to drizzle. I turned up the collar of my coat.

It was a soft rain; one of those things that comes down at the end of summer, making its own music like a dull concert you think will have no end. It drove people indoors until even the cabs didn't bother to cruise. The cars that went by had their windows steamed into opaque squares, the drivers peering through the hand-wiped panes.

I jumped a streetcar when one came along, took it downtown, and got off again. And I was back with the people I knew and the places made for them. Bucky was on his usual stool and I wondered if it was a little too late. He had that all-gone look in his face and his fingers were caressing a tall amber-colored glass.

When I sat down next to him his eyes moved, giving me a glassy stare. It was like the cars on the street, they were cloudy with mist, then a hand seemed to reach out and rub them clear. They weren't glass any more. I could see the white in his fingers as they tightened around the glass and he said, "You did it fancy, kiddo. Get out of here."

"Scared, Bucky?"

His eyes went past me to the door, then came back again. "Yes. You said it right. I'm scared. Get out. I don't want to be around when they find you."

"For a guy who's crocked most of the time you seem to know a lot about what happens."

"I think a lot. I figure it out. There's only one answer."

"If you know it why don't you write it?"

"Living's not much fun anymore, but what there is of it, I like. Beat it, kid."

This time I grinned at him, a big fat grin and told the bartender to get me an orange. Large. He shoved it down, picked up my dime, and went back to his paper.

I said, "Let's hear about it, Bucky." I could feel my mouth changing the grin into something else. "I don't like to be a target either. I want to know the score."

Bucky's tongue made a pass over dry lips. He seemed to look back inside himself to something he had been a long time ago, dredging the memory up. He found himself in the mirror behind the back bar, twisted his mouth at it and looked back at me again.

"This used to be a good town."

"Not that," I said.

He didn't hear me. "Now anybody who knows anything is scared to death. To death, I said. Let them talk and that's what they get. Death. From one side or another. It was bad enough when Renzo took over, worse when Carboy came in. It's not over yet." His shoulders made an involuntary shudder and he pulled the drink halfway down the glass. "Friend Gulley had an accident this afternoon. He was leaving town and was run off the road. He's dead."

I whistled softly, "Who?"

For the first time a trace of humor put lines at the corner of his lips. "It wasn't Renzo. It wasn't Phil Carboy. They were all accounted for. The tire marks are very interesting. It looked like the guy wanted to stop friend Gulley for a chat but Gulley hit the ditch. You could call it a real accident without lying." He finished the rest of the drink, put it down and said, "The boys are scared stiff." He looked at me closely then. "Vetter," he said.

"He's getting close."

Bucky didn't hear me. "I'm getting to like the guy. He does what should have been done a long time ago. By himself he does it. They know who killed Gonzales. One of Phil's boys saw it happen before he ran for it. There's a guy with a broken neck who was found out on the highway and they know who did that and how." He swirled the ice around in his glass. "He's taking good care of you, kiddo."

I didn't say anything.

"There's just one little catch to it, Joe. One little catch."

"What?"

"That boy who saw Gonzales get it saw something else. He saw you and Johnny tangle over the package. He figures you got it. Everybody knows and now they want you. It can't happen twice. Renzo wants it and Carboy wants it. You know who gets it?"

I shook my head.

"You get it. In the belly or in the head. Even the cops want you that bad. Captain Gerot even thinks that way. You better get out of here, Joe. Keep away from me. There's something about you that spooks me. Something in the way your eyes look. Something about your face. I wish I could see into that mind of yours. I always thought I knew people, but I don't know you at all. You spook me. You should see your own eyes. I've seen eyes like yours before but I can't remember where. They're familiar as hell, but I can't place them. They don't belong in a kid's face at all. Go on, Joe, beat it. The boys are all over town. They got orders to do just one thing. Find you. When they do I don't want you sitting next to me."

"When do you write the big story, Bucky?"

"You tell me."

My teeth were tight together with the smile moving around them. "It won't be long."

"No...maybe just a short obit. They're tracking you fast. That hotel was no cover at all. Do it smarter the next time."

The ice seemed to pour down all over me. It went down over my shoulders, ate through my skin until it was in the blood that pounded through my body. I grabbed his arm and damn near jerked him off the stool. "What about the hotel?"

All he did was shrug. Bucky was gone again.

I cursed silently, ran back into the rain again and down the block to the cabstand.

The clerk said he was sorry, he didn't know anything about room 612. The night man had taken a week off. I grabbed the key from his hand and pounded up the stairs. All I could feel was that mad frenzy of hate swelling in me and I kept saying her name over and over to myself. I threw the door open, stood there breathing fast while I called myself a dozen different kinds of fool.

CHAPTER TWENTY-TWO

She wasn't there. It was empty.

A note lay beside the telephone. All it said was, *"Bring it where you brought the first one."*

I laid the note down again and stared out the window into the night. There was sweat on the backs of my hands. Bucky had called it. They thought I had the package and they were forcing a trade. Then Mark Renzo would kill us both. He thought.

I brought the laugh up from way down in my throat. It didn't sound much like me at all. I looked at my hands and watched them open and close into fists. There were calluses across the palms, huge things that came from Gordon's junk carts. A year and a half of it, I thought. Eighteen months of pushing loads of scrap iron for pennies, then all of a sudden I was part of a multi-million dollar operation. The critical part of it. I was the enigma. Me, Joey the junk pusher. Not even Vetter now. Just me. Vetter would come when they had me out of the way.

For a while I stared at the street. That tiny piece of luck that chased me caught up again and I saw the car stop and the men jump out. One was Phil Carboy's right hand man. In a way it was funny. Renzo was always a step ahead of the challenger, but Phil was coming up fast. He'd caught on too and was ready to pull the same deal. He didn't know it had already been pulled.

But that was all right too.

I reached for the pen on the desk, lifted a sheet of cheap stationery out of the drawer and scrawled across it, *"Joe…be back in a few hours. Stay here with the package until I return. I'll have the car ready."* I signed it, *Helen,* put it by the phone, and picked up the receiver.

The clerk said, "Yes?"

I said, "In a minute some men will come in looking for the blonde and me. You think the room is empty, but let them come up. You haven't seen me at all yet. Understand?"

"Say…"

"Mister, if you want to walk out of here tonight you'll do what you're told. You're liable to get killed otherwise. Understand that?"

I hung up and let him think about it. I'd seen his type before and I wasn't worried a bit. I got out, locked the door, and started up the stairs to the roof. It didn't take me longer than five minutes to reach the street and when I turned the corner the light was back on in the room I had just left. I gave it another five minutes and the tall guy came out again, spoke to the driver of the car and the fellow reached in and shut off the engine. It had worked. The light in the window went out. The vigil had started and the boys could afford to be pretty patient. They thought.

The rain was a steady thing coming down just a little bit harder than it had. It was cool and fresh with the slightest nip in it. I walked, putting the pieces together in my head. I did it slowly, replacing the fury that had been there, deliberately wiping out the gnawing worry that tried to grow. I reached the deserted square of the park and picked out a bench under a tree and sat there letting the rain drip down around me. When I looked at my hands they were shaking.

I was thinking wrong. I should have been thinking about fat, ugly, faces; rat faces with deep voices and whining faces. I should have been thinking about the splashes of orange a rod makes when it cuts a man down and blood on the street. Cops who want the big payoff. Thinking of a town where even the press was cut off and the big boys came from the city to pick up the stuff that started more people on the long slide down to the grave.

Those were the things I should have thought of.

All I could think of was Helen. Lovely Helen who had been all things to many men and hated it. Beautiful Helen who didn't want me to be hurt, who was afraid the dirt would rub off. Helen who found love for the first time…and me. The beauty in her face when I told her. Beauty that waited to be kicked and wasn't because I loved her too much and didn't give a damn what she had been. She was different now. Maybe I was too. She didn't know it, but she was the good one, not me. She was the child that needed taking care of, not me. Now she was hours away from being dead and so was I. The thing they wanted, the thing that could buy her life, I saw floating in the water beside the dock. It was like having a yacht with no fuel aboard.

The police? No, not them. They'd want me. They'd think it was a phony. That wasn't the answer. Not Phil Carboy either. He was after the same thing Renzo was.

I started to laugh, it was so damn, pathetically funny. I had it all in my hand and couldn't turn it around. What the devil does a guy have to do? How many times does he have to kill himself? The answer. It was right there but wouldn't come through. It wasn't the same answer I had started with, but a better one.

So I said it all out to myself. Out loud, with words. I started with the night I brought the note to Renzo, the one that promised him Vetter would cut his guts out. I even described their faces to myself when Vetter's name was mentioned. One name, that's all it took, and you could see the fear creep in because Vetter was deadly and unknown. He was the shadow that stood there, the one they couldn't trust, the one they all knew in the society that stayed outside the law. He was a high-priced killer who never missed and always got more than he was paid to take. So deadly they'd give anything to keep him out of town, even to doing the job he was there for. So deadly they could throw me or anybody else to the wolves just to finger him. So damn deadly, they put an army on him, yet so deadly he could move behind their lines without any trouble at all.

Vetter.

I cursed the name. I said Helen's. Vetter wasn't important any more. Not to me.

The rain lashed at my face as I looked up into it. The things I knew fell into place and I knew what the answer was. I remembered something I didn't know was there, a sign on the docks by the fishing fleet that said, "Season Lockers."

Jack Cooley had been smart by playing it simple. He even left me the ransom.

I got up, walked to the corner, and waited until a cab came by. I flagged him down, got in, and gave the address of the white house where Cooley had lived.

CHAPTER TWENTY-THREE

The same guy answered the door. He took the bill from my hand and nodded me in. I said, "Did he leave any old clothes behind at all?"

"Some fishing stuff downstairs. It's behind the coal bin. You want that?"

"I want that," I said.

He got up and I followed him. He switched on the cellar light, took me downstairs, and across the littered pile of refuse a cellar can collect. When he pointed to the old set of dungarees on the nail in the wall, I went over and felt through the pockets. The key was in the jacket. I said thanks and went back upstairs. The taxi was still waiting. He flipped his butt away when I got in, threw the heap into gear, and headed toward the smell of the water.

I had to climb the fence to get on the pier. There wasn't much to it. The lockers were tall steel affairs, each with somebody's name scrawled across it in chalk. The number that matched the key didn't say Cooley, but it didn't matter anymore either. I opened it up and saw the cardboard box that had been jammed in there so hard it had snapped one of the rods in the corner. Just to be sure I pulled one end open, tore through the other box inside, and tasted the white powder it held.

Heroin.

They never expected Cooley to do it so simply. He had found a way to grab their load and stashed it without any trouble at all. Friend Jack was good at that sort of thing. Real clever. Walked away with a couple million bucks' worth of stuff and never lived to convert it. He wasn't quite smart enough. Not quite as smart as Carboy, Gerot, Renzo…or even a kid who pushed a junk cart. Smart enough to grab the load, but not smart enough to keep on living.

I closed the locker and went back over the fence with the box in my arms. The cabbie found me a phone in a gin mill and waited while I made my calls. The first one got me Gerot's home number. The second got me Captain Gerot himself, a very annoyed Gerot who had been pulled out of bed.

I said, "Captain, this is Joe Boyle and if you trace this call you're going to scramble the whole deal."

So the captain played it smart. "Go ahead," was all he told me.

"You can have them all. Every one on a platter. You know what I'm talking about?"

"I know."

"You want it that way?"

"I want you, Joe. Just you."

"I'll give you that chance. First you have to take the rest. There won't be any doubt this time. They won't be big enough to crawl out of it. There isn't enough money to buy them out either. You'll have everyone of them cold."

"I'll still want you."

I laughed at him. "I said you'll get your chance. All you have to do is play it my way. You don't mind that, do you?"

"Not if I get you, Joe."

I laughed again. "You'll need a dozen men. Ones you can trust. Ones who can shoot straight and aren't afraid of what might come later."

"I can get them."

"Have them stand by. It won't be long. I'll call again."

I hung up, stared at the phone a second, then went back outside. The cabbie was working his way through another cigarette. I said, "I need a fast car. Where do I get one?"

"How fast for how much?"

"The limit."

"I got a friend with a souped-up Ford. Nothing can touch it. It'll cost you."

I showed him the thing in my hand. His eyes narrowed at the edges. "Maybe it won't cost you at that," he said. He looked at me the same way Helen had, then waved me in.

We made a stop at an out-of-the way rooming house. I kicked my clothes off and climbed into some fresh stuff, then tossed everything else into a bag and woke up the landlady of the place. I told her to mail it to the post office address on the label and gave her a few bucks for her trouble. She promised me she would, took the bag into her room and I went outside. I felt better in the suit. I patted it down to make sure everything was set. The cabbie shot me a half smile when he saw me and held the door open.

I got the Ford and it didn't cost me a thing unless I piled it up. The guy grinned when he handed me the keys and made a familiar gesture with his hand. I grinned back. I gave the cabbie his fare with a little extra and got in the Ford with my box. It was almost over.

A mile outside Mark Renzo's roadhouse I stopped at a gas station and while the attendant filled me up all around, I used his phone. I got Renzo on the first try and said, "This is Joe, fat boy."

His breath in the phone came louder than the words. "Where are you?"

"Never mind. I'll be there. Let me talk to Helen."

I heard him call and then there was Helen. Her voice was tired and all the hope was gone from it. She said, "Joe..."

It was enough. I'd know her voice any time. I said, "Honey...don't worry about it. You'll be okay."

She started to say something else, but Renzo must have grabbed the phone from her. "You got the stuff, kid?"

"I got it."

"Let's go, sonny. You know what happens if you don't."

"I know," I said. "You better do something first. I want to see the place of yours empty in a hurry. I don't feel like being stopped going in. Tell them to drive out and keep on going. I'll deliver the stuff to you, that's all."

"Sure, kid, sure. You'll see the boys leave."

"I'll be watching," I said.

Joke.

I made the other call then. It went back to my hotel room and I did it smart. I heard the phone ring when the clerk hit the room number, heard the phone get picked up and said as though I were in one big hurry, "Look, Helen, I'm hopping the stuff out to Renzo's. He's waiting for it. As soon as he pays off we'll blow. See you later."

When I slapped the phone back I laughed again, then got Gerot again. This time he was waiting. I said, "Captain...they'll all be at Renzo's place. There'll be plenty of fun for everybody. You'll even find a fortune in heroin."

"You're the one I want, Joe."

"Not even Vetter?"

"No, he comes next. First you." This time he hung up on me. So I laughed again as the joke got funnier and made my last call.

The next voice was the one I had come to know so well. I said, "Joe Boyle. I'm heading for Renzo's. Cooley had cached the stuff in a locker and I need it for a trade. I have a light blue Ford and need a quick way out. The trouble is going to start."

"There's a side entrance," the voice said. "They don't use it any more. If you're careful you can come in that way and if you stay careful you can make it to the big town without getting spotted."

"I heard about Gulley," I said.

"Saddening. He was a wealthy man."

"You'll be here?"

"Give me five minutes," the voice told me. "I'll be at the side entrance. I'll make sure nobody stops you."

"There'll be police. They won't be asking questions."

"Let me take care of that."

"Everybody wants Vetter," I said.

"Naturally. Do you think they'll find him?"

I grinned. "I doubt it."

The other voice chuckled as it hung up.

CHAPTER TWENTY-FOUR

I saw them come out from where I stood in the bushes. They got into cars, eight of them and drove down the drive slowly. They turned back toward town and I waited until their lights were a mile away before I went up the steps of the club.

At that hour it was an eerie place, a dimly lit ghost house showing the signs of people that had been there earlier. I stood inside the door, stopped, and listened. Up the stairs I heard a cough. It was like that first night, only this time I didn't have somebody dragging me. I could remember the stairs and the long, narrow corridor at the top, and the oak paneled door at the end of it. Even the thin line of light that came from under the door. I snuggled the box under my arm and walked in.

Renzo was smiling from his chair behind the desk. It was a funny kind of a smile like I was a sucker. Helen was huddled on the floor in a corner holding a hand to the side of her cheek. Her dress had been shredded down to the waist, and tendrils of tattered cloth clung to the high swell of her breasts, followed the smooth flow of her body. Her other hand tried desperately to hide her nakedness from Renzo. She was trembling, and the terror in her eyes was an ungodly thing.

And Renzo grinned. Big, fat Renzo. Renzo the louse, whose eyes were now on the package under my arm, with the grin turning to a slow sneer. Renzo the killer who found a lot of ways to get away with murder and was looking at me as if he were seeing me for the first time.

He said, "You got your going-away clothes on, kid."

"Yeah."

"You won't be needing them."

He made the sneer bigger, but I wasn't watching him. I was watching Helen, seeing the incredible thing that crossed her face.

"I'm different, Helen?"

She couldn't speak. All she could do was nod.

"I told you I wasn't such a kid. I just look that way. Twenty…twenty-one you thought?" I laughed and it had a funny sound. Renzo stopped sneering. "I got ten years on that, honey. Don't worry about being in love with a kid."

Renzo started to get up then. Slowly, a ponderous monster with hands spread apart to kill something. "You two did it. You damn near ruined me. You know what happens now?" He licked his lips and the muscles rolled under his shirt.

My face was changing shape and I nodded. Renzo never noticed. Helen saw it. I said, "A lot happens now, fat boy." I dropped the package on the floor and kicked it to one side. Renzo moved out from behind the desk. He wasn't thinking any more. He was just seeing me and thinking of his empire that had almost toppled. The package could set it up again. I said, "Listen, you can hear it happen."

Then he stopped to think. He turned his head and you could hear the whine of engines and the shots coming clear across the night through the rain. There was a frenzy about the way it was happening, the frenzy and madness that go into a *banzai* charge and above it the moan of sirens that seemed to go ignored.

It was happening to Renzo too, the kill hate in his eyes, the saliva that made wet paths from the corners of his tight mouth. His whole body heaved and when his head turned back to me again, the eyes were bright with the lust of murder.

I said, "Come here, Helen," and she came to me. I took the envelope out of my pocket and gave it to her, and then I took off my jacket, slipping it over her shoulders. She pulled it closed over her breasts, the terror in her eyes fading. "Go out the side...the old road. The car is waiting there. You'll see a tall guy beside it, a big guy all around and if you happen to see his face, forget it. Tell him this. Tell him I said to give the report to the Chief. Tell him to wait until I contact him for the next assignment then start the car and wait for me. I'll be in a hurry. You got that?"

"Yes, Joe." The disbelief was still in her eyes.

Renzo moved slowly, the purpose plain in his face. His hands were out and he circled between me and the door. There was something fiendish about his face.

The sirens and the shooting were getting closer.

He said, "Vetter won't get you out of this, kid. I'm going to kill you and it'll be the best thing I ever did. Then the dame. The blonde. Weber told me he saw a blonde at Gulley's and I knew who did this to me. The both of you are going to die, kid. There ain't no Vetter here now."

I let him have a long look at me. I grinned. I said, "Remember what that note said? It said Vetter was going to spill your guts all over the floor. You remember that, Renzo?"

"Yeah," he said. "Now tell me you got a gun, kid. Tell me that and I'll tell you you're a liar. I can smell a rod a mile away. You had it, kid. There ain't no Vetter here now."

Maybe it was the way I let myself go. I could feel the loosening in my shoulders and my face was a picture only Renzo could see. "You killed too many men, Renzo, one too many. The ones you peddle the dope to die slowly, the ones who take it away die quick. It's still a lot of men. You killed them, Renzo, a whole lot of them. You know what happens to killers in this country? It's a funny law, but it works. Sometimes to get what it wants, it works in peculiar fashion. But it works.

"Remember the note. Remember hard what it said." I grinned and what was in it stopped him five feet away. What was in it made him frown, then his eyes opened wide, too wide and he had the expression Helen had had the first time.

I said to her, "Don't wait, Helen," and heard the door open and close. Renzo was backing away, his feet shuffling on the carpet.

Two minutes at the most.

CHAPTER TWENTY-FIVE

"I'm Vetter," I said. "Didn't you know? Couldn't you tell? Me…Vetter. The one everybody wonders about, even the cops. Vetter, the puzzle. Vetter, the one who's there but isn't there." The air was cold against my teeth. "Remember the note Renzo. No, you can't smell a gun because I haven't got one. But look at my hand. You're big and strong…you're a killer, but look at my hand and find out who the specialist really is and you'll know that there was no lie in that note you read the first night."

Renzo tried to scream, stumbled, and fell. I laughed again and moved in on him. He was reaching for something in the desk drawer knowing all the time that he wasn't going to make it and the knife in my hand made a nasty little snick and he screamed again so high it almost blended with the sirens.

Maybe one minute left, but it would be enough and the puzzle would always be there and the name when mentioned would start another ball rolling and the country a little cleaner and the report when the Chief read it would mean one more done with…done differently, but done.

THE END

If you've enjoyed this book, you will not want to miss these terrific titles...

ARMCHAIR MYSTERY-CRIME DOUBLE NOVELS, $12.95 each

- **B-16** **KISS AND KILL** by Richard Deming
  THE DEAD STAND-IN by Frank Kane
- **B-17** **DANGEROUS LADY** by Octavus Roy Cohen
  ONE HOUR LATE by William O'Farrell
- **B-18** **LOVE ME AND DIE!** by Day Keene
  YOU'LL GET YOURS by Thomas Wills
- **B-19** **EVERYBODY'S WATCHING ME** by Mickey Spillane
  A BULLET FOR CINDERELLA by John D. MacDonald
- **B-20** **WILD OATS** by Harry Whittington
  MAKE WAY FOR MURDER by A. A. Marcus
- **B-21** **THE ART STUDIO MURDERS** by Edward Ronns
  THE CASE OF JENNIE BRICE by Mary Roberts Rinehart
- **B-22** **THE LUSTFUL APE** by Bruno Fisher
  KISS THE BABE GOODBYE by Bob McKnight
- **B-23** **SARATOGA MANTRAP** by Dexter St. Claire
  CLASSIFICATION: HOMICIDE by Jonathan Craig

ARMCHAIR SCI-FI & HORROR DOUBLE NOVELS, $12.95 each

- **E-5** **THE IDOLS OF WULD** by Milton Lesser
  PLANET OF THE DAMNED by Harry Harrison
- **E-6** **BETWEEN WORLDS** by Garret Smith
  PLANET OF THE DEAD by Rog Phillips
- **E-7** **DAUGHTER OF THOR** by Edmond Hamilton
  TALENTS, INCORPORATED by Murray Leinster
- **E-8** **ALL ABOARD FOR THE MOON** by Harold M. Sherman
  THE METAL EMPEROR by Raymond A. Palmer
- **E-9** **DEATH HUNT** by Robert Gilbert
  THE BEST MADE PLANS by Everett B. Cole
- **E-10** **GIANT KILLER** by Dwight V. Swain
  GOLDEN AMAZONS OF VENUS by John Murray Reynolds

ARMCHAIR SCI-FI & HORROR GEMS SERIES, $12.95 each

- **G-21** **SCIENCE FICTION GEMS, Vol. Eleven**
  Gordon R. Dickson and others
- **G-22** **HORROR GEMS, Vol. Eleven**
  Thorp McClusky and others

THEN CAME THE DARK...

They lay on their sides, facing each other. In the half-light of the cave he could see the sheen of her eyes, the slow curve of her waist.

"So we wait," she said.
"And we'll have to be very careful," he answered. "He likes the night. He even likes us right now, waiting for us to come out, to give him the pleasure of killing us. Killing…that's really his only pleasure."

She rolled onto her back. Her voice was soft. "We're going to make it," she said. "We've got the money, and we'll get the car and then there's Buenos Aires, Paris and…"

They were quiet for a while until suddenly he heard her breath begin to quicken. She turned toward him and he pulled her close. There was time…

AUTHOR PORTRAIT

John D. MacDonald, 1916-1986

A BULLET FOR CINDERELLA

By
JOHN D. MacDONALD

ARMCHAIR FICTION
PO Box 4369, Medford, Oregon 97504

*The original text of this novel was first
published as a Dell First Edition Book*

Armchair Edition, Copyright 2016 by Gregory J. Luce
All Rights Reserved

*For more information about Armchair Books and products, visit our
website at…*

www.armchairfiction.com

Or email us at…

armchairfiction@yahoo.com

CHAPTER ONE

A steady April rain was soaking the earth. It hadn't been bad to drive through until dusk came. In the half-light it was hard to see the road. The rain was heavy enough to reflect my headlights back against the wind-shield. My mileage on the speedometer told me I couldn't be very far from Hillston.

When I saw the motel sign ahead on the right I slowed down. It looked fairly new. I turned in. The parking area was paved with those round brown pebbles that crunch under the tires. I parked as close to the office as I could get and ran from the car into the office. A woman with the bright cold eyes and thin sharp movements of a water bird rented me a room far back from the highway sound. She said the place was just four miles from the Hillston city limits.

Once I saw the room I decided that it would do. It would be a good place to stay while I did what had to be done in Hillston. I stretched out on the bed and wondered if I had been smart to use my right name on the motel register. But if I could find the money, there would be no one to say that I was the one who had taken it. And using my right name wouldn't make any difference at all.

When at last the rain eased up I went and found a small roadside restaurant. The girl behind the counter told me where I could buy a bottle of liquor. She seemed open to any invitation to help me drink it up, but though she was reasonably pretty I was not interested. I had this other thing on my mind and I wanted to go back alone and have some drinks and think about it and wonder how I could do it.

Maybe you saw pictures of us, the ones who were really bad off when the prisoners were exchanged. I was one of the litter cases. My stomach had stopped digesting the slop they fed us, and I was down to ninety-three pounds. One more week and I would have been buried up there beyond the river like so many others were. I was in bad shape. Not only physically but mentally. I was too sick to be flown back. Memory was all shot.

I went right into hospital and they started feeding me through a tube.

It was during the months in the military hospital back in this country that I began to sort things out and began to remember more of the details about Timmy Warden of Hillston. When the intelligence people had interrogated me I had told them how Timmy died but nothing more than that. I didn't tell them any of the stuff Timmy had told me.

We were both captured at the same time in that action near the reservoir. I'd known him casually. He was in a different platoon. We were together most of the time after we were captured. Enough has already been written about how it was. It wasn't good.

That prison camp experience can change your attitude toward life and toward yourself. It did that to Timmy Warden. His one thought was to survive. It was that way with all of us, but Timmy seemed more of a fanatic than anybody else. He had to get back.

He told me about it one night. That was after he'd gotten pretty weak. I was still in fair shape. He told me about it in the dark, whispering to me. I couldn't see his face.

"Tal, I've got to get back and straighten something out. I've got to. Every time I think about it I'm ashamed. I thought I was being smart. I thought I was getting what I wanted. Maybe I've grown up now. I've got to get it straightened out."

"What was it you wanted?"

"I wanted it and I got it, but I can't use it now. I wanted her too, and had her, but she's no good to me now."

"I'm not following this so good, Timmy."

He told me the story then. He had been in business with his brother George Warden. George was older by six years. George took him in as a partner. George had a flair for salesmanship and promotion. Timmy was good on the books, as he had a natural knack for figure work. They had a building supply business, a retail hardware outlet, a lumberyard, and several concrete trucks.

And George had a lush, petulant, amoral, discontented young wife named Eloise.

"I didn't make any play for her, Tal. It just seemed to happen. She was my brother's wife and I knew it was bad, but I couldn't stop. We had to sneak around behind his back. Hillston isn't a very big city. We had to be very careful. I guess I knew all the time what she was. But George thought she was the best thing that ever walked. She was the one who talked me into running away with her, Tal. She was the one who said we'd have to have money. So I started to steal."

He told me how he did it. A lot of the gimmicks didn't make much sense to me. He did all the ordering, handled the bank accounts and deposits. It was a big and profitable operation. He took a little bit here, a little bit there, always in cash. All the time he was doing it he was carrying on the affair with Eloise. He said it took nearly two years to squirrel away almost sixty thousand dollars. The auditors didn't catch it.

"I couldn't open a bank account with the money, and I knew better than to put it in a safety-deposit box. I put the money in those old-fashioned jars. The kind with the red rubber washer and the wire that clamps the top on. I'd fill them and bury them. George kept worrying about why we weren't making more money. I kept lying to him. Eloise was getting more restless all the time and more careless. I was afraid George would find out, and I didn't know what he'd do. She had me sort of hypnotized. We finally set the date when we were going to run away. Everything was planned. And then they called me up. I was reserve. There wasn't a damn thing I could do about it. I told Eloise that when I got out we'd go through with it the way we planned. But now I'm stuck here. And now I don't want to go through with it. I want to get back there and give the money back to George and tell him the whole thing. I've had too much chance to think it over."

"How do you know she hasn't taken the money and left?"

"I didn't tell her where I put it. It's still there. Nobody can find it."

His story gave me a lot to think about. Timmy Warden sank lower and lower. By that time those of us who were left alive had become expert on how long the dying would last. And I knew that Timmy was one of the dying. I knew he'd never leave there alive. I tried to find out where the money was buried. But I'd waited a little too long. He was out of his head. I listened to him rave. I listened to every word he said.

But in his raving he never gave away the hiding place. It was in a moment of relative lucidity that he told me. It was afternoon and he caught my wrist with his wasted hand. "I'm not going to make it, Tal."

"You'll make it."

"No. You go back there and straighten it out. You can do that. Tell George. Give him the money. Tell him everything."

"Sure. Where is the money?"

"Tell him everything."

"Where's the money hidden?"

"Cindy would know," he said, suddenly breathless with weak, crazy laughter. "Cindy would know." And that's all I could get out of him. I was still strong enough then to use a shovel. I helped dig the hole for Timmy Warden that night.

Back in the stateside hospital I thought about that sixty thousand dollars. I could see those fruit jars with the tight rolls of bills inside the glass. I would dig them out and rub the dirt off and see the green gleam of the money. It helped pass the time in the hospital.

Finally they let me out. The thought of the money was no longer on the surface of my mind. It was hidden down underneath. I would think about it, but not very often. I went back to my job. It seemed pretty tasteless to me. I felt restless and out of place. I'd used up a lot of emotional energy in order to stay alive and come back to this, back to my job and back to Charlotte, the girl I had planned to marry. Now that I was back neither job nor girl seemed enough.

Two weeks ago they let me go. I don't blame them. I'd been doing my job in a listless way. I told Charlotte I was going away for a while. Her tears left me completely untouched. She was just a girl crying, a stranger. I told her I didn't know where I was going. But I knew I was going to Hillston. The money was there. And somebody named Cindy who would know how to find it.

I had started the long trip with an entirely unrealistic anticipation of success. Now I was not so confident. It seemed that I was searching for more than the sixty thousand dollars. It seemed to me that I was looking for some meaning or significance to my life. I had a thousand dollars in traveler's checks and everything I owned with me. Everything I owned filled two suitcases.

Charlotte had wept, and it hadn't touched me. I had accepted being fired without any special interest. Ever since the repatriation, since the hospital, I had felt like half a man. It was as though the other half of me had been buried and I was coming to look for it—here in Hillston, a small city I had never seen. Somehow I had to begin to live again. I had stopped living in a prison camp. And never come completely to life again.

I drank in the motel room until my lips felt numb. There was a pay phone in the motel office. The bird woman looked at me with obvious disapproval but condescended to change three ones into change for the phone.

I had forgotten the time difference. Charlotte was having dinner with her people. Her mother answered the phone. I heard the coldness in her mother's voice. She called Charlotte.

"Tal? Tal, where are you?"

"A place called Hillston."

"Are you all right? You sound so strange."

"I'm okay."

"What are you doing? Are you looking for a job?"

"Not yet."

She lowered her voice so I could barely hear her. "Do you want me to come there? I would, you know, if you want me. And no—no strings, Tal darling."

"No. I just called so you'd know I'm all right."

"Thank you for calling, darling."

"Well…good-by."

"Please write to me."

I promised and hung up and went back to my room. I wanted things to be the way they had once been between us. I did not want to hurt her. I did not want to hurt myself. But I felt as if a whole area in my mind was dead and numb. The part where she had once been. She had been loyal while I had been gone. She was the one who had the faith I would return. She did not deserve this.

On the following morning, Thursday morning, Hillston lay clean and washed by the night rains, bright and glowing in the April sunshine. Timmy had often talked about the city.

"It's more town than city. There isn't much of a transient population. Everybody seems to know everybody. It's a pretty good place, Tal."

It lay amid gentle hills, and the town stretched north-south, following the line of Harts River. I drove up the main street, Delaware Street. Traffic had outgrown the narrowness of the street. Standardization had given most of our small cities the same look. Plastic and glass brick store fronts. Woolworth's and J. C. Penney and Liggett and Timely and the chain grocery. The essential character of Hillston had been watered down by this standardization and yet there was more individuality left than in many other cities. Here was a flavor of leisure, of mild manners and quiet pleasures. No major highway touched the city. It was in an eddy apart from the great current.

Doubtless there were many who complained acidly about the town being dead on its feet, about the young people leaving for greater opportunities. But such human irritants did not change the rather smug complacency of the city. The population was twenty-five thousand and Timmy had told me that it had not changed very much in the past twenty years. There was the pipe mill and a small electronics industry and a plant that made cheap hand tools. But the money in town was the result of its being a shopping center for all the surrounding farmland.

I had crossed the country as fast as I could, taking it out on the car, anxious to get to this place. The car kept stalling as I stopped for the lights on Delaware Street. When I spotted a repair garage I turned in.

A man came up to me as I got out of the car. "I think I need a tune-up. It keeps stalling. And a grease job and oil change."

He looked at the wall clock. "About three this afternoon be okay?"

"That'll be all right."

"California plates. On your way through?"

"Just on a vacation. I stopped here because I used to know a fellow from this town. Timmy Warden."

He was a gaunt man with prematurely white hair and bad teeth. He picked a cigarette out of the top pocket of his coveralls. "Knew Timmy, did you? The way you say it, I guess you know he's dead."

"Yes. I was with him when he died."

"There in the camp, eh? Guess it was pretty rough."

"It was rough. He used to talk about this place. And about his brother George. I thought I'd stop and maybe see his brother and tell him about how it was with Timmy."

The man spat on the garage floor. "I guess George knows how it was."

"I don't understand."

"There's another man came here from that camp. Matter of fact he's still here. Came here a year ago. Name of Fitzmartin. Earl Fitzmartin. He works for George at the lumberyard. Guess you'd know him, wouldn't you?"

"I know him," I said.

Everybody who survived the camp we were in would know Fitzmartin. He'd been taken later, had come in a month after we did. He was a lean man with tremendously powerful hands and arms. He had pale colorless hair, eyes the elusive shade of wood smoke. He was a Texan and a Marine.

I knew him. One cold night six of us had solemnly pledged that if we were ever liberated we would one day hunt down Fitzmartin and kill him. We had believed then that we would. I had forgotten all about it. It all came back.

Fitz was not a progressive. Yet he was a disrupting influence. In the camp we felt that if we could maintain a united front it would improve our chances for survival. We organized ourselves, appointed committees, assigned responsibilities. There were two retreads who had been in Jap camps in another war who knew the best organizational procedures.

Fitz, huskier and quicker and craftier than anyone else in camp, refused to take any part in it. He was a loner. He had an animal instinct for survival. He kept himself clean and fit. He ate anything that was organically sound. He prowled by himself and treated us with icy contempt and amusement. He was no closer to us than to his captors. He was one of the twelve quartered in the same hut with Timmy and me.

Perhaps that does not seem to constitute enough cause to swear to kill a man. It wouldn't, in a normal situation. But in captivity minor resentments become of major importance. Fitz wasn't with us so he was against us. We needed him and every day he proved he didn't need us.

At the time of the exchange Fitzmartin was perhaps twenty pounds lighter. But he was in good shape. Many had died but Fitz was in fine shape. I knew him.

"I'd like to see him," I told the garage man. "Is the lumberyard far from here?"

It was north of town. I had to take a bus that crossed a bridge at the north end of town and walk a half mile on the shoulder of the highway—past junk yards, a cheap drive-in movie, rundown rental cabins. I kept asking myself why Fitz should have come to Hillston. He couldn't know about the money. But I could remember the slyness of the man, his knack of moving without a sound.

The lumberyard was large. There was an office near the road. There was a long shed open on the front where semi-fabricated pieces were kept in bins in covered storage. I heard the whine of a saw. Beyond the two buildings were tall stacks of lumber. A truck was being loaded back there. In the open shed a clerk was helping a customer select window frames. An office girl with thin face and dark hair looked up from an adding machine and told me I could find Fitzmartin out in the back where they were loading the truck.

I went back and saw him before he saw me. He was heavier but otherwise unchanged. He stood with another man watching two men loading a stake truck. He wore khakis and stood with his fists in his hip pockets. The man said something and Earl Fitzmartin laughed. The sound startled me. I had never heard him laugh in the camp.

He turned as I approached him. His face changed. The smoke eyes looked at me, wary, speculative. "I've got the name right, haven't I? Tal Howard."

"That's right." There was, of course, no move toward shaking hands.

He turned to the other man. "Joe, you go right ahead here. Leave this slip in the office on your way out."

Fitzmartin started walking back through the lot between the stacked lumber. I hesitated and followed him. He led the way to a shed on the back corner of the lot. An elderly Ford coupé was parked by the shed. He opened the door and gestured and I went into the shed. It was spotlessly clean. There was a bunk, table, chair, shelf with hot plate and dishes. He had a supply of canned goods, clean clothes hanging on hooks, a pile of magazines and paper-bound books near the head of the bunk. There was a large space heater in the corner, and through an open door I could see into a small bathroom with unfinished walls.

There was no invitation to sit down. We faced each other.

"Nice to see any old pal from north of the river," he said.

"I heard in town you work here."

"You just happened to be in town and heard I work here."

"That's right."

"Maybe you're going around looking all the boys up. Maybe you're writing a book."

"It's an idea."

"My experiences as a prisoner of war. Me and Dean."

"I'd put you in the book, Fitz. The big ego. Too damn impressed with himself to try to help anybody else."

"Help those gutless wonders? You types stone me. You wanted to turn it into a boys' club. I watched a lot of you die because you didn't have the guts or will or imagination to survive."

"With your help maybe a couple more would have come back."

"You sound like you think that would be a good thing."

There was an amused sneer in his tone that brought it all vividly back. That was what we had sensed about him. He hadn't cared if we had all been buried there, just so Fitzmartin got out of it with a whole skin. I had thought my anger and outrage had been buried, had thought I was beyond caring. Perhaps he, too, misjudged the extent of the contempt that made me careless of his physical power.

I struck blindly, taking him almost completely by surprise, my right fist hitting his jaw solidly. The impact jarred my arm and shoulder and back. It knocked him back a full step. I wanted him on the floor. I swung again and hit a thick, hard arm. He muffled the third blow and caught my left wrist, then grabbed my right wrist. I tried to snap my wrists free, but he was far too powerful. I was able to resist the grinding twisting force for several seconds. His face was quite impassive. I was slowly forced down onto my knees, tears of anger and humiliation stinging my eyes.

He released my wrists suddenly and gave me a casual open-handed slap across the side of my head that knocked me down onto the bare floor. I scrambled to the chair and tried to pick it up to use it as a weapon. He twisted it out of my hands, put a foot against my chest and shoved me back so that I rolled toward the door. He put the chair back in place, went over and sat on the bunk, and lighted a cigarette. I got up slowly.

He looked at me calmly. "Out of your system?"

"God damn you!"

He looked bored. "Shut up. Sit down. Don't try to be the boy hero, Howard. I'll mark you up some if that's what you want."

I sat in the chair. My knees were weak and my wrists hurt. He got up quickly, went to the door and opened it and looked out, closed it and went back to the bunk. "We'll talk about Timmy Warden, Howard."

"What about Timmy?"

"It's too damn late for games. Information keeps you alive. I did a lot of listening in that camp. I made a business of it. I know that Timmy stole sixty thousand bucks from his brother and stashed it away in jars. I know Timmy told you that. I heard him tell you. So don't waste our time trying to play dumb about it. I'm here and you're here, and that's the only way it adds up. I got here first. I got here while you were still in the hospital. I haven't got the money. If I had it, I wouldn't still be here. That's obvious. I figured Timmy might have told you where he hid it. I've been waiting for you. What kept you?"

"I don't know any more about it than you do. I know he hid it, but I don't know where."

He was silent as he thought it over. "Maybe I won't buy that. I came here on a long shot. I didn't have much to go on. I wanted to be here and all set when you came after it. It was a long shot, but one town is the same as another to me. I can't see you coming here to find the money and not knowing any more than I do. You're a more conservative type, Howard. You know something I want to know."

"That's right," I said. "I know exactly where it is. I can go and dig it up right now. That's why I waited a year before I came here. And that's why I came here to see you instead of going and digging it up."

"Why come at all?"

I shrugged. "I lost my job. I remembered the money. I thought I'd come here and look around."

"I've spent a year looking around. I know a hell of a lot more about Timmy Warden, the way he lived, the way his mind worked, than you'll ever know. And I can't find it."

"Then I won't be able to either, will I?"

"Then you better take off, Howard. Go back where you came from."

"I think I'll stay around."

He leaned forward. "Then you do have some little clue that I don't have. Maybe it isn't a very good one."

"I don't know any more than you do. I just have more confidence in myself than I have in you."

That made him laugh. The laughter stung my pride. It was a ludicrous thought to him that I could do anything in the world he couldn't do.

"You've wasted better than a year on it. At least I haven't done that," I said hotly.

He shrugged. "I have to be somewhere. It might as well be here. What's wasted about it? I've got a good job. Let's pool everything we know and can remember, and if we can locate it I'll give you a third."

"No," I said, too quickly.

He sat very still and watched me. "You have something to work on."

"No. I don't."

"You can end up with nothing instead of a third."

"Or all of it instead of a third."

"Finding it and taking it away from here are two different problems."

"I'll take that chance."

He shrugged. "Well, suit yourself. Go and say hello to George. Give him my regards."

"And Eloise?"

"You won't be able to do that. She took off while we were still behind the wire. Took off with a salesman, they say."

"Maybe she took the money with her."

"I don't think so."

"But she knew Timmy was hiding it, had hidden a big amount. From what he said about her, she wouldn't leave without it."

"She did," he said, smiling. "Take my word. She left without it."

CHAPTER TWO

The lumberyard had looked reasonably prosperous. The retail hardware store was not what I expected. From talks with Timmy I had expected a big place with five or six clerks and a stock that ranged from appliances and cocktail trays to deep-well pumps and pipe wrenches.

It was a narrow, dingy store, poorly lighted. There was an air of dust and defeat about it. It was on a side street off the less prosperous looking end of Delaware Street. A clerk in a soiled shirt came to help me. I said I wanted to see Mr. Warden. The clerk pointed back toward a small office in the rear where through glass I could see a man hunched over a desk.

He looked up as I walked back to the office. The door was open. I could see the resemblance to Timmy. But Timmy just before and for a short time after we were taken, had a look of bouncing vitality, good spirits. This man looked far older than the six years difference Timmy had told me about. He was a big man, as Timmy had been. The wide, high forehead was the same, and the slightly beaked nose and the strong, square jaw. But George Warden looked as though he had been sick for a long time. His color was bad. The stubble on the unshaven jaw was gray. His eyes were vague and troubled, and there was a raw smell of whisky in the small office.

"Something I can do for you?"

"My name is Tal Howard, Mr. Warden. I was a friend of Timmy's."

"You were a friend of Timmy's." He repeated it in an odd way. Apathetic and yet somehow cynical.

"I was with him when he died."

"So was Fitz. Sit down, Mr. Howard. Drink?"

I said I would have a drink. He pushed by my chair and went out to a sink. I heard him rinsing out a glass. He came back and picked a bottle off the floor in the corner and put a generous drink in each glass.

"Here's to Timmy," he said.

"To Timmy."

"Fitz got out of it. You got out of it. But Timmy didn't make it."

"I almost didn't make it."

"What did he actually die of? Fitz couldn't say."

I shrugged. "It's hard to tell. We didn't have medical care. He lost a lot of weight and his resistance was down. He had a bad cold. He ran a fever and his legs got swollen. He began to have trouble breathing. It hurt him to breathe. A lot of them went like that. Nothing specific. Just a lot of things. There wasn't much you could do."

He turned the dirty glass around and around. "He should have come back. He would have known what to do."

"About what?"

"I guess he told you about how we were doing before he left."

"He said you had a pretty good business."

"This store used to be over on Delaware. We moved about six months ago. Sold the lease. Sold my house too. Still got the yard and this. The rest of it is gone."

I felt uncomfortable. "Business is bad, I guess."

"It's pretty good for some people. What business are you in?"

"I'm not working right now."

He smiled at me in a mirthless way. "And I suppose you plan on sticking around awhile."

"I'd thought of it."

"Did Fitz send for you?"

"I don't know what you mean. I didn't know he was here."

"But you talked to him. He phoned me and said you'd probably be in for a little chat. And that you're an old friend of Timmy's. He's been working for me for nearly a year. I don't see how I can give you a job. There just isn't enough coming in. I couldn't swing it."

"I don't want a job, Mr. Warden."

He kept smiling. His eyes were funny. I had the feeling that he was either very drunk or out of his head. "Maybe something nice out of the store? We still have some nice things. I could unlock the gun rack for you. Need a nice over and under, with gold inlay, French walnut stock? On the house."

"No thanks. I don't understand, Mr. Warden. I knew Timmy and I thought maybe it would be the right thing to do to just stop in and chat."

"Sure. But you went out to the yard first."

"Yes. I went out there because I put my car in a garage here and I told the man I'd known Timmy in prison camp. He said there was another man here who'd been in the same place. Earl Fitzmartin. So I went out there and saw him. Then I came here. I could have come here first and then gone out there. I don't know why you think you have to give me a job or a gun or anything."

He looked at me and then bent over and picked up the bottle again. He put some in both glasses. "Okay," he said. "So it's just like that. Pay no attention to me. Hardly anybody does any more. Except Fitz. He's a good worker. The yard makes a little money. That's a good thing, isn't it?"

"Yes, I guess it is."

It wasn't anything like the conversation I had expected. He was a strange man. He seemed defeated and yet amused, as though amused at his own defeat.

"Timmy talked a lot about Hillston," I said.

"I guess he did. He lived here most of his life."

Though I didn't feel right about it, I took the plunge. "We had a lot of time to talk. They made us go to lectures and read propaganda and write reports on what we read, but the rest of the time we talked. I feel as though I know Hillston pretty well. Even know the girls he used to go with. Ruth Stamm. Janice Currier. Cindy somebody."

"Sure," he said softly, half smiling. "Ruthie Stamm. And it was Judith not Janice Currier. Those were two of them. Nice girls. But the last couple of years before he went away he stopped running around so much. Stuck closer to the business. Lots of nights he'd work on the books. He was getting almost too serious to suit me."

"Wasn't there one named Cindy?"

He frowned and thought and shook his head. "No Cindy I know of. Either of those other two would have made him a good wife. Ruthie is still around town, still single. Judy got married and moved away. El Paso, I think. Either one of them would have made him a better wife than the one I got stuck with. Eloise. He talk about her?"

"He mentioned her a few times."

"She's gone."

"I know. Fitz told me."

"Lovely little Eloise. Two-faced bitch. While you're around, stop in again any time. We'll have a nice little chat. I'm usually here. Hell, I used to have a lot of other things to do. Zoning board. Chamber of Commerce. Rotary. Always on the run. Always busy. Now I have a lot of time. All the time in the world."

I was dismissed. I walked back through the narrow store to the street door. The clerk leaned against one of the counters near the front, picking his teeth with a match. It felt good to get back out into the sunlight. The cheap liquor had left a bad taste in my mouth. It was too early to go after the car. I went into the nearest bar I could find and ordered an ale. It was a dark place, full of brown and violet shadows, with deer antlers on the wall and some dusty mounted fish. Two elderly men played checkers at a corner table. The bartender was a dwarf. The floor was built up behind the bar to bring him up to the right height.

I sipped the ale and thought about Fitz, about my own unexpectedly violent reaction that had been made ludicrous by his superior strength. I had not thought that I cared enough. It was a long time since camp. But he had brought it all back. The time with him had not been pure fiasco, however. I sensed that I had won a very small victory in the talk that had followed the one-sided fight. He was not certain of where I stood, how much I knew. The talk with George had canceled that small victory. George puzzled me. There was a curious under-current in his relationship with Fitz, something I could not understand.

Bartenders are good sources of information. I sensed that the little man was watching me, trying to figure out who I was. I signaled for a refill. When he brought my glass back from the beer tap I said, "What do people do for excitement around this town?"

He had a high, thin voice. "Stranger in town, are you? It's pretty quiet. Saturday night there's things going on here and there. Not much on a weekday. There's some that drive all the way to Redding. There's gambling there, but it's crooked. Then it's easier to meet women there than here. You a salesman?"

I needed a quick answer and I suddenly remembered something that Fitz had said to give me my gimmick, ready-made, and reasonably plausible. "I'm working on a book."

He showed a quick interest. "Writer, are you? What's there here to write about? Historical stuff?"

"No. It's a different kind of a book. I was taken prisoner in Korea. Some of the boys died there, boys I knew. This book is a sort of personal history of those boys. You know, the way they lived, what they did, what they would have come back to if they'd lived. One of them is from this town. Timmy Warden."

"Hell, did you know Timmy? My God, that was a shame. There was a good kid."

"I've been talking to his brother, George, just down the street."

The little man clucked and shook his head. "George has just plain gone to hell the last year or so. He and Timmy had a pretty good setup too. Couple of good businesses. But then George's wife left him. Then he got word Timmy was dead. It took the heart out of him, I guess. He's got about one tenth the business he used to have, and he won't have that long if he keeps hitting the bottle. Buck Stamm's girl has been trying to straighten him out, but she's wasting her time. But that Ruthie is stubborn. I tell you, if Timmy had made it back and if he'd waited until now, he'd have a long uphill fight. George has been selling stuff off and piddling away the money he gets. Lives in a room at White's Hotel. Gets drunk enough to be picked up every now and then. For a while there they'd just take him home because he used to be an important man in this town. Now they let him sober up in the can."

One of the old men playing checkers said, "Stump, you talk too damn much."

"Watch your game," Stump said. "Get some kings. Let smart people talk in peace, Willy."

He turned back to me and said, "How do you figure on writing up Timmy?"

"Oh, just the way he lived. Where he was born. Interview his schoolteachers. Talk to the girls he dated."

Stump glanced at the checker players and then hunched himself over the bar and spoke in a tone so low they couldn't hear him. Stump wore a sly smirk as he talked. "Now I wouldn't stand back of this, and it isn't anything you could put in your book, but I heard it from a pretty good source that before Timmy took off into the army, he and that Eloise Warden were a little better than just plain friends. Know what I mean? She was a good-looking piece, and you can hardly blame the kid, if she was right there asking for it. She was no good, anyway. She took off with a salesman and nobody's seen or heard from her since."

He backed away and gave me a conspiratorial smile. "Of course, George wouldn't know anything about it. Like they say, he'd be the last to know."

"Are there any other relatives in town, beside George?"

"Not a one. Their daddy died six or seven years ago. George got married right after that. Then the three of them, George, Timmy, and Eloise stayed right on in the old Warden place. George sold that this year. Man named Syler bought it. He chopped it up into apartments, I hear."

I talked with him for another half hour, but he didn't have very much to add. He asked me to stop around again. I liked the atmosphere of his bar, but I didn't like him. He was a little too eager to prove he knew everything, particularly the unsavory details.

When I got back to the garage a little after three my car was ready. I paid for the work. It ran smoothly on the way back to the motel south of town. Once I was in my room with the door shut I reviewed everything that had happened. Though I had told my lie about writing up Timmy on impulse, I couldn't see how it could hurt anything. In fact it might make things a good deal easier. I decided that I'd better buy some kind of pocket notebook and write things down so that my story would stand up a little better.

There was no reason why Timmy and the others like him shouldn't be written up. I remembered that a magazine had done the same sort of thing with the progressives who refused repatriation. So why not the dead. They would be more interesting than the turncoats, who, almost without exception, fell into two groups. They were either ignorant and very nearly feeble-minded, or they were neurotic, out-of-balance, with a lifelong feeling of having been rejected. The dead were more interesting.

My one abortive attempt to find Cindy had failed. Using the cover story of writing up Timmy, I should be able to find her. From what Timmy had said, she was a girl who would know of a special hiding place. And the money was there.

Unless Eloise had taken it. I was puzzled by Fitz's insistence that she hadn't taken it.

When I went back into town for dinner I bought a notebook in a drugstore. At dinner I filled three pages with notes. I could have filled more. Timmy had talked a lot. There hadn't been much else to do. I went to a movie, but I couldn't keep my mind on it. The next person to talk to was Ruth Stamm. I could see her the next morning.

But back in the motel room I took another look at Ruth Stamm. I took her picture out of the back of my wallet. Tomorrow, Friday, I would see her for the first time in the flesh. I had looked at this picture a thousand times. Timmy had showed it to me in camp. I remembered the day we sat with our backs against a wall in watery sunshine and he took the picture out and showed it to me.

"That's the one, Tal. I didn't have sense enough to stay with her. That's the good one, Tal. Ruthie Stamm."

They had taken my papers away from me, including the shots of Charlotte. I held the picture of Ruthie Stamm, turning it toward the pale sunshine. It was cracked but none of the cracks touched her face. It was in color and the colors had faded and changed. She sat on her heels and scratched the joyous belly of a blond cocker while she laughed up into the camera eye. She wore yellow shorts and a halter top, and her laughter was fresh and good and shared.

In some crazy way it became our picture—Timmy's and mine. I took it off his body after he died and it became mine. It represented an alien world of sanity and kindness and strength. I looked at it often.

Now I took it out again and lay on the motel bed and looked at it in the lamplight. And felt a tingle of anticipation. For the first time I permitted myself to wonder if this pilgrimage to Hillston was in part due to the picture of a girl I had never seen. And to wonder if this picture had something to do with the death of love for Charlotte.

I put the picture away. It took a long time to get to sleep. But the sleep that came was deep and good.

CHAPTER THREE

On Friday morning it was not until I opened the bureau drawer to take out a clean shirt that I knew somebody had been in the room. I had stacked the clean shirts neatly in one corner of the big middle drawer. They were scattered all over the drawer as if stirred by a hasty hand. I went over all my things and saw more and more evidence of quick, careless search. There was nothing for anyone to find. I had written down nothing about the elusive Cindy.

It did not seem probable that the maid or the woman who had rented me the room had done this. Nor did it seem probable that it had occurred on the previous day while I was out. I checked the door. I distinctly remembered locking it. It was unlocked. That meant someone had come in while I had slept. Fortunately, from long habit, I had put my wallet inside the pillowcase. My money was safe. Some cool morning air came through the door, chilling my face and chest, and I realized I was sweating lightly. I remembered how Fitz could move so quietly at night. I did not like the thought of his being in the room, being able to unlock the door. I did not see how it could have been anyone else. I wondered how he had found the motel so easily. I had given the address to no one. Yet it could not have taken too long on the phone. Maybe an hour or an hour and a half to find where I was registered. It would take patience. But Fitzmartin had waited over a year.

I had breakfast, looked up an address and drove off to see the girl of the cracked, treasured picture—the girl who, unknown to herself, had eased great loneliness, and strengthened frail courage.

Dr. Buck Stamm was a veterinary. His home and place of business was just east of town, a pleasant old frame house with the animal hospital close by. Dogs made a vast clamor when I drove up. They were in individual runways beside the kennels. There were horses in a corral beyond the house.

Dr. Stamm came out into the waiting-room when the bell on the door rang. He was an enormous man with bushy red hair that was turning gray. He had a heavy baritone voice and an impressive frown.

"We're not open around here yet unless it's an emergency, young man."

"No emergency. I wanted to see your daughter for a minute."

"What about?"

"It's a personal matter. I was a friend of Timmy Warden."

He did not look pleased. "I guess I can't stop you from seeing her. She's at the house, wasting time over coffee. Go on up there. Tell her Al hasn't showed up yet and I need help with the feeding. Tell her Butch died in the night and she'll have to phone the Bronsons. Got that?"

"I can remember it."

"And don't keep her too long. I need help down here. Go around to the back door. She's in the kitchen."

I went across the lawn to the house and up the back steps. It was a warm morning and the door was open. The screens weren't on yet. The girl came to the back door. She was medium tall. Her hair was dark red, a red like you can see in old furniture made of cherry wood, oiled and polished so the sun glints fire streaks in it. She wore dungarees and a pale blue blouse. Her eyes were tilted gray, her mouth a bit heavy and quite wide. She had good golden skin tones instead of the blotched pasty white of most redheads. Her figure was lovely. She was twenty-six, or perhaps twenty-seven.

There are many women in the world as attractive as Ruth Stamm. But the expression they wear for the world betrays them. Their faces are arrogant, or petulant, or sensuous. That is all right because their desirability makes up for it, and you know they will be good for a little time and when you have grown accustomed to the beauty, there will be just the arrogance or the petulance left.

But Ruth wore her own face for the world—wore an expression of strength and humility and goodness. Should you become accustomed to her loveliness, there would still be all that left. This was a for-keeps girl. She couldn't be any other way because all the usual poses and artifices were left out of her. This was a girl you could hurt, a girl who would demand and deserve utter loyalty.

"I guess I'm staring," I said.

She smiled. "You certainly are." She tried to make smile and words casual, but in those few moments, as it happens so very rarely, a sharp awareness had been born, an intense and personal curiosity.

I took the picture out of my pocket and handed it to her. She looked at it and then looked sharply at me, eyes narrowed. "Where did you get this?"

"Timmy Warden had it."

"Timmy! I didn't know he had this. Were you at—that place?"

"In the camp with him? Yes. Wait a minute. Your father gave me some messages for you. He says Al hasn't showed up and he needs help with the feeding. And you're to phone the Bronsons that Butch died during the night."

Her face showed immediate concern. "That's too bad."

"Who was Butch?"

"A nice big red setter. Some kid in a jalopy hit him, and didn't even stop. I should phone right away."

"I would like to talk to you when you have more time. Could I take you to lunch today?"

"What do you want to talk to me about?"

The lie was useful again. "I'm doing a book on the ones who didn't come back. I thought you might help fill me in on Timmy. He mentioned you many times."

"We used to go together. I—yes, I'll help all I can. Can you pick me up at twelve-fifteen here?"

"I'll be glad to. And—may I have the picture back?"

She hesitated and then handed it to me. "The girl in this picture was eighteen. That's a long time ago—" She frowned. "You didn't tell me your name yet."

"Howard. Tal Howard."

Our glances met for a few seconds. Again there was that strong awareness and interest. I believe it startled her as much as it did me. The figure in the picture was a girl. This was a woman, a fulfillment of all the promises in the picture—a mature and lovely woman—and we were shyly awkward with each other. She said good-by and went into the house. I drove back into town. For a long time I had carried the picture in the photograph in my mind. Now reality was superimposed on that faded picture. I had imagined that I had idealized the photo image, given it qualities it did not possess. Now at last I knew that the reality was stronger, more persuasive than the dreaming.

I found the old Warden house and chatted for a time with the amiable Mr. Syler who had purchased it from George Warden. It was a big, high-shouldered frame house and he had cut it into four apartments. Mr. Syler needed no encouragement to talk. In fact, it was difficult to get away from him. He complained of the condition of the inside of the house when he took it over. "That George Warden lived here alone for a while and that man must have lived like a darn bear."

In addition he complained about the yard. "When I took it over I didn't expect much grass. But the whole darn place had been spaded up like somebody was going to plant every inch of it and then just left it alone."

That was a clue to some of Fitzmartin's activities. He was a man who would do a good job of searching. And the isolation of the house behind high plantings would give him an uninterrupted opportunity to dig.

I drove back out through April warmth and picked up Ruth Stamm at the time she suggested. She had changed to a white sweater and a dark green skirt. She seemed more reserved, as if she had begun to doubt the wisdom of coming along with me. As we got into the car I said, "How did the Bronsons take it?"

"Very hard. I thought they would. But I talked them into getting another dog right away. That's the best way. Not the same breed, but a new pup, young enough to need and demand attention."

"Where should we have lunch? Where we can talk."

"The coffee shop at the Hillston Inn is nice."

I remembered seeing it. I was able to park almost in front. She led the way back through a bleak lobby and down a half flight of stairs to the coffee shop. It had big dark oak booths upholstered in red quilted plastic. They were doing a good business. The girls were brisk, starched. There was a good smell of steaks and chops.

She accepted the offer of a drink before lunch, and said she'd like an old-fashioned, so I ordered two of them. There was an exceptionally fresh clean look about her. She handled herself casually and well.

"How well did you know Timmy?" she asked me.

"Pretty well. In a deal like that you get to know people well. Whatever they are, it shows. You knew him well, too, I guess."

"We went steady. It started seven years ago. Somehow it seems like longer than seven years. We were seniors in high school when it started. He'd been going with a friend of mine. Judy Currier. They had a sort of spat and they were mad at each other. I was mad at the boy I'd been going with. When he wanted to take me out I went. And we went together from then on. When we graduated we both went up to state college at Redding. He only went two years and then came back to help George. When he quit, I quit, too. We came back here and everybody thought we were going to get married." She smiled a small wry smile. "I guess I did, too. But then things changed. I guess he lost interest. He worked very hard. We drifted apart."

"Were you in love with him?"

She gave me a slightly startled glance. "I thought I was, of course. Otherwise we wouldn't have been as close. But—I don't know as I can explain it. You see, Timmy was very popular in high school. He was a good athlete, and everybody liked him. He was president of the senior class. I was popular, too. I was queen of the senior pageant and all that sort of thing. We both liked to dance and we were good at it. It was as if people *expected* us to go together. It seemed right to other people. And that sort of infected us, I guess. Maybe we fell in love with the way we looked together, and felt the responsibility of what other people wanted us to be. We made a good team. Do you understand that?"

"Of course."

"When it finally ended it didn't hurt as badly as I would have thought it would. If it hadn't ended, we would have gone on and gotten married and—I guess it would have been all right." She looked puzzled.

"What kind of a guy was he, Ruth?"

"I told you. Popular and nice and—"

"Underneath."

"I don't want to feel—disloyal or anything."

"Another drink?"

"No. We better order, thanks." After we had given the order, she frowned beyond me and said, "There was something weak about Timmy. Things had come too easily. His mind was good and his body was good and he made friends without trying. He'd never been—tested. I had the feeling that he thought that things would always be that easy all his life. That he could always get whatever he wanted. It worried me because I'd learned the world isn't like that. It was as though nothing had ever happened to him to make him grow up. And I used to wonder what would happen when things started to go wrong. I knew he'd either turn into a man, or he'd start to whine and complain."

"He turned into a man, Ruth."

There was a sudden look of tears in her eyes. "I'm glad to hear that. I'm very glad to hear that. I wish he'd come back."

"I think you would have seen that I'm right. After he stopped going with you, who did he go with before he went into the army?"

Her eyes were evasive. "No one."

I lowered my voice. "He told me about Eloise."

Her face became more pale. "So it was true, then. I couldn't be completely certain. But I suspected it. It made me sick to think that could be going on. And it was part of the pattern. Everything came so easily. I don't think he even realized what he was doing to himself and to George. She was trash. Everybody was sorry and shocked when George married her."

"Timmy told me about Eloise and he told me he was sorry about it. He wanted to come back so he could make things right. I guess he knew he couldn't turn the clock back and make things like they were before, but he wanted to be able to make amends of some sort."

"I don't think George has ever suspected. But even if he knew now it couldn't hurt too much. He knows what she is now."

"What was she like?"

"Quite pretty in a sort of full-blown way. A tawny blonde, with a kind of gypsy-looking face. I don't know where she got those features. They're not like the other people in her family. She was a year ahead of me in school at first, and then in the same year, and then a year behind me. She never did graduate from high school. She was dumb as a post as far as schoolwork is concerned. But smart in other ways. Very smart. She was sloppy. You know, soiled collars, bare dirty ankles. She always soaked herself in perfume. She had a very sexy walk, full hips and a tiny waist and nice legs. She had a lot of little provocative mannerisms. Boys used to follow her around like stupid dogs, their eyes glazed and their tongues out. We used to make fun of her, but we hated her, and in some funny way we were jealous of her. She did as she pleased. She always seemed to be mocking everybody. It was a very good marriage for her, to marry George. Then the three of them were living in that house. I guess she got bored. Being right there in the house, once she got bored Timmy had as much chance as—hamburger in a panther cage. I guess they were careful, but in a place this size people get to know things. Quite a few people were talking by the time Timmy went away. I hadn't had a date with Timmy for over two years when he went away."

"Then Eloise went off with a salesman."

"That was so stupid of her. She had everything she wanted. George believed in her. The man's name was Fulton. He was a big red-faced man who drove a gray Studebaker and came to Hillston about once every six months. Eloise ran off almost— no, it's over two years ago. George had to be out of town on business. People saw Eloise and Mr. Fulton right here in this place having dinner one night, bold as can be. They must have left that night. When George came back they were gone."

"Did he try to trace her?"

"He didn't want to. He was too badly hurt. She'd packed her prettiest things, and taken the house money and gone without even leaving a note. I'll bet that some day she's going to come crawling back here."

"Would George take her back?"

"I don't know. I don't know what he'd do. I've been trying to help George." She blushed. "Dad always teases me about the way I keep bringing kittens and homeless dogs back to the place. He says my wards eat up all the profits. It's sort of the same with George. He hasn't got anyone now. Not a soul. Not anyone in the world. He's drinking all the time and he's lost most of his business. I do what little I can. Cook for him sometimes. Get his room cleaned up. Get his clothes in shape. But I can't seem to make him wake up. He just keeps going down and down. It makes me sick."

"I saw him at the store. He wasn't in very good shape. He acted strange."

"The store is doing almost no business at all."

"The lumberyard looks all right. I was out there to talk to Fitzmartin. He was in the same camp."

"I know. He told me that. I—is he a good friend of yours?"

"No."

"I don't like him, Tal. He's a strange man. I don't know why George hired him. It's almost as if he had some hold over George. And I have the feeling he keeps pushing George downhill. I don't know how, or why he should. He kept bothering me. He kept coming to see me to talk about Timmy. It seemed very strange."

"What did he want to talk about?"

"It didn't make much sense. He wanted to know where Timmy and I used to go on picnics when we were in high school. He wanted to know if we ever went on hikes together. And he acted so sly about it, so sort of insinuating that the last time he came it made me mad and I told him I wouldn't talk to him any more. It seemed like such a queer thing for him to keep doing. He's creepy, you know. His eyes are so strange and colorless."

"Has he stayed away?"

"Oh yes. I got very positive about it... He had such an unhealthy kind of interest in Timmy I wondered if it was the same sort of thing with you. But if you're going to write about him I can understand your wanting to know things."

The honesty in her level eyes made me feel ashamed. There was an awkward pause in our conversation. She fiddled with her coffee spoon and then, not looking up, said, "Timmy told you about Eloise. Did he tell you about me?" She was blushing again.

"He mentioned you. He didn't say much. I could make something up to make you feel better, but I don't want to do that."

She raised her head to look directly at me, still blushing. "This isn't anything to go in your book. But it's nothing I'm ashamed of. And maybe you can understand him better, or me better, if I tell you. We went steady during our senior year here. A lot of the kids, a lot of our friends, who went steady, taking it for granted that they were going to get married as soon as they could, they slept together. It was almost—taken for granted. But Timmy and I didn't. Then we both went up to Redding. We were both away from home. We were lonely and in a new environment. It—just happened. It got pretty intense for a few months, but we began to realize that it wasn't helping anything. We stopped. Oh, we had a few lapses, accidents. Times it wasn't meant to happen. But we stopped, and felt very proud of our character and so on. You know, I sometimes wonder if that is what spoiled things for us. It's a pretty Victorian attitude to think that way, but you can't help wondering sometimes."

I felt ill at ease with her. I had never come across this particular brand of honesty. She had freely given me an uncomfortable truth about herself, and I felt bound to reciprocate.

I said, too quickly, "I know what you mean. I know what it is to feel guilty from the man's point of view. When they tapped my shoulder I had thirty days grace before I had to report. I had a girl. Charlotte. And a pretty good job. We wondered if we ought to get married before I left. We didn't. But I took advantage of all the corny melodrama. Man going to the wars and so on. I twisted it so she believed it was actually her duty to take full care of the departing warrior. It was a pretty frantic thirty days. So off I went. Smug about the whole thing. What soft words hadn't been able to accomplish, the North Koreans had done. She's a good kid."

"But you're back and you're not married?"

"No. I came back in pretty bad shape. My digestive system isn't back to par yet. I spent quite a while in an army hospital. I got out and went back to my job. I couldn't enjoy it. I used to enjoy it. I couldn't do well at it. And Charlotte seemed like a stranger. At least I had enough integrity not to go back to bed with her. She was willing, in the hopes it would cure the mopes.

I was listless and restless. I couldn't figure out what was wrong with me. Finally they got tired of the way I was goofing off and fired me. So I left. I started this—project. I feel guilty as hell about Charlotte. She was loyal all the time I was gone. She thought marriage would be automatic when I got back. She doesn't understand all this. And neither do I. I only know that I feel guilty and I still feel restless."

"What is she like, Tal?"

"Charlotte? She's dark-haired. Quite pretty. Very nice eyes. She's a tiny girl, just over five feet and maybe a hundred pounds sopping wet. She'd make a good wife. She's quick and clean and capable. She has pretty good taste, and her daddy has yea bucks stashed."

"Maybe you shouldn't feel guilty."

I frowned at her. "What do you mean, Ruth?"

"You said she seems like a stranger. Maybe she is a stranger, Tal. Maybe the *you* who went away would be a stranger to you, too. You said Timmy changed. You could have changed, too. You could have grown up in ways you don't realize. Maybe the Charlotte who was ample for that other Tal Howard just isn't enough of a challenge to this one."

"So I break her heart."

"Maybe better to break her heart this way than marry her and break it slowly and more thoroughly. I can explain better by talking about Timmy and me."

"I don't understand."

"When Timmy lost interest the blow was less than I thought it would be. I didn't know why. Now after all this time I know why. Timmy was a less complicated person than I am. His interests were narrower. He lived more on a physical level than I do. Things stir me. I'm more imaginative than he was. Just as you are more imaginative than he was. Suppose I'd married him. It would have been fine for a time. But inevitably I would have begun to feel stifled. Now don't get the idea that I'm sort of a female long-hair. But I do like books and I do like good talk and I do like all manner of things. And Timmy, with his beer and bowling and sports page attitude, wouldn't have been able to share. So I would have begun to feel like sticking pins in him. Do you understand?"

"Maybe not. I'm the beer, bowling, and sports page type myself."

She watched me gravely. "Are you, Tal?"

It was an uncomfortable question. I remembered the first few weeks back with Charlotte when I tried to fit back into the pattern of the life I had known before. Our friends had seemed vapid, and their conversation had bored me. Charlotte, with her endless yak about building lots, and what color draperies, and television epics, and aren't these darling shoes for only four ninety-five, and what color do you like me best in, and yellow kitchens always look so cheerful—Charlotte had bored me, too.

My Charlotte, curled like a kitten against me in the drive-in movie, wide-eyed and entranced at the monster images on the screen who traded platitudes, had bored me.

I began to sense where it had started. It had started in the camp. Boredom was the enemy. And all my traditional defenses against boredom had withered too rapidly. The improvised game of checkers was but another form of boredom. I was used to being with a certain type of man. He had amused and entertained me and I him. But in the camp he became empty. He with his talk of sexual exploits, boyhood victories, and Gargantuan drunks, he had made me weary just to listen.

The flight from boredom had stretched my mind. I spent more and more time in the company of the off-beat characters, the ones who before capture would have made me feel queer and uncomfortable, the ones I would have made fun of behind their backs. There was a frail headquarters type with a mind stuffed full of things I had never heard of. They seemed like nonsense at first and soon became magical. There was a corporal, muscled like a Tarzan, who argued with a mighty ferocity with a young, intense, mustachioed Marine private about the philosophy and ethics of art, while I sat and listened and felt unknown doors open in my mind.

Ruth's quiet question gave me the first valid clue to my own discontent. Could I shrink myself back to my previous dimensions, I could once again fit into the world of job and

Charlotte and blue draperies and a yellow kitchen and the Saturday night mixed poker game with our crowd.

If I could not shrink myself, I would never fit there again. And I did not wish to shrink. I wished to stay what I had become, because many odd things had become meaningful to me.

"Are you, Tal?" she asked again.

"Maybe not as much as I thought I was."

"You're hunting for something," she said. The strange truth of that statement jolted me. "You're trying to do a book. That's just an indication of restlessness. You're hunting for what you should be, or for what you really are." She grinned suddenly, a wide grin and I saw that one white tooth was entrancingly crooked. "Dad says I try to be a world mother. Pay no attention to me. I'm always diagnosing and prescribing and meddling." She looked at her watch. "Wow! He'll be stomping and thundering. I've got to go right now."

I paid the check and we went out to the car. On the way back I steered the conversation to the point where I could say, "And I remember him talking about a girl named Cindy. Who was she?"

Ruth frowned. "Cindy? I can remember some—No there wasn't any girl named Cindy in this town, not that Timmy would go out with. I'm sure he never knew a pretty one. And for Timmy a girl had to be pretty. Are you certain that's the right name?"

"I'm positive of it."

"But what did he say about her?"

"He just mentioned her casually a few times, but in a way that sounded as though he knew her pretty well. I can't remember exactly what he said, but I got the impression he knew her quite well."

"It defeats me," Ruth said. I turned into the driveway and stopped in front of the animal hospital and got out as she did. We had been at ease and now we were awkward again. I wanted to find some way of seeing her again, and I didn't know exactly how to go about it. I hoped her air of restraint was because she was hoping I would find a way. There had been too many little signs and hints of a surprising and unexpected closeness between us. She could not help but be aware of it.

"I want to thank you, Ruth," I said and put my hand out. She put her hand in mine, warm and firm, and her eyes met mine and slid away and I thought she flushed a bit. I could not be certain.

"I'm glad to help you, Tal. You could—let me know if you think of more questions."

The opening was there, but it was too easy. I felt a compulsion to let her know how I felt. "I'd like to be with you again even if it's not about the book."

She pulled her hand away gently and faced me squarely, chin up. "I think I'd like that, too." She grinned again. "See? A complete lack of traditional female technique."

"I like that. I like it that way."

"We better not start sounding too intense, Tal."

"Intense? I don't know. I carried your picture a long time. It meant something. Now there's a transition. You mean something."

"Do you say things like that just so you can listen to yourself saying them?"

"Not this time."

"Call me," she said. She whirled and was gone. Just before she went in the door I remembered what I meant to ask her. I called to her and she stopped and I went up to her.

"Who should I talk to next about Timmy?"

She looked slightly disappointed. "Oh, try Mr. Leach. Head of the math department at the high school. He took quite an interest in Timmy. And he's a nice guy. Very sweet."

I drove back into town, full of the look of her, full of the impact of her. It was an impact that made the day, the trees, the city, all look more vivid. Her face was special and clear in my mind—the wide mouth, the one crooked tooth, the gray slant of her eyes. Her figure was good, shoulders just a bit too wide, hips just a shade too narrow to be classic. Her legs were long, with clean lines. Her flat back and the inswept lines of her waist were lovely. Her breasts were high and wide spaced, with a flavor of impertinence, almost arrogance. It was the coloring of her though that pleased me most. Dark red of the hair, gray of the eyes, golden skin tones.

It was nearly three when I left her place. I tried to put her out of my mind and think of the interview with Leach. Leach might be the link with Cindy.

I must have been a half mile from the Stamm place when I began to wonder if the Ford coupé behind me was the one I had seen beside Fitz's shed. I made two turns at random and it stayed behind me. There was no attempt at the traditional nuances of shadowing someone. He tagged along, a hundred feet behind me. I pulled over onto the shoulder and got out. I saw that it was Fitz in the car. He pulled beyond me and got out, too.

I marched up to him and said, "What the hell was the idea of going through my room."

He leaned on his car. "You have a nice gentle snore, Howard. Soothing."

"I could tell the police."

"Sure. Tell them all." He squinted in the afternoon sunlight. He looked lazy and amused.

"What good does it do you to follow me?"

"I don't know yet. Have a nice lunch with Ruthie? She's a nice little item. All the proper equipment. She didn't go for me at all. Maybe she likes the more helpless type. Maybe if you work it right you'll get a chance to take her to—"

He stopped abruptly, and his face changed. He looked beyond me. I turned just in time to see a dark blue sedan approaching at a high rate of speed. It sped by us and I caught a glimpse of a heavy balding man with a hard face behind the wheel, alone in the car. The car had out-of-state plates but it was gone before I could read the state.

I turned back to Fitz. "There's no point in following me around. I told you I don't know any more—" I stopped because there was no point in going on. He looked as though I had become invisible and inaudible. He brushed by me and got into his car and drove on. I watched it recede down the road. I got into my own car. The episode made no sense to me.

I shrugged it off my mind and began to think about Leach again.

Though the high-school kids had gone, the doors were unlocked and a janitor, sweeping green compound down the dark-red tiles of the corridor, told me I could probably find Mr. Leach in his office on the ground floor of the old building. The two buildings, new and old, were connected. Fire doors separated the frame building from the steel and concrete one. My steps echoed in the empty corridor with a metallic ring. A demure little girl came out of a classroom and closed the door behind her. She had a heavy armload of books. She looked as shy and gentle and timid as a puppy in a strange yard. She looked at me quickly and hurried on down the corridor ahead of me, moccasin soles slapping, meager horsetail bobbing, shoulders hunched.

I found the right door and tapped on it. A tired voice told me to come in. Leach was a smallish man with a harsh face, jet eyebrows, a gray brushcut. He sat at a table marking papers. His desk, behind him, was stacked with books and more papers.

"Something I can do for you?"

"My name is Tal Howard. I want to talk to you about a student you used to have."

He shook hands without enthusiasm. "An ex-student who is in trouble?"

"No. It's—"

"I'm refreshed. Not in trouble? Fancy that. The faculty has many callers. Federal narcotics people. Parole people. Prison officials. County police. Lawyers. Sometimes it seems that we turn out nothing but criminals of all dimensions. I interrupted you."

"I don't want to impose on you. I can see how busy you are. I'm gathering material about Timmy Warden. Ruth Stamm suggested I talk to you."

He leaned back and rubbed his eyes. "Timmy Warden. Gathering material. That has the sound of a book. Was he allowed to live long enough to give you enough material?"

"Timmy and some others. They all died there in the camp. I was there, too. I almost died, but not quite."

"Sit down. I'm perfectly willing to talk about him. I take it you're not a professional."

"No, sir."

"Then this, as a labor of love, should be treated with all respect. Ruth knows as much about Timmy as any person alive, I should say."

"She told me a lot. And I got a lot from Timmy. But I need more. She said you were interested in him."

"I was. Mr. Howard, you have probably heard of cretins who can multiply two five digit numbers mentally and give the answer almost instantaneously."

"Yes, but—"

"I know. I know. Timmy was no cretin. He was a very normal young man. Almost abnormally normal if you sense what I mean. Yet he had a spark. Creative mathematics. He could sense the—the rhythm behind numbers. He devised unique short cuts in the solution of traditional class problems. He had that rare talent, the ability to grasp intricate relationships and see them in pure simple form. But there was no drive, no dedication. Without dedication, Mr. Howard, such ability is merely facility, an empty cleverness. I hoped to be a mathematician. I teach mathematics in a high school. Merely because I did not have enough of what Timmy Warden was born with. I hoped that one day he would acquire the dedication. But he never had time."

"I guess he didn't."

"Even if he had the time I doubt if he would have gone any further. He was a very good, decent young man. Everything was too easy for him."

"It wasn't easy at the end."

"I don't imagine it was. Nor easy for hundreds of millions of his contemporaries anywhere in the world. This is a bad century, Mr. Howard. Bad for the young. Bad for most of us."

"What do you think would have become of him if he'd lived, Mr. Leach?"

The man shrugged. "Nothing exceptional. Marriage, work, children. And death. No contribution. His name gone as if it never existed. One of the faceless ones. Like us, Mr. Howard." He rubbed his eyes again, then smiled wanly. "I'm not usually so depressing, Mr. Howard. This has been a bad week. This is one of the weeks that add to my conviction that something is eating our young. This week the children have seemed more sullen, dangerous, dispirited, inane, vicious, foolish, and impossible than usual. This week a young sophomore in one of my classes went into the hospital with septicemia as the result of a self-inflicted abortion. And a rather pleasant boy was slashed. And last Monday two seniors died in a head-on collision while on their way back from Redding, full of liquor. The man in the other car is not expected to recover. When Timmy was here in school I was crying doom. But it was not like it is now. By comparison, those were the good old days, recent as they are."

"Was Timmy a disciplinary problem?"

"No. He was lazy. Sometimes he created disturbances. On the whole he was co-operative. I used to hope Ruth would be the one to wake him up. She's a solid person. Too good for him, perhaps."

"I guess he was pretty popular with the girls."

"Very. As with nearly everything else, things were too easy for him."

"He mentioned some of them in camp. Judy, Ruth, Cindy."

"I couldn't be expected to identify them. If I remember correctly, I once had eight Judys in one class. Now that name, thank God, is beginning to die out a little. There have never been too many Cindys. Yet there has been a small, constant supply."

"I want to have a chance to talk to the girls he mentioned. I've talked to Ruth. Judy has moved away. I can't remember Cindy's last name. I wonder if there is any way I could get a look at the list of students in hopes of identifying her."

"I guess you could," he said. "The administration office will be empty by now. You could ask them Monday. Let me see. Timmy graduated in forty-six. I keep old yearbooks here. They're over there on that bottom shelf. You could take the ones for that year and the next two years and look them over, there by the window if you like. I have to get on with these papers. And I really can't tell you much more about Timmy. I liked him and had hopes for him. But he lacked motivation. That seems to be the trouble with too many of the children lately. No motivation.

They see no goal worth working for. They no longer have any dreams. They are content with the manufactured dreams of N.B.C. and Columbia."

I sat by the windows and went through the yearbooks. There was no Cindy in the yearbook for '46. There was one in the '47 yearbook. I knew when I saw her picture that she could not be the one. She was a great fat girl with small, pinched, discontented features, sullen, rebellious little eyes. There was a Cindy in the '48 yearbook. She had a narrow face, protruding teeth, weak eyes behind heavy lenses, an expression of overwhelming stupidity. Yet I marked down their names. It would be worth a try, I thought.

I went back to the '46 yearbook and went through page after page of graduates more thoroughly. I came to a girl named Cynthia Cooper. She was a reasonably attractive snub-nosed blonde. I wondered if Timmy could possibly have said Cynthy. It would be an awkward nickname for Cynthia. And even though his voice by that time had been weak and blurred, I was certain he had said Cindy. He had repeated the name. But I wrote her down, too.

Ruth Stamm's yearbook picture was not very good. But the promise of her, the clear hint of what she would become, was there in her face. Her activities, listed under the picture, made a long list. It was the same with Timmy. He grinned into the camera.

Mr. Leach looked up at me when I stood near his table. "Any luck?"

"I took down some names. They might help."

I thanked him for his help. He was bent over his papers again before I got to the door. Odd little guy, with his own strange brand of dedication and concern. Pompous little man, but with an under-current of kindness.

I got to the Hillston Inn at a little after five. I got some dimes from the cashier and went over to where four phone booths stood flanked against the lobby wall. I looked up the last name of the fat girl, Cindy Waskowitz. There were two Waskowitzes in the book. John W. and P. C. I tried John first. A woman with a nasal voice answered the phone.

"I'm trying to locate a girl named Cindy Waskowitz who graduated from Hillston High in nineteen forty-seven. Is this her home?"

"Hold it a minute," the woman said. I could hear her talking to someone else in the room. I couldn't make out what she was saying. She came back on the line. "You want to know about Cindy."

"That's right. Please."

"This wasn't her home. But I can tell you about her. I'm her aunt. You want to know about her?"

"Please."

"It was the glands. I couldn't remember the word. My daughter just told me. The glands. When she got out from high school she weighed two hundred. From there she went up like balloons. Two hundred, two fifty, three hundred. When she died in the hospital she was nearly four hundred. She'd been over four hundred once, just before she went in the hospital. Glands, it was."

I remembered the rebellious eyes. Girl trapped inside the prison of white, soft flesh. A dancing girl, a lithe, quick-moving girl forever lost inside that slow inevitable encroachment. Stilled finally, and buried inside her suet prison.

"Is your daughter about the same age Cindy would have been?"

"A year older. She's married and three kids already." The woman chuckled warmly.

"Could I talk to your daughter?"

"Sure. Just a minute."

The daughter's voice was colder, edged with thin suspicion. "What goes on anyhow? Why do you want to know about Cindy?"

"I was wondering if she was ever friendly in high school with a boy named Timmy Warden."

"Timmy is dead. It was in the papers."

"I know that. Were they friendly?"

"Timmy and Cindy? Geez, that's a tasty combination. He would have known who she was on account of her being such a tub. But I don't think he ever spoke to her. Why should he? He had all the glamour items hanging around his neck. Why are you asking all this?"

"I was in the camp with him. Before he died he gave me a message to deliver to a girl named Cindy. I wondered if Cindy was the one."

"Not a chance. Sorry. You just got the wrong one."

"Was there another Cindy in the class?"

"In one of the lower classes. A funny-looking one. That's the only one I can remember. All teeth. Glasses. A sandy sort of girl. I can't remember her last name, though."

"Cindy Kirschner?"

"That's the name. Gosh, I don't know where you'd find her. I think I saw her downtown once a year ago. Maybe it's in the book. But I don't think she'd fit any better than my cousin. I mean Timmy Warden ran around with his own group, kind of. Big shots in the school. That Kirschner wasn't in that class, any more than my cousin. Or me."

The bitterness was implicit in her tone. I thanked her again. She hung up.

I tried Kirschner. There was only one in the book. Ralph J. A woman answered the phone.

"I'm trying to locate a Cindy Kirschner who graduated from Hillston High in nineteen forty-eight."

"That's my daughter. Who is this calling, please?"

"Could you tell me how I could locate her?"

"She married, but she doesn't have a phone. They have to use the one at the corner store. She doesn't like to have people call her there because it's a nuisance to the people at the store. And she has small children she doesn't like to leave to go down there and answer the phone. If you want to see her, you could go out there. It's sixteen ten Blackman Street. It's near the corner of Butternut. A little blue house. Her name is Mrs. Rorick now. Mrs. Pat Rorick. What did you say your name is?"

I repeated the directions and said, "Thanks very much, Mrs. Kirschner. I appreciate your help. Good-by."

I hung up. I was tempted to try Cynthia Cooper, but decided I had better take one at a time, eliminate one before starting the next. I stepped out of the booth. Earl Fitzmartin stepped out of the adjoining booth. He smiled at me almost genially.

"So it's got something to do with somebody named Cindy."

"I don't know what you're talking about."

"'I was in camp with Timmy. Before he died he gave me a message to deliver to a girl named Cindy.' So you try two Cindy's in a row. And you know when they graduated. Busy, aren't you?"

"Go to hell, Fitz."

He stood with his big hard fists on his hips, rocking back and forth from heel to toe, smiling placidly at me. "You're busy, Tal. Nice little lunch with Ruth. Trip to the high school. Tracking down Cindy. Does she know where the loot is?"

He was wearing a dark suit, well cut. It looked expensive. His shoes were shined, his shirt crisp. I wished I'd been more alert. It's no great trick to stand in one phone booth and listen to the conversation in the adjoining one. I hadn't even thought of secrecy, of making certain I couldn't be overheard. Now he had almost as much as I did.

"How did you get along with George, Howard?"

"I got along fine."

"Strange guy, isn't he?"

"He's a little odd."

"And he's damn near broke. That's a shame, isn't it?"

"It's too bad."

"The Stamm girl comes around and holds his hand. Maybe it makes him feel better. Poor guy. You know he even had to sell the cabin. Did Timmy ever talk about the cabin?"

He had talked about it when we were first imprisoned. I'd forgotten about it until that moment. I remembered Timmy saying that it was on a small lake, a rustic cabin their father had built. He and George had gone there to fish, many times.

"He mentioned it," I said.

"I heard about it after I got here. It seemed like a good place. So I went up there with my little shovel. No dice, Tal. I dug up most of the lake shore. I dug a hundred holes. See how nice I am to you? That's one more place where it isn't. Later on

George let me use it for a while before he sold it. It's nice up there. You'd like it. But it's clean."

"Thanks for the information."

"I'm keeping an eye on you, Tal. I'm interested in your progress. I'll keep in touch."

"You do that."

"Blackman runs east off Delaware. It starts three blocks north of here. Butternut must be about fourteen blocks over. It's not hard to find."

"Thanks."

I turned on my heel and left him. It was dusk when I headed out Blackman. I found Butternut without difficulty. I found the blue house and parked in front.

As I went up the walk toward the front door the first light went on inside the house. I pushed the bell and she opened the door and looked out at me, the light behind her, child in her arms.

"Mrs. Rorick?"

"I'm Mrs. Rorick," she said. Her voice was soft and warm and pleasant.

"You were Cindy Kirschner then. I was a friend of Timmy Warden in prison camp."

She hesitated for a moment and then said, "Won't you come in a minute."

When I was inside and she had turned toward the light I could see her better. The teeth had been fixed. Her face was fuller. She was still a colorless woman with heavy glasses, but now there was a pride about her, a confidence that had been lacking in the picture I had seen. Another child sat on a small tricycle and gave me a wide-eyed stare. Both children looked very much like her. Mrs. Rorick did not ask me to sit down.

"How well did you know Timmy, Mrs. Rorick?"

"I don't think he ever knew I was alive."

"In camp, before he died, he mentioned a Cindy. Could you have been the one?"

"I certainly doubt that."

It confused me. I said, "When I mentioned him you asked me to come in. I thought—"

She smiled. "I guess I'll have to tell you. I had the most fantastic and awful crush on him. For years and years. It was pathetic. Whenever we were in the same class I used to stare at him all the time. I wrote letters to him and tore them up. I sent him unsigned cards at Easter and Valentine Day and Christmas and on his birthday. I knew when his birthday was because once a girl I knew went to a party at his house. It was really awful. It gave me a lot of miserable years. Now it seems funny. But it wasn't funny then. It started in the sixth or seventh grade. He was two grades ahead. It lasted until he graduated from high school. He had a red knit cap he wore in winter. I stole it from the cloakroom. I slept with it under my pillow for months and months. Isn't that ridiculous?"

She was very pleasant. I smiled back at her. "You got over it."

"Oh, yes. At last. And then I met Pat. I'm sorry about Timmy. That was a terrible thing. No, if he mentioned any Cindy it wasn't me. Maybe he would know me by sight. But I don't think he'd know my name."

"Could he have meant some other Cindy?"

"It would have to be some other Cindy. But I can't think who. There was a girl named Cindy Waskowitz but it couldn't have been her, either. She's dead now."

"Can you think of who it could be?"

She frowned and shook her head slowly. "N—No, I can't. There's something in the back of my mind, though. From a long time ago. Something I heard, or saw. I don't know. I shouldn't even try to guess. It's so vague. No, I can't help you."

"But the name Cindy means something?"

"For a moment I thought it did. It's gone now. I'm sorry."

"If you remember, could you get in touch with me?"

She smiled broadly. "You haven't told me who you are."

"I'm sorry. My name is Howard. Tal Howard. I'm staying at the Sunset Motel. You could leave a message there for me."

"Why are you so interested in finding this Cindy?"

I could at least be consistent. "I'm writing a book. I need all the information about Timmy that I can get."

"Put in the book that he was kind. Put that in."

"In what way, Mrs. Rorick?"

She shifted uneasily. "I used to have dreadful buck teeth. My people could never afford to have them fixed. One day—that's when I was in John L. Davis School, that's the grade school where Timmy went, too, and it was before they built the junior high, I was in the sixth grade and Timmy was in the eighth. A boy came with some funny teeth that stuck way out like mine. He put them in his mouth in assembly and he was making faces at me. I was trying not to cry. A lot of them were laughing. Timmy took the teeth away from the boy and dropped them on the floor and smashed them under his heel. I never forgot that. I started working while I was in high school and saving money. I had enough after I was out to go to get my teeth straightened. But it was too late to straighten them then. So I had them taken out. I wanted marriage and I wanted children, and the way I was no man would even take me out." She straightened her shoulders a little. "I guess it worked," she said.

"I guess it did."

"So put that in the book. It belongs in the book."

"I will."

"And if I can remember that other, I'll phone you, Mr. Howard."

I thanked her and left. I drove back toward the center of town. I began to think of Fitz again. Ruth was right when she used the word creepy. But it was more than that. You sensed that Fitz was a man who would not be restrained by the things that restrain the rest of us. He had proved in the camp that he didn't give a damn what people thought of him. He depended on himself to an almost psychopathic extent. It made you feel helpless in trying to deal with him. You could think of no appeal that would work. He couldn't be scared or reasoned with. He was as primitive and functional as the design of an ax. He could not even be anticipated, because his logic was not of normal pattern. And then, too, there was the startling physical strength.

In camp I had seen several minor exhibitions of that power, but only one that showed the true extent of it. Those of us who saw it talked about it a long time. The guards who saw it treated Fitz with uneasy respect after that. One of the supply trucks became mired inside the compound, rear duals down to the hubs. They broke a towline trying to snake it out. Then they rounded up a bunch of us to unload the supply truck. The cases aboard had obviously been loaded on with a winch. We got all the stuff off except one big wooden packing case. We never did learn what was in it. We only knew it was heavy. We were trying to get a crude dolly under it, but when we tilted it, we couldn't get the dolly far enough back. Every guard was yelling incomprehensible orders. I imagine Fitz lost patience. He jumped up into the bed of the truck, put his back against the case, squatted and got his fingers under the edge. Then he came up with it, his face a mask of effort, cords standing out on his throat. He lifted it high enough so the dolly could be put under it. He lowered it again and jumped down off the truck, oddly pale and perspiring heavily.

Once it was rolled to the tail gate on the dolly, enough men could get hold of it to ease it down. When it was on the ground one of the biggest of the guards swaggered up, grinning at his friends, and tried to do what Fitz had done. He couldn't budge it. He and one of his friends got it up a few inches, but not as high as Fitz had. They were humiliated and they took it out on the rest of us, but not on Fitz. He was left alone.

Back in town I decided I would have a drink at the Inn and a solitary meal and try to think of what the next step should be. I was picked up in front of the Inn, ten steps from my car.

CHAPTER FIVE

There were two of them. One was a thin, sandy man in uniform and the other was a massive middle-aged man in a gray suit with a pouched, florid face.

"Your name Howard?"

"Yes, it is."

"Police. Come on along."

"What for?"

"Lieutenant wants to talk to you."

I went along. They put me in a police sedan and drove about eight blocks and turned into an enclosed courtyard through a gray stone arch. Other cars were parked there. They took me through a door that was one of several opening onto the courtyard. We went up wide wooden stairs that were badly worn to the second floor. It was an old building with an institutional smell of dust, carbolic, and urine. We went by open doors. One door opened onto a big file room with fluorescent lights and gray steel filing cases. Some men played cards in another room. I could hear the metallic gabbling voice of some sort of communication system.

We turned into a small office where a thin, bald man sat behind a desk that faced the door. His face was young, with a swarthy Indian harshness about it, black brows. His hands were large. He looked tall. A small wooden sign on his desk said *Det. Lt. Stephen D. Prine*. The office had cracked buff plaster walls. Books and pamphlets were piled in disorder in a glass-front bookcase. A smallish man with white hair and a red whisky face sat half behind Lieutenant Prine, on the small gilded radiator in front of the single window.

One of the men behind me gave me an unnecessary push that made me thump my knee against the front of the desk and almost lose my balance. Prine looked at me with complete coldness.

"This is that Howard," one of the men behind me said.

"Okay." The door behind me closed. I glanced back and saw that the man in uniform had left. The big man in the gray suit leaned against the closed door. "Empty your pockets onto the desk," Prine said. "Everything."

"But—"

"Empty your pockets." There was no threat in the words. Cold, bored command.

I put everything on the desk. Wallet, change, pen and pencil, notebook, cigarettes, lighter, penknife, folder of traveler's checks. Prine reached a big hand over and separated the items into two piles, notebook, wallet, and checks in one pile that he pulled toward him.

"Put the rest of that stuff back in your pockets."

"Could I ask why—"

"Shut up."

I stood in uncomfortable silence while he went through my wallet. He looked carefully at every card and piece of paper, at the photograph of Charlotte, at the reduced Photostat of my discharge laminated in plastic. He went through the notebook and then examined the traveler's checks.

"Now answer some questions." He opened a desk drawer, flipped a switch, and said, "April 20, seven-ten p.m., interrogation by Lieutenant Prine of suspect picked up by Hillis and Brubaker in vicinity of Hillston Inn. What is your full name?"

"Talbert Owen Howard."

"Speak a little louder. Age and place of birth."

"Twenty-nine. Bakersfield, California."

"Home address."

"None at the present time."

"What was your last address?"

"Eighteen Norwalk Road, San Diego."

"Are you employed?"

"No."

"When were you last employed and by who?"

"Up until two and a half weeks ago. By the Guaranty Federated Insurance Company. I had a debit. Health and life. I was fired."

"For what reason?"

"I wasn't producing."

"How long did you work for them?"

"Four years all together. Three and a half before the Korean war. The rest of it since I got back."

"Are you married? Have you ever been married?"

"No."

"Parents living?"

"No."

"Brothers or sisters?"

"One sister. Older than I am. She lives in Perth, Australia. She was a Wave and she married an Aussie during the war."

"Do you have any criminal record?"

"N—No."

"You don't seem sure."

"I don't know if you'd call it a criminal record. It was when I was in school. One of those student riots. Disturbing the peace and resisting an officer."

"Were you booked and mugged and fingerprinted and found guilty?"

"Yes. I paid a fine and spent three days in jail."

"Then you have a criminal record. How long have you been in Hillston?"

"I arrived here—Wednesday night. Two days."

"What is your local address?"

"The Sunset Motel."

"On this vehicle registration, do you own the vehicle free and clear?"

"Yes."

"You have a little over a thousand dollars. Where did you get it?"

"I earned it. I saved it. I'm getting a little sick of all this. It's beginning to make me sore."

"Why did you come to Hillston?"

"Do I have to have a reason?"

"Yes. You need a reason."

"I knew Timmy Warden in prison camp. And I knew others there that didn't come back. I'm going to write a book about them. There's my notes. You have them there."

"Why didn't you tell George Warden that?"

"I didn't know how he'd take it."

"You didn't tell Fitzmartin, either?"

"He has no reason to know my business."

"But you went out there to see him. And you were both in the same camp with Timmy Warden. It would seem natural to tell him."

"I don't care how it seems. I didn't tell him."

"If a man came to town with a cooked-up story about writing a book, it would give him a chance to nose around, wouldn't it?"

"I guess it would."

"What else have you written?"

"Nothing else."

"Are you familiar with the state laws and local ordinances covering private investigators?"

I stared at him blankly. "No."

"Are you licensed in any state?"

"No. I don't know what—"

"If you were licensed, it would be necessary for you to find out whether this state has any reciprocal agreement. If so, you would merely have to make a courtesy call and announce your presence in this county and give the name of your employer."

"I don't know what you're talking about."

"Do you know a woman named Rose Fulton?"

"No. I've never heard of her."

"Were you employed by Rose Fulton to come to Hillston?"

"No. I told you I never heard of her."

"We were advised a month ago that Rose Fulton had hired an investigator to come here on an undercover assignment. We've been looking for the man. He would be the third one she's sent here. The first two made a botch of their job. There was no job here for them in the first place. Rose Fulton is a persistent and misguided woman. The case, if there was any case, was completely investigated by this department. Part of our job is to keep citizens of Hillston from being annoyed and persecuted by people who have no business here. Is that clear to you?"

"I don't understand what you're talking about. I really don't."

He looked at me for what seemed a long time. Then he said, "End of interrogation witnessed by Brubaker and Sparkman. Copies for file. Prine." He clicked the switch and closed the desk drawer. He leaned back in his chair and yawned, then pushed my wallet, checks, and notebook toward me. "It's just this, Howard. We get damned tired of characters nosing around here. The implication is that we didn't do our job. The hell we didn't. This Rose Fulton is the wife of the guy who ran off with George Warden's wife, Eloise."

"That name Fulton sounded familiar, but I didn't know why."

"It happened nearly two years ago. The first inquiry came from the company Fulton worked for. We did some hard work on it. Fulton was in town for three days. He was registered at the Hillston Inn. He stayed there every time he was in town. On the last night he was here, Friday night, he had dinner at the hotel with Eloise Warden. She waited in the lobby and he checked out. They got in his car. They drove to the Warden house. Eloise went in. Fulton waited out in the car. It was the evening of the eleventh of April. A neighbor saw him waiting and saw her come out to the car with a big suitcase. They drove off. George Warden hadn't reported it to us. He knew what the score was when he got back to town and saw the things she'd taken. It was an open and shut situation. It happens all the time. But Rose Fulton can't bring herself to believe that her dear husband would take off with another woman. So she keeps sicking these investigators on us. You could be the third. I don't think so. No proof. Just a hunch. She thinks something happened to him here. We know nothing happened to him here. I've lost patience, so this time we're making it tough. You can go. If I happen to be wrong, if you happen to be hired by that crazy dame, you better keep right on going, friend. We've got a small force here, but we know our business."

The big middle-aged man moved away from the door to let me out. There was no offer of a ride back to where they had picked me up. I walked. The walk wasn't long enough. By the time I got to the Inn I was still sore at Prine and company. I could grudgingly admit that maybe he thought he had cause to swing his weight around. But I didn't like being picked up like that. And it had irritated me to have to tell them I had no job, no permanent residence. I wasn't certain what legal right they had to take that sort of a statement from me.

I had a drink at the dark bar at the end of the cocktail lounge at the Inn. Business was light. I nursed my drink and wondered how they had picked me up so quickly. I guessed it was from the motel register. I'd had to write down the make of my car and the license number. They'd known who I'd talked to and what had been said. It was a small city and they acted like men who made a business of knowing what was going on.

Just as I ordered the second drink I saw a big man come in and stand at the other end of the bar. He looked like the man I had seen in the blue sedan. But I couldn't be certain. I had forgotten him and the effect he had had on Fitzmartin. He became aware of my interest. He turned and gave me a long look and turned back to the drink the bartender put in front of him. He had moved his head slowly when he turned to look at me. His eyes were in shadow. I had a sudden instinctive premonition of danger. Fitz was danger, but a known quantity. I did not know this man or where he fitted in. I did not want to attempt to ask him. He finished his drink quickly and left. I looked down into my drink and saw myself lying dead, sprawled, cold. It was a fantasy that had been with me in the prison camp and later. You think of your own death. You try to imagine how it will be—to just cease, abruptly, eternally. It is a chilling thought, and once you have started it, it is difficult to shake off.

The depression stayed with me the rest of the evening. Thoughts of Ruth, of the new emphasis she had brought into my life, did little to relieve the blackness and the hint of fear. My mission in Hillston seemed pointless. It was part of running away from myself. There was no chance of finding the money and even if there was and I did find it, I couldn't imagine it changing anything. Somehow I had become a misfit in my world, in my time. I had been jolted out of one comfortable rut, and there seemed to be no other place where I could fit. Other than Charlotte—and, too optimistically, Ruth—I could think of no one who gave a special damn whether I lived or died.

After the light was out I lay in darkness and surrendered myself to the great waves of bathos and self-pity. I wondered what would become of me. I wondered how soon I would be dead. I wondered how many other lonely beds there would be, and where they would be. Finally I fell asleep.

CHAPTER SIX

Saturday morning was dreary, with damp winds, low, scudding clouds, lights on in the stores. I couldn't get a better line on the Cooper girl until the administration office at the high school opened on Monday. The few leads had faded away into nothing. I wondered what I would do with the day.

After buying some blades and some tooth paste, I drove around for a while and finally faced the fact that I was trying to think of a good excuse to see Ruth Stamm. I went without an excuse. She was in the reception office at the animal hospital. She gave me a quick, warm smile as I walked in. A woman sat holding a small shivering dog, waiting her turn. There was a boy with a Siamese cat on a leash. The cat, dainty and arrogant, purposefully ignored the shivering dog.

Ruth, smiling, asked in a low voice, "More questions?"

"No questions. Just general depression."

"Wrong kind of hospital, Tal."

"But the right kind of personnel."

"Need some kind of therapy?"

"Something like that."

She looked at her watch. "Come back at twelve. We close at noon on Saturday. I'll feed you and we'll cook up something to do."

The day was not as dreary when I drove away. I returned at twelve. I went up to the house with her, and the three of us ate in the big kitchen. Dr. Buck Stamm was a skilled storyteller. Apparently every misfortune that could happen to a veterinary had happened to him. He reviled his profession, and his own stupidity in getting into it in the first place. After a cigar he went off to make farm calls. I helped Ruth with a few dishes.

"How about a plain old tour of the surrounding country," she suggested. "There are parts that are very nice."

"Then dinner tonight and a movie or something?"

"Sold. It's Saturday night."

She changed to slacks and a tweed jacket over a yellow sweater and we took my car. She gave me the directions. We took small back roads. It was pretty country, with rolling hills and spines of rock that stuck out of the hills. In the city the day had been gloomy. Out in the country it was no better, but the breeze seemed moist with spring. The new leaves were a pale green. She sat slouched in the seat with one knee up against the glove compartment and pointed out the farms, told me about the people, told me about the history of the area.

At her suggestion I took a back road that led to a place called Highland Lake. She told me when to slow down. When we came to a dirt road we turned right. A mile down the slippery, muddy road was a sign that said *B. Stamm*. I went cautiously down an overgrown drive through the woods until we came to a small cabin with a big porch overlooking a small lake less than a mile long and half as wide. I could see other cabins in the trees along the lake shore.

We went onto the cabin porch and sat on the railing and smoked and talked and watched the quick winds furrow the lake surface.

"We don't get up here as much as we used to when Mother was alive. Dad talks about selling it, but I don't think he will. He hunts up here in the fall. It's only eighteen miles from town, the shortest way. It's pretty primitive, but you know, Tal, this would be a good place to write."

I felt again a quick, sharp pang of guilt.

Her enthusiasm grew. "Nobody is using it. There's no electricity, but there are oil lamps and a Coleman lantern. There's plenty of wood in the shed, and one of those little gasoline stoves. The bunks are comfortable and there's lots of blankets. It would save paying rent. I know Dad wouldn't mind a bit."

"Thanks, Ruth, but really I couldn't—"

"Why not? It's only a half hour to town."

"I don't think I'll be here long enough to make it worth while moving in."

"Well, then," she said, "okay." And I thought I detected some disappointment in her tone. "I'd like you to see it, anyhow." The key was hidden on one of the roof supports near the door. We went inside. It was bare, but it looked clean and comfortable. There were fish rods on a wall rack, and a big stone fireplace.

"It's nice," I said.

"I've always loved it. I'd make a wild row if Dad ever tried to sell it. The first time I came up here they had to bring play pen and high chair. I learned to swim here. I broke my collarbone falling out of one of those top bunks in there."

She smiled at me. We were standing quite close together. There was something both warm and wistful about her smile. There was a long silence in the room. I could hear birds and a far-off drone of an outboard motor. Our eyes locked once more and her smile faded as her mouth softened. There was a heaviness about her eyes, a look almost of drowsiness. We took a half step toward each other and she came neatly, graciously into my arms as though it were an act we had performed many times. The kiss was gentle at first and then fierce and hungry; as she strained upward against me my hands felt the long smoothness of her back, and her arm was crooked hard around my neck.

We wavered in dizzy balance and I side-stepped quickly to catch our balance and we parted awkwardly, shy as children.

"Tal," she said. "Tal, I—" Her voice was throaty and unfocused.

"I know," I said. "I know."

She turned away abruptly and walked slowly to the window and looked out across the lake. I followed her and put my hands lightly on her shoulders. I felt shamed by all this, shamed by my lies, and afraid of what would happen when she found out about me.

I felt new tension in her body and she leaned closer to the window and seemed to peer more intently.

"What's the matter?"

"Look. Isn't that some kind of animal over there? Directly across. That was the Warden camp before George sold it. The one with the green roof. Now look just to the right of the porch." I looked and saw something bulky, partially screened by brush. It looked as if it could be a bear. She brushed by me and came back with a pair of binoculars. She focused them and said, "It's a man. Here. You look."

I adjusted them to my eyes. The man was getting to his feet. He was a big man in a brown suit. He was hatless and his hair was thin on top and he had a wide, hard-looking face. It was the man who had driven by Fitz and me in the blue sedan, the man who had come into the bar at the Inn. He brushed the knees of his brown suit and dusted his hands together. He bent over and picked up what looked to be a long dowel or a piece of reinforcing rod.

"Let me look," she said and took the binoculars again. "I know the people who bought the camp from George. That isn't the man."

"Maybe he's a service man of some kind."

"I don't think so. I know most of them. Now he's going up on the porch. He's trying the door. Hey! He broke a window right next to the door. Now he's getting it up. Now he's stepping in over the sill." She turned to me, her eyes wide. "How about that? Tal, he's a thief! We better go over there."

"Anything you say. But how about the law?"

"Wait a minute." She hurried into the bedroom. She came back with a .22 target pistol and a box of shells. It was a long-barreled automatic. She thumbed the clip out and loaded it expertly, snapped the clip back in and handed me the gun. "You'll be more impressive with it than I would. Come on."

There was no road that led directly around the lake. We had to go about four miles out of our way to get to the road on the other side of the lake. A dark blue sedan was parked at the head of the driveway, facing out. There wasn't room to drive by. I parked and we went down the trail toward the camp. I turned and motioned her to stay back. I went ahead but I heard her right behind me. The man came walking around the corner of the camp, frowning. He stopped short when he saw me, his eyes flicking toward the gun and then toward Ruth.

"Why did you break into that camp?" Ruth demanded angrily.

"Take it easy, lady. Put the gun away, friend."

"Answer the question," I said, keeping the gun on him.

He acted so unimpressed that I felt ridiculous holding the gun.

"I'm a licensed private investigator, friend. Don't put any hole in me while I'm getting my wallet. I'll show you."

He took the wallet out. He took out a card encased in plastic and nipped it toward us. Ruth picked it up. It had his picture and a thumb print and two official looking countersignatures and it said he was licensed by the State of Illinois. His name was Milton D. Grassman. The card said he was forty-one years old, six foot one, and weighed two hundred and five.

"But what are you investigating?" Ruth asked.

He smiled. "Just investigating. And who are you, lady? Maybe you're trespassing." His smile was half good humor, half contempt.

"You're working for Rose Fulton, aren't you?" I asked.

The smile was gone instantly. He didn't seem to move or breathe. I had the impression that a very good mind behind that flat, tough face was working rapidly.

"I'm afraid I don't know the name," he said. But he had waited too long. "Who are you, friend?"

"We're going to report this to the police," Ruth said.

"Go ahead, lady. Be a good citizen. Give them the word."

"Come on, Tal," she said. We went back up the trail. When we got into the car I looked back and saw him standing by his car, watching us. He didn't take his eyes off us while he lit a cigarette and shook the match out.

Ruth was oddly silent as I drove back toward the Stamm camp. Finally I said, "What's the matter?"

"I don't know. At first I thought you lied to me. Then I believed you. Now I don't know."

"How come?"

"You know what I'm thinking. You asked him about a Rose Fulton. It shocked him when you asked him that. Anybody could see that. Eloise Warden ran away with a man named Fulton. What would make you think to ask that Mr. Grassman that question?" She turned to face me. "What are you doing in Hillston, Tal? If that's your name."

"I told you what I'm doing."

"Why did you ask that man that question?"

"The police picked me up last night. They had word that Rose Fulton had hired another man to come here. This will be the third. They thought I was that man. They interrogated me and then they let me go. So I guessed that maybe he was the man."

We got out of the car. She was still looking at me oddly. "Tal, if you're here to write up Timmy, I think you would have told me that before now. It's a cute and interesting little story if you were here just to write up Timmy. And I can't believe that you could have forgotten it."

"I just didn't—think of telling it."

"That's no good, Tal."

"I know it isn't."

"What's wrong? Is it something you can't tell me?"

"Look, Ruth. I—There is another reason why I came. I lied to you. I don't want to tell you why I came here. I'd rather not."

"But it has something to do with Timmy."

"That's right."

"He is dead, isn't he?"

"He's dead."

"But how can I know when you're lying and when you're not?"

"I guess you can't," I said helplessly.

She locked the camp and, on the way back, told me which turns to take. She had nothing else to say. I drove into her place. She opened the door quickly to get out.

"Wait a minute, Ruth."

Her right foot was on the ground. She sat on the corner of the seat and turned and looked back at me. "Yes?"

"I'm sorry about this."

"You've made me feel like a fool. I talked a lot to you. I believed you and so I told you things I've never told anybody. Just to help you when you had no intention of writing up Timmy."

"I tell you, I'm sorry."

"That doesn't do very much good. But I'll give you this much benefit of the doubt, Tal. Look right at me and tell me that you have no reason to be ashamed of why you came here."

I looked into the gray eyes and, like Grassman, I hesitated too long. She slammed the car door and went to the house without looking back. Saturday night was no longer a nice thing to think about. Somehow, through impulsiveness and through awkwardness, I had trapped myself. I felt as if I had lost a great deal more than a Saturday night date. She was not a girl you could lie to. She was not a girl you would want to lie to. My little cover story now seemed soiled and dingy. I drove into town. I started my drinking at the Hillston Inn.

Before I left the Inn I cashed two traveler's checks. I hit a great many bars. It was Saturday night. The city seemed alive. I can remember seeing the dwarf bartender. There was a woman I bought drinks for. At one time I was in a men's room and four of us were singing. The door was locked and somebody was pounding on it. We were making fine music. I was sick in a hedge and I couldn't find my car. I wandered a long time before I found it. I don't know what time it was. It was late. I had to keep one eye closed as I drove cautiously out to the motel. Otherwise the center line was double.

I parked the car in front of my motel room and went, unwashed, to bed. Sunday was a replica, a sodden day in town, a drunken day.

It was eleven when I got up on Monday morning. A half dozen glasses of water made me feel bloated but didn't quench my thirst. My head pounded in a dull, ragged rhythm. I shaved slowly, painfully. The shower made me feel a little better. I decided that it was time to go. Time to leave this place. I didn't know where I would head for. Any place. Any kind of a job. Some kind of manual labor. Get too bushed to think.

I packed my two bags. I left them inside the door and went out to unlock the trunk. All the transient cars were gone. A big dog stood with his feet against the side of my car, looking in the side window. The cold, thin, birdlike woman was carrying sheets and towels out of one of the other rooms and dumping them into a hamper on wheels.

The dog jumped back as I walked out. He stood twenty feet away and whined in a funny way. I made as though to throw gravel at him and he went farther back. I didn't know what attracted him to my car.

I happened to glance inside as I was heading to unlock the trunk. I stopped and looked for a long time. It seemed an effort to take my eyes away. A big body was on the floor in the back, legs bent, head tilted sideways. It was Milton Grassman. He still wore the brown suit. The knees showed traces of pale dried mud. The forehead, in the area where the thin hairline had started, was broken jelly, an ugly, sickening depression. No man could have lived more than a moment with a wound like that.

I realized the woman was calling to me in her thin voice.

I turned and said, "What?"

"I said are you staying another day?"

"Yes. Yes, I'm staying another day."

She went into another room. She was working her way toward mine. I hurried back in. I put one bag in the closet, opened the other one, put my toilet articles back in the bathroom. I slammed the door and went out. The dog was standing by the car again, whining. I got behind the wheel and drove out of there. I drove away from town. I didn't want to be stopped by a traffic light where anybody could look down into the back of the car. I remembered an old tarp in the back. I pulled off onto the shoulder and got the tarp. I waited while traffic went by and then spread the tarp over Grassman. I tried not to look at him while I did it. But I couldn't help seeing his face. The slackness of death had ironed everything out of it, all expression.

I drove on aimlessly and then stormed again on the shoulder of the highway. I wanted to be able to think. I could feel the dreadful presence of the body behind me. My brain felt frozen, numbed, useless. It did no good to wonder when the body had been put there. I couldn't even remember the places where I had parked.

Why had it been put in my car? Somebody wanted to get rid of it. Somebody wanted to divert suspicion from himself. From the look of the wound, murder had been violent and unplanned. One tremendous, skull-smashing blow. It was inevitable that I should begin to think of Fitz. Of the people I knew in Hillston, he was the one capable of murder, and both quick and brutal enough to have killed a man like Grassman. From what I had seen of him, Grassman looked tough and capable.

But why would Fitz want to implicate me? The answer was quick and chilling. It meant that he had traced the right Cindy, the Cindy who would know where Timmy had buried the money. He might already have the money.

The immediate problem was to get rid of the body. It should be a place where there would be no witness, no one to remember having seen my car. I couldn't go to the police. "I was here before. Unemployed. No permanent address. A criminal record, according to your definition. It so happens I have a body in my car. It got in there somehow last night. Was I drunk? Brother, you can find a dozen witnesses to how drunk I was. I was a slobbering mess, the worst I've ever been in my life. Worse even than the night before."

There would be no glimmer of understanding in the cold official eyes of Lieutenant Prine.

A state road patrol car passed me, going slowly. The trooper behind the wheel stared curiously at me as I sat there. He stopped and backed up. Maybe they were already looking for me.

He leaned across the empty seat and said, "What's the trouble?"

"Nothing. I mean I was overheating. I thought I'd let it cool off. Is it far to a gas station?"

"Mile or so. It'll cool off quicker if you open the hood."

"Will it? Thanks."

"And get it a little farther off the road, doc."

He went on. I moved the car farther off the road. I opened the hood. I wondered if he would be bothered by the way I had acted and come back to check my license and look the car over. I wondered if I should make a U-turn and get as far away from him as I could. But it made some sense to risk the outside chance of his coming back and stay right there until I could plan what to do with the body.

The noon sun was warm. There was a subtle, sour odor in the car that sickened me. A dark-red tractor moved back and forth across a distant hillside. Drainage water bubbled in the ditch beside the shoulder. A truck went by at high speed, the blast of its passage shaking my car.

I found that a two-day drunk gives your mind a flavor of unreliability. Memory is shaky and dreams become mixed with reality. I began to wonder if I had imagined the body. When there was no traffic I looked into the back seat again. The tarp was there. The body was covered. It was not covered very well. I saw a thick ankle, a dark green sock, a brown scuffed shoe, cracked across the instep, with laces tied in a double knot, the way my mother used to tie my shoelaces when I was very small to keep them from coming untied. It made Grassman more believable as a person, as the person who had sat on the edge of a bed and tied those laces and then had gone out and become a body, and the laces would eventually be untied by somebody else, somebody with a professional coolness and an unthinking competence. I whirled around when I heard traffic coming. When the road was clear again I pulled the tarp to cover the ankle and shoe, but it pulled clear of his head and my stomach spasmed and I could not look at him.

After a while I fixed the tarp properly. I got out of the car. I did not want to look in again. But I found myself staring in at the side window.

I had to get rid of it somewhere. I had to get rid of it soon. The very nearness of the body kept me from thinking clearly.

The lake? I could find it again. But I could be seen there as readily as Ruth saw Grassman. I could hunt for obscure roads at random and dump the body out when I came to what seemed to be a good place. But the body was going to be found and it was going to be identified and it was going to be in the paper with the right name. And Ruth was going to remember the odd question I had asked the man and remember his telltale response to that question.

The minutes were ticking by and I was getting nowhere. Fitzmartin's trap was wide and deep, lined with sharp stakes. I wished I could put the body back on his doorstep. Give it right back to him. Let him sweat.

At first glance the idea seemed absurd. But the more I thought about it the better it seemed. I would be seen driving into the yard. But if questioned I could say that I was going to see Fitzmartin. And I would see Fitzmartin. I would leave the body in the yard somewhere between the piles of stacked lumber.

No. That would do no good. No man would be so stupid as to kill another man and leave the body at the place where he worked. Yet if some attempt was made to conceal the body— Perhaps then they would assume it was a temporary hiding place until Fitzmartin could think of another.

On the other hand, would any man be so stupid as to kill another man and then drive the body to the police station in his car and claim he didn't do it? Maybe that was my best out. Maybe that was the best innocent reaction.

My hands were icy cold and sweaty. They left wet marks where I touched the steering wheel. I was trying to think of every alternative, every possible plan of action. I could go back and check out and head west and try to leave the body where it would never be found. Buy a shovel. Dig a desert grave. I could put the body in the seat beside me and run into something. My ideas were getting worse instead of better. The very presence of the body made thinking as laborious as trying to run through waist-deep water. I did not want to panic, but I knew I had to get rid of it as soon as possible. And I could not see myself going to Prine for tender mercy. There had been a reason why Grassman had been killed. Hiding the body would give me a grace period. I would have to assume it would be traced to me eventually. By the time they caught up with me, I would have to know why he had been killed. Knowing why would mean knowing who. I knew it was Fitz. Why did Fitz kill Grassman?

I shut the hood and started the car and drove. I was five miles from the court and about nine miles from town when I found a promising looking road that turned left. It was potholed asphalt, ravaged by winter, torn by tractor lugs. It climbed mild hills and dipped into forgotten valleys. It came out of a heavy wooded area, and ahead on the left, set well back from the road, I saw a tall stone chimney where a house had burned long ago. The weathered gray barn had half collapsed. It looked like a great gray animal with a broken back, its hind legs dragging. The road was empty. I turned in where the farm road had once been. Small trees bent over under my front bumper, dragged along the underside of the car, and half rose again behind me. I circled the foundation of the house and parked behind the barn near a wild tangle of berry bushes. I could not be seen from the road. I had to risk being seen from distant hillsides. It seemed very quiet with the motor off. A crow went over, hoarse and derisive.

I opened the rear door of the car. I made myself grasp his heavy ankles. Rigor had begun to set in. It took all my strength to pull the bulky body free of the cramped space between the back seat and the back of the front seat. It came free suddenly, thudding to the ground. I released the ankles and staggered back. There had been something under the body. Friction had pulled it toward me. It rested on the car floor, half in and half out of the car—a short, bright length of galvanized pipe with a dark brown smear at one end. I left the body there and went to see where I would put it. There was a great splintered hole in the back of the barn. I stepped up and through the hole. The floor felt solid. Daylight came brightly through the holes in the roof.

I went back to the body again. It was not hard to drag it to the hole. But getting it inside the barn was difficult. I had to lift it about three feet. I puzzled over how to do it. Finally I turned him around and propped him up in a sitting position, his back to the hole. I climbed up over him, then reached down and got his wrists. I pulled him up over the edge and then dragged him back into the darkness. There was some hay on the floor, musty and matted. I covered the body with it. I went out and got the piece of pipe, using a dry leaf to pick it up. I dropped it into the hay that covered the body. I went back out into the sunlight.

I wondered about Grassman. I wondered what compulsion had made him choose his line of work. Dirty, monotonous, and sometimes dangerous work. From the look of the man as he talked to us up at the lake, I guessed that he had no idea it would end like this. He had looked tough and confident. This body under the straw was a far cry from the fictional private eyes, the smart ones and the suave ones and the gamy ones. His story had ended. He would not sit up, brush the straw out of his eyes and reach for either blonde or bottle. Leaving him there had about it the faint flavor of burial, as though solemn words should be said.

I inspected the car. The floor rug was stained and spotted in four places. I couldn't see any on the seat, or on the insides of the doors. I took the floor rug out and rolled it up. I put it beside me in the front seat. I sat and listened to the quietness, straining to hear any sound of car motor laboring on the hills. I heard only the birds and the sound of wind.

I drove back out and I did not head back the way I had come. A car seen going and returning was more likely to be remembered on a country road than a car that went on through. In about three miles I came to a crossroads. I turned north. I thought the road was paralleling the main highway, but in five miles it joined the main highway, coming into it at a shallow angle. I took the next secondary road that turned right. I was closer to the city. Soon, as I had hoped and expected, I came to a place where a lot of trash had been dumped. I put the rolled rug in with the bed springs and broken scooters and kicked some cans over it.

By the time I passed the motel, heading toward the city, I was surprised to find that it was only quarter after one. I ate at a small restaurant on Delaware Street. When I left I met Mrs. Pat Rorick on the sidewalk. She had an armful of bundles. She smiled and said "Hello, Mr. Howard."

"Did you remember anything, Mrs. Rorick?"

"I don't know if this is any use to you, but I did remember one little thing. It was a skit the eighth grade did and Timmy was in it. It was based on Cinderella. I can't remember the girl who played the part, but I remember how funny it sounded the way it was written, with Timmy calling the girl Cindy. It probably doesn't mean anything."

"It might. Thanks."

"I'm glad I met you. I was wondering whether to call you about anything that sounds so stupid. I've got to run. There comes my bus."

"I'll drive you home."

"No. Don't bother."

I convinced her I had nothing to do. We got into the car. She had her packages piled on her lap. I wondered how she'd feel if she'd known about my last passenger.

"How should I go about finding out who that girl was?"

"Gee, I don't know. It was a long time ago. I don't know if anybody would remember. The eighth-grade home-room teacher was Miss Major. I had her too, later. She was real cute. I think she wrote that skit they did. I don't know what happened to her. I think she got married and moved away. They might know at the school. It's John L. Davis School. On Holly Street, near the bridge."

CHAPTER SEVEN

The John L. Davis School was an ancient red-brick building with an iron picket fence enclosing the schoolyard. As I went up the steps to the door, I could hear a class of small voices chanting something in unison. It was a sleepy, nostalgic, afternoon sound.

In the wide wooden hallway there were drinking fountains which looked absurdly low. A small boy came down the hall, tapping himself gently and wistfully on the head with a ruler. He gave me an opaque stare and continued on his way.

There was a nervous young woman in the outer office of the principal's office. She was typing and chewing her lip and when she looked up at me she was obviously irritated by the interruption.

"I'm trying to find a Miss Major who used to teach here. She taught eighth-grade subjects, I believe."

"We only go through the sixth. Then the children go to the junior high."

"I know that. But you used to have the seventh and eighth here."

"Not for a long time. Not since I've been here."

"Aren't there any records? Isn't there any place you could look?"

"I wouldn't know where to look. I wouldn't know anything like that."

"Are there any teachers here who would have been here when Miss Major was here?"

"I guess there probably are. I guess there would be some. How long ago was she here?"

"About twelve years ago."

"Mrs. Stearns has been teaching here twenty-two years. Third grade. Room sixteen. That's on this floor just around the corner."

"I wouldn't want to interrupt a class."

"Any minute now they'll all be going home. Then you could ask her. I wouldn't know anything like that. I wouldn't know where to look or anything."

I waited outside room sixteen. There was a lull and then somebody started a record player. Sousa filled the halls with brass, at peak volume. There was a great scurrying in all the rooms. The doors opened. All the small denizens marched into the hall and stood in impatient ragged double lines, stomping their feet in time to the music. The floor shook. Weary teachers kept a cautious eye on the lines. The upstairs rooms marched down the stairs and out the double doors. Then the main floor marched out, yelling as soon as they hit the sunlight. The school was emptied. Sousa blared on for a few moments and died in the middle of a bar.

"Mrs. Stearns?"

"Yes, I'm Mrs. Stearns." She was a round, pale woman with hair like steel wool and small, sharp, bright dark eyes.

"My name is Howard, Talbert Howard. Did you know a Miss Major who used to teach here?"

"Of course. I knew Katherine very well. That reminds me, I should stop by and see how she's getting along these days."

"She's in town?"

"Oh, yes, the poor thing."

"Is she ill?"

"Oh, I thought you knew. Katherine went blind quite suddenly about ten years ago. It was a shock to all of us. I feel guilty that I don't call on her more often. But after a full day of the children, I don't feel like calling on anyone. I don't seem to have the energy any more."

"Could you tell me where she lives?"

"Not off hand, but it's in the phone book. She's on Finch Avenue, in an apartment. I know the house but I can't remember the number. She lives alone. She's very proud, you know. And she really gets along remarkably well, considering."

It was a small ground-floor apartment in the rear of an old house. Music was playing loudly in the apartment. It was a symphony I didn't recognize. The music stopped moments after I knocked at the door.

Miss Major opened the door. She wore a blue dress. Her hair was white and worn in a long page boy. Her features were strong. She could have once been a beautiful woman. She was still handsome. When I spoke to her, she seemed to focus on my face. It was hard to believe those eyes were sightless.

I told her my name and said I wanted to ask her about a student she had had in the eighth grade.

"Please come in, Mr. Howard. Sit there in the red chair. I was having tea. Would you care for some?"

"No, thank you."

"Then one of these cookies. A friend of mine bakes them. They're very good."

She held the plate in precisely the right spot. I took one and thanked her. She put the plate back on the table and sat facing me. She found her teacup and lifted it to her lips.

"Now what student was it?"

"Do you remember Timmy Warden?"

"Of course I remember him! He was a charmer. I was told how he died. I was dreadfully sorry to hear it. A man came to see me six or seven months ago. He said he'd been in that prison camp with Timmy. I never could quite understand why he came to see me. His name was Fitzmartin and he asked all sorts of odd questions. I couldn't feel at ease with him. He didn't seem—quite right if you know what I mean. When you lose one sense you seem to become more aware of nuances."

"I was in that camp too, Miss Major."

"Oh, I'm so sorry. Probably Mr. Fitzmartin is a friend of yours."

"No, he's not."

"That's a relief. Now don't tell me you came here to ask odd questions too, Mr. Howard."

"Fairly odd, I guess. In camp Timmy spoke about a girl named Cindy. I've been trying to track her down for—personal reasons. One of your other students, Cindy Kirschner, told me that you wrote a skit based on Cinderella for the eighth grade when you had Timmy in the class. Timmy wasn't—very well when he mentioned this Cindy. I'm wondering if he could have meant the girl who played the part in the play."

"Whatever has happened to Cindy Kirschner, Mr. Howard? Such a shy, sweet child. And those dreadful teeth."

"The teeth have been fixed. She's married to a man named Pat Rorick and she has a couple of kids."

"That's good to hear. The other children used to be horrible to her. They can be little animals at times."

"Do you remember who played the part of Cindy in the skit?"

"Of course I remember. I remember because it was sort of an experiment. Her name was Antoinette Rasi. Wait a moment. I'll show you something." She went into the other room. She was gone nearly five minutes. She came back with a glossy photograph.

"I had a friend help me sort these out after I learned Braille. I've marked them all so I know this is the right one. It's a graduation picture. I've kept the graduation pictures of all my classes, though what use I have for pictures, I'll never know."

She handed it to me and said, "I believe Antoinette is in the back row toward the left. Look for a girl with a great mass of black hair and a pretty, rather sullen face. I don't imagine she was smiling."

"I think I've found her."

"Antoinette was a problem. She was a little older than the others. Half French and half Italian. She resented discipline. She was a rowdy, a troublemaker. But I liked the child and I thought I understood her. Her people were very poor and I don't think she got much attention at home. She had an older brother who had been in trouble with the police and I believe an older sister. She came to school inadequately dressed when the weather was cold. She had a lot of spirit. She was a very alive person. I think she was sensitive, but she hid it very carefully. I can't help but wonder sometimes what has happened to the child. The Rasis lived north of the city where the river widens out. I believe that Mr. Rasi had a boat and bait business in the summer and did odd jobs in the wintertime. Their house was a shack. I went out there once after Antoinette had missed a whole week of school. I found she hadn't come because she had a black eye. Her brother gave it to her. I gave her the part of Cinderella in an attempt to get her to take more interest in class activities. I'm afraid it was a mistake. I believe she thought it was a reflection on the way she lived."

"Was Timmy friendly with her?"

"Quite friendly. I sometimes wondered if that was a good thing. She seemed quite—precocious in some departments. And Timmy was a very sweet boy."

"He could have called her Cindy because of the skit?"

"I imagine so. Children dote on nicknames. I remember one poor little boy with a sinus condition. The other children made him unhappy by calling him Rumblehead."

"I want to thank you for your help, Miss Major."

"I hope the information is of some use to you. When you find Antoinette, tell her I asked about her."

"I'll do that."

She went with me to the door. She said, "They're bringing me a new Braille student at four. He seems to be a little late. Mr. Howard, are you in some kind of trouble?"

The abrupt *non sequitur* startled me. "Trouble? Yes, I'm in trouble. Bad trouble."

"I won't give you any chin-up lecture, Mr. Howard. I've been given too much of that myself. I was just checking my own reactions. I sensed trouble. An aura of worry. As with that Mr. Fitzmartin I detected an aura of directed evil."

When I got out in front, a woman was helping a young boy out of a car. The boy wore dark glasses. His mouth had an ill-tempered look, and I heard the whine in his voice as he complained about something to her.

I felt that I had discovered Cindy. There had been a hint as to what she was like in the very tone of Timmy's voice. Weak as he was, there had been a note of fond appreciation—the echo of lust. Cindy would know. The phrasing was odd. Not *Cindy knows. Cindy would know.* It would be a place known to her.

I sat in my car for a few moments. I did not know how long my period of grace would last. I did not know whether I should continue in search of the elusive Cindy or try to make sense of the relationship between Fitz and Grassman. It came to me that I had been a fool not to search the body. There might have been notes, papers, letters, reports—something to indicate why he had been slain. Yet I knew I could not risk going back there, and it was doubtful that the murderer would have been so clumsy as to leave anything indirectly incriminating on the body itself.

I did not know where to start. I didn't think anything could be gained by going to Fitzmartin, facing him. He certainly would answer no questions. Why had it been necessary to kill Grassman? Either it was related to Grassman's job, or it was something apart from it. Grassman's job had apparently been due to Rose Fulton's conviction that her husband had come to some harm here in Hillston.

Prine's investigation had evidently been thorough. He was satisfied that Fulton and Eloise Warden had run off together. He had a witness to the actual departure. Yet Grassman had been poking around the cabin the Wardens used to own. I could not imagine what he hoped to gain.

I could not help but believe that Grassman's death was in some way related to the sixty thousand dollars. I wondered if Grassman had somehow acquired the information that a sizable sum had disappeared from the Warden business ventures over a period of time, and had added two and two together. Or if, in looking for Fulton's body, he had stumbled across the money. Maybe at the same time Fitz was looking for it. Many murders have been committed for one tenth that amount. There was only one starting place with Grassman. That was Rose Fulton. Maybe Grassman had sent her reports. She was probably a resident of Illinois.

I wondered who would know her address. It would have to be someone whose suspicions would not be aroused. I wondered if there was any way of finding out without asking anyone. If the police investigation had been reported in the local paper, Fulton's home town would probably have been given, but not his street address.

I realized that I did not dare make any effort to get hold of Mrs. Fulton. It would link me too closely to Grassman.

Antoinette Rasi then. I would look for her.

The shack was on the riverbank. It had a sagging porch, auto parts stamped into the mud of the yard, dingy Monday washing flapping on a knotted line, a disconsolate tire hanging from a tree limb, and a shiny new television aerial. A thin, dark boy of about twelve was carefully painting an overturned boat, doing a good job of it. A little dark-headed girl was trying to harness a fat, humble dog to a broken cart. A toddler in diapers watched her. Some chickens were scratching the loose dirt under the porch.

The children looked at me as I got out of the car. A heavy woman came to the door. She bulged with pregnancy. Her eyes and expression were unfriendly. The small girl began to cry. I heard her brother hiss at her to shut up. The woman in the doorway could have once been quite pretty. She wasn't any more. It was hard to guess how old she might be.

"Is your name Rasi?" I asked.

"It was once. Now it's Doyle. What do you want?"

"I'm trying to locate Antoinette Rasi."

"For God's sake, shut up sniveling, Jeanie. This man isn't come to take the teevee." She smiled apologetically at me. "They took it away once, and to Jeanie any stranger comes after the same thing. Every night the kids watch it. No homework, no nothing. Just sit and look. It drives me nuts. What do you want Antoinette for?"

"I've got a message for her. From a friend."

The woman sniffed. "She makes a lot of friends, I guess. She doesn't hang around here any more. She's up in Redding. I don't hear from her any more. She never gets down. God knows I never get up there. The old man is dead and Jack is in the federal can in Atlanta, and Doyle can't stand the sight of her, so why should she bother coming down here. Hell, I'm only her only sister. She sends money for the kids, but no messages. No nothing."

"What does she do?"

She gave me a wise, wet smile. "She goes around making friends, I guess."

"How do I get in touch with her?"

"Cruise around. Try the Aztec, and the Cub Room. And try the Doubloon, too. I heard her mention that. You can probably find her."

It was sixty miles to Redding, and dark when I got there. It was twice the size of Hillston. It was a town with a lot of neon. Lime and pink. Dark, inviting blue. Lots of uniforms on the night streets. Lots of girls on the dark streets. Lots of cars going nowhere too fast, horns blowing, Bermuda bells ringing, tires wailing. I asked where the Aztec and the Cub Room and the Doubloon were. I was directed to a wide highway on the west edge of town, called, inevitably, the Strip. There the neon really blossomed. There wasn't as much sidewalk traffic. But for a Monday night there were enough cars in the lots. Enough rough music in the air. Enough places to lose your money. Or spend it. Or have it taken away from you.

I went to the Aztec and I went to the Cub Room and I went to the Doubloon. In each place I asked a bartender about Antoinette Rasi. On each occasion I received a blank stare and a shrug and a, "Never heard of her."

"Dark-haired girl?"

"That's unusual? Sorry, buster."

The cadence of the evening was beginning to quicken. All three places were glamorous. They were like the lounges of the hotels along Collins Avenue on Miami Beach. And like the bistros of Beverly Hills. The lighting was carefully contrived. There was a Las Vegas tension in those three places, a smell of money. Here the games were hidden. But not hard to find.

The way Mrs. Doyle had spoken of her sister gave me reason to believe I could get assistance from the police. They were in a brand new building. The sergeant looked uncomfortable behind a long curve of stainless steel.

I told him what Mrs. Doyle had said about how to find her.

"There ought to be something on her. Let me check it out. Wait a couple minutes."

He got on the phone. He had to wait quite a while. Then he thanked the man on the other end and hung up. "He knows her. She's been booked a couple times as Antoinette Rasi. But the name she uses is Toni Raselle. She calls herself an entertainer. He says he thinks she did sing for a while at one place. She's a fancy whore. The last address he's got is the Glendon Arms. That's a high-class apartment hotel on the west side, not too far from the Strip. Both times she was booked last it was on a cute variation of the old badger game. So cute they couldn't make it stick. So watch yourself. She plays with rough people. We got rough ones here by the dozen."

I thanked him and left. It was nearly ten when I got back to the Strip. I went into the Aztec first. I went to the same bartender. "Find that girl yet?" he asked.

"I found she calls herself Toni Raselle."

"Hell, I know her. She comes in every once in a while. She may show here yet tonight. You an old friend or something?"

"Not exactly."

I tried the other two places. They knew the name there also, but she hadn't been in. I had a steak sandwich in the Doubloon. A girl alone at the bar made a determined effort to pick me up. She dug through her purse looking for matches, unlit cigarette in her mouth. She started a conversation a shade too loudly with the bartender and tried to drag me into it. She was a lean brunette with shiny eyes and trembling hands. I ordered a refill for her and moved onto the bar stool next to her.

We exchanged inanities until she pointed up at the ceiling with her thumb and said, "Going to try your luck tonight? I'm always lucky. You know there's some fellas I know they wouldn't dare try the crap table without they give me some chips to get in the game."

"I don't want to gamble."

"Yeah, sometimes I get tired of it, too. I mean when you just can't seem to get any action out of your money."

"Do you know a girl around town named Toni Raselle?"

She stopped smiling. "What about her? You looking for her?"

"Somebody mentioned her. I remembered the name. Is she nice?"

"She's damn good looking. But she's crazy. Crazy as hell. She doesn't grab me a bit."

"How come you think she's crazy, Donna?"

"Well, dig this. There's some important guys around here. Like Eddie Larch that owns this place. Guys like Eddie. They really got a yen for her. A deal like that you can fall into. Everything laid on. Apartment, car, clothes. They'd set you up. You know? Then all you got to do is be nice and take it easy. Not Toni. She strictly wants something going on all the time. She wants to lone wolf it. And she keeps getting in jams that way. My Christ, you'd think she liked people or something. If I looked like her, I'd parlay that right into stocks and bonds, believe you me. But that Toni. She does as she damn pleases. She don't like you, you're dead. So you can have hundred-dollar bills out to here, you're still dead. She wouldn't spit if your hair was on fire. That's how she's crazy, man."

"I think I see what you mean."

Donna sensed she'd made some sort of tactical error. She smiled broadly and said, "Don't take me serious, that about parlaying it into stocks and bonds. I'm not that type girl. I like a few laughs. I like to get around. My boy friend is away and I got lonesome tonight so I thought I'd take a look around, see what's going on. You know how it is. Lonesome? Sure you wouldn't want to see if you're lucky?"

"I guess not."

She pursed her lips and studied her half-empty glass. She tried the next gambit. "You know, at a buck a drink, they must make a hell of a lot out of a bottle. If a person was smart they'd do their drinking at home. It would be a lot cheaper."

"It certainly would."

"You know, if we could get a bottle, I got glasses and ice at my place. We could take our hair down and put our feet up and watch the teevee and have a ball. What do you say?"

"I don't think so."

"My boy friend won't be back in town until next weekend. I got my own place."

"No thanks, Donna."

"What *do* you want to do?"

"Nothing in particular."

"Joey," she called to the bartender. "What kind of place you running? You got a dead customer sitting here. He's giving me the creepers." She moved over two stools and wouldn't look at me. Within fifteen minutes two heavy, smiling men came in. Soon she was in conversation with them. The three of them went upstairs together to try the tables. I hoped her luck was good.

After she was gone the bartender came over and said in a low voice, "The boss gives me the word to keep her out of here. She used to be a lot better looking. Now she gets drunk and nasty. But when he isn't around, I let her stay. What the hell. It's old times, like they say. You know how it is."

"Sure."

"She can sure get nasty. And she won't make any time with that pair. Did you dig those country-style threads? A small beer says they don't have sixteen bucks between the pair of them. She's losing her touch. Last year this time she'd have cut off their water before they said word one. Old Donna's on the skids."

"What will she do?"

He shrugged. "I don't know where they go. She can always sign for a tour." He winked. "See the world. See all the ports in S.A. I don't know where they go."

I wandered back to the Aztec. My bartending friend told me that Toni Raselle was out in the casino in back, escorted by a general. He said she was wearing a white blouse and dark-red skirt, and had an evening scarf that matched her skirt.

I tipped him and went out into the casino. I bought chips through the wicket just inside the door. The large room was crowded. It was brightly, whitely lighted, like an operating amphitheater. The light made the faces of the people look sick. The cards, the chips, the dice, the wheels were all in pitiless illumination. I spotted the uniform across the room. The general was big-chested. He held his face as though he thought he resembled MacArthur. He did a little. But not enough. He had three rows of discreetly faded ribbons.

Antoinette Rasi stood beside him and laughed up at him. It was the face of the high-school picture, matured, not as sullen. Her tumbled hair was like raw blue-black silk. She held her folded *rebozo* over her arm. Her brown shoulders were bare. She was warm within her skin, moving like molten honey, teeth white in laughter against her tan face. Wide across the cheekbones. Eyes deep set. Nose broad at the bridge. Feral look. Gypsy look. A mature woman so alive she made the others in the room look two dimensional, as though they had been carefully placed there to provide their drab contrast to Toni's look of greedy life.

They were at the roulette table. I stood across the table. The general was solemnly playing the black. When he lost Toni laughed at him. He didn't particularly like it, but there wasn't much he could do about it. I had twenty one-dollar chips. I began playing twenty-nine, and watching her instead of the wheel. I won thirty-six dollars on the fourth spin. I began to play the red, and kept winning. Toni became aware of my interest in her.

So did the general. He gave me a mental command to throw myself on my sword. Toni gave me a few irritated glances.

Finally the general had to go back to the window to buy more chips. They didn't sell them at the table. As soon as he was gone I said, "Antoinette?"

She looked at me carefully. "Do I know you?"

"No. I want a chance to talk to you."

"How do you know my name?"

"Antoinette Rasi. Through Timmy Warden. Remember him?"

"Of course. I can't talk now. Phone me tomorrow. At noon. Eight three eight nine one. Can you remember that?"

"Eight three eight nine one. I'll remember."

The general came back, staring at me with bitter suspicion. I went away, taking with me the memory of her dark eyes and her low, hoarse, husky voice.

I drove back through the night to Hillston. It was well after midnight when I got there. I wondered if they would be waiting for me at the motel. But the *No Vacancy* sign was lighted and my room was dark.

I went to bed and went to sleep at once. An hour later I awakened abruptly from a nightmare. I was drenched with sweat. I had dreamed that Grassman rode my back, his legs clamped around my waist, his heavy arms around my throat. I walked down a busy street with him there, asking, begging for help. But they would scream and cover their eyes and shrink away from me. And I knew that Grassman's face was more horrible than I had remembered. No one would help me. Then it was not Grassman any more. It was Timmy who rode there. I could smell the earth we had buried him in. I woke up in panic and it took me a long time to quiet down again.

CHAPTER EIGHT

I called her at noon and she answered on the tenth ring just as I was about to give up.

Her voice was blurred with sleep. "Whozit?"

"Tal Howard."

"Who?"

"I spoke to you last night at the Aztec. About Timmy Warden. You said to phone."

I could hear the soft yowl of her complete yawn. "Oh, sure. You go have some coffee or something and then stop around here. I live at a place called the Glendon Arms. Give me about forty minutes to wake up."

I wasted a half hour over coffee and a newspaper, and then found the Glendon Arms without difficulty. It was as pretentious as its name, with striped canopy, solid glass doors, mosaic tile lobby floor, desk clerk with dreary sneer. He phoned and told me I could go right up to Miss Raselle's apartment, third floor, 3A. The elevator was self-service. The hallway was wide. I pushed the button beside her door.

She opened the door and smiled as she let me in. She wore a white angora sleeveless blouse, slacks of corduroy in a green plaid. I had expected her to be puffy, blurred by dissipation, full of a morning surliness. But she looked fresh, golden, shining and clean. The great mop of black hair was pulled sleekly back and fastened into an intricate rosette.

"Hi, Tal Howard. Can you stand more coffee? Come along."

There was a small breakfast terrace with sliding doors that opened onto it from the bedroom and the kitchen. The sun was warm on the terrace. We had coffee and rolls and butter on a glass-topped table.

"Last night was a waste," she said. "He was a friend of a friend. A stuffed uniform until drink number ten. And then what. He goes with his hands like so. Zoom. Dadadadadada. Gun noises. Fighter planes. I'm too old for toys."

"He had a lot of ribbons."

"He told me what they were for. Several times. How did you track me down, Tal Howard?"

"Through your sister."

"Dear God. Anita has turned into a real slob. It's that Doyle. Doyle allows that the sun rises and sets on Doyle. The kids are nice, though. I don't know how they made it, but they are. What's with Timmy? He was my first love. How is that cutie?"

"He's dead, Toni."

Her face lost its life. "You certainly didn't waste any time working up to that. How?"

"He was taken prisoner by the Chinese in Korea. So was I. We were in the same hut. He got sick and died there and we buried him there."

"What a stinking way for Timmy to go. He was a nice guy. We got along fine, right up into the second year of high school, and then he started considering his social position and brushed me off. I don't blame him. He was too young to know any better. He left me to take a big hack at the dancing-school set. My reputation wasn't exactly solid gold." She grinned. "Nor is it yet."

"He mentioned you while we were in camp."

"Did he?"

"He called you Cindy."

For a long moment she looked puzzled, and then her face cleared. "Oh, that. You know, I'd just about forgotten that. It was sort of a gag. In that eighth grade we had a teacher who was all hopped up about class activities. I was the rebel. She stuck me in a play as Cinderella. Timmy was the prince. He called me Cindy for quite a while after that. A year maybe. A pretty good year, too. I was a wild kid. I didn't know what I wanted. I knew that what I had, I didn't want. But I didn't know how to make a change. I was too young. Gee, I'm sorry about Timmy. That's depressing. It makes me feel old, Tal. I don't like to feel old."

"I came back and tried to find a Cindy. I didn't know your right name. I found a couple. Cindy Waskowitz—"

"A great fat pig. But nothing jolly about her. Brother, she was as nasty as they come."

"She's dead, too. Glandular trouble of some kind."

"Couldn't you go around wearing a wreath or singing hymns like Crossing the Bar?"

"I'm sorry. Then there was Cindy Kirschner."

"Kirschner. Wait a minute. A younger kid. Teeth like this?"

"That's right. But she had them fixed. Now she has a husband and a couple of kids."

"Good for her."

"She was the one who remembered the class play or skit or whatever it was. And the name of the eighth-grade teacher. Miss Major. She couldn't remember who played Cinderella. So I found Miss Major. She went blind quite a while ago and—"

"For God's sake, Tal! I mean really!"

"I'm sorry. Anyway, she identified you. I went out and saw your sister. I came here hunting for Antoinette Rasi. The way your sister spoke about you, when I couldn't find you, I tried the police. They told me the name you use. Then it was easy."

She looked at me coldly and dubiously. "Police, eh? They give you all the bawdy details?"

"They told me a few things. Not much."

"But enough. Enough so that when you walked in here you had to act like a little kid inspecting a leper colony. What the hell did you expect to find? A room all mirrors? A turnstile?"

"Don't get sore."

"You look stuffy to me, Tal Howard. Stuffy people bore me. So what the hell was this? A sentimental journey all the way from prison camp to dig up poor little me?"

"Not exactly. And I'm not stuffy. And I don't give a damn what you are or what you do."

The glare faded. She shrugged and said, "Skip it. I don't know why I should all of a sudden get sensitive. I'm living the way I want to live. I guess it's just from talking about Timmy. That was a tender spot. From thinking about the way I was. At thirteen I wanted to lick the world with my bare hands. Now I'm twenty-eight. Do I look it?"

"No, you really don't."

She rested her cheek on her fist. She looked thoughtful. "You know, Tal Howard, another reason why I think I jumped on you. I think I'm beginning to get bored. I think I'm due for some kind of a change."

"Like what?"

"More than a new town. I don't know. Just restless. Skip that. You said this wasn't exactly a sentimental journey. What is it?"

"There's something else involved."

"Mystery, hey? What's with you?"

"How do you mean?"

"What do you do? You married?"

"I'm not doing anything right now. I'm not married. I came here from the west coast. I haven't got any permanent address."

"You're not the type."

"How do you mean that?"

"That information doesn't fit you, somehow. So it's just a temporary thing with you. You're between lives, aren't you? And maybe as restless as I am?"

"I could be."

She winked at me. "And I think you've been taking yourself too seriously lately. Have you noticed that?"

"I guess I have."

"Now what's the mystery?"

"I'm looking for something. Timmy hid something. Before he left. I know what it is. I don't know where it is. Before he died, not very many hours before he died, Timmy said, 'Cindy would know.' That's why I'm here."

"Here from the west coast, looking for Cindy. He hid something nice, then. Like some nice money?"

"If you can help me, I'll give you some money."

"How much?"

"It depends on how much he hid."

"Maybe you admitted too fast that it was money, Tal. I am noted for my fondness for money. It pleases me. I like the feel of it and the smell of it and the look of it. I'm nuts about it. I like all I can get, maybe because I spent so much time without any of it. A psychiatrist friend told me it was my basic drive. I can't ever have too much."

"If that was really your basic drive, you wouldn't say it like that, I don't think. It's just the way you like to think you are."

She was angry again. "Why does every type you meet try to tell you what you really are?"

"It's a popular hobby."

"So all right. He hid something. Now I've got a big fat disappointment for you. I wouldn't have any idea where he hid something. I don't know what he means."

"Are you sure?"

"Don't look at me like that. I know what you're thinking. You're thinking I *do* know and I won't tell you because I want it all. Honestly, Tal, I don't know. I can't think what he could have meant."

I believed her.

"This sun is actually getting too hot. Let's go inside," she said. I helped carry the things in. She rinsed the dishes. Having seen her the previous evening I would not have thought she had the sort of figure to wear slacks successfully. They were beautifully tailored and she looked well in them. We went into the living-room. It was slightly overfurnished. The lamps were in bad taste. But it was clean and comfortable.

She sat on the couch and pulled one leg up and locked her hands around her knee. "Want to hear about Timmy and me? The sad story? Not sad, I guess."

"If you want to tell it."

"I've never told anybody. Maybe it's time. I turned fifteen before I got out of the eighth grade. I was older than the other kids. Timmy was fourteen. He was the biggest boy in class. We never had anything to do with each other until that skit. We practiced a couple of times. We got to be friends. It wasn't a girl-friend-boy-friend thing. More like a couple of boys. I wasn't the most feminine creature in the world, believe me. I could run like the wind and I could fight with my fists.

"I didn't want Timmy to come out to the house. I was ashamed of where I lived. I never wanted any of the kids to see how and where I lived. My God, we lived like animals. It wasn't so bad until my mother died but from then on it was pretty bad. You saw the place?"

"I saw it."

"The old man kept pretty well soaked in his *vino*. My brother was completely no good. My sister slept with anybody who took the trouble to ask her. We lived in filth. We were on the county relief rolls. The do-gooders brought us food and clothing at Thanksgiving and Christmas. I was proud as hell inside. I couldn't see any way out. The best I could do was try to keep myself clean as a button and not let any of the kids come out there."

She came over and took one of my cigarettes, bent over for me to light it. "Timmy came out there. It nearly killed me. Then I saw that it was all right. He didn't pay any attention to the way things were. I mean it didn't seem to mean much to him. That's the way they were, so that's the way they were. He was my friend. After that I was able to talk to him. He understood. He had his dreams, too. We talked over our dreams.

"When school was out that summer he came out a lot. He used to cut lawns and make money and we'd go to the movies. We used to swim in the river. He'd come out on his bike. He got hold of a broken-down boy's bike for me. He fixed it up and I painted it. Then we could get around better. The relief people gave the old man a hard ride for buying me a bike. I had to explain how I got it and prove I didn't steal it. I can still remember the sneaky eyes on that cop.

"When it happened to us it was sudden. It was in late August. I'd gotten a job in the dime store by lying about my age and filling out the forms wrong. I was squirreling the money away. I spent Sundays with Timmy. His brother and his father didn't like him to see me, but he managed it.

"He had a basket on the front of his bike and we went off on a Sunday picnic. We went a long way into the country. Fifteen miles, I guess. We walked the bikes up a trail. We found a place under trees where it was like a park. It was far away from anybody. We could have been alone in the world. Maybe we were. We ate and then we stretched out and talked about how high school would be when it started in September. It was hot. We were in the shade. He went to sleep. I watched him while he was sleeping, the way his eyelashes were, and the way he looked like a little kid when he slept. I felt a big warmth inside me. It was a new way to feel toward him. When I couldn't stand it any longer, I slipped my arm under his neck and half lay across him and kissed him. He woke up with me kissing him.

"He was funny and kind of half scared and sort of half eager at the same time. I'd had a pretty liberal education as you can well imagine. I guess it was pretty sad. Two kids being as awkward and fumbling as you can possibly imagine, there on that hill in the shade. But awkward as we were, it happened.

"We hardly talked at all on the way back. I knew enough to be damn scared. But fortunately nothing happened. From then on we were different with each other. It got to be something we did whenever we had a chance. It got better and better for us. But we weren't friends the way we were before. Sometimes we seemed almost to be enemies. We tried to hurt each other. It was a strong hunger. We found good places to go. It lasted for a year and a half. We never talked about marriage or things like that. We lived for now. There was one place we would go. We'd take one of the boats and—"

She stopped abruptly. We looked into each other's eyes.

"Now you know where he meant?" I asked her softly.

"I think I do."

"Where?"

"I don't think we can handle it that way, do you?"

"How do you mean?"

"I think we better go there together, don't you?"

"There's nothing to keep you from going there by yourself, Antoinette."

"I know that. What would it mean if I told you I won't?"

"In spite of the money hunger?"

"I would be honest with a thing like this. I would. Believe me. I'd have known nothing about it. How much is there?"

I waited several moments, measuring her and the situation. I couldn't get to it without her. "Nearly sixty thousand, he said."

She sat down abruptly, saying a soundless *Oh*. "How—how would Timmy get hold of money like that?"

"He did all the book work for the four companies he and his brother owned. He took over two years milking that much in cash out of the four companies."

"Why would he do that to George? It doesn't sound like Timmy."

"He planned to run off with Eloise."

"That thing George married? That pig. I knew her. Where is she?"

"She went off with another man two years ago."

"Maybe she took the money with her."

"Timmy said she didn't know where he buried it."

"And she'd hardly be able to find it. I can guarantee that. So—this is George's money then, isn't it?"

I waited a moment. "Yes, it is."

"But it was already stolen."

"That's right."

"And nobody knows about it. George doesn't suspect. Nobody knows about it but you and me, Tal."

"There's another one who knows about it. A man named Earl Fitzmartin. He was in the camp, too. He didn't know about the name Cindy. Now he does. He's smart. He may be able to trace the name to you."

"What's he like?"

"He's smart and he's vicious."

"So are a lot of my friends."

"I don't think they're like Fitz. I don't think you could go with Fitz and find it and come back from wherever you went to find it, that is if it was a quiet place and he could put you where he dug up the money."

"Like that?"

"I think so. I think there's something wrong in his head. I don't think he's very much like other people."

"Can you and I—can we trust each other, Tal?"

"I think we can." We shook hands with formal ceremony.

She looked at me quizzically. "How about you, Tal? Why are you after the money?"

"Like they say about climbing mountains. Because it's there."

"What will it mean to you?"

"I don't know. I have to find it first."

"And then all of a sudden it's going to be some kind of an answer to everything?"

"Maybe."

"What fouled you up, Tal? What broke your wagon?"

"I don't know."

"I can place most people. I can't quite place you. You look like one type. You know. Played ball in school. Sells bonds or something. Working up to a ranch-type house, a Brooks wardrobe, and some day winter vacations in Bermuda after the kids are in college. You look like that all except the eyes. And the eyes don't look like that at all."

"What do they look like?"

"The eyes on the horse that knows they're going to shoot him because he was clumsy and busted his leg."

"When do we go after the money?"

She stepped to the kitchen door and looked at the clock. "You'd feel better if we stayed together until we get it, wouldn't you?"

"I guess I would. But it isn't essential."

"Your faith is touching. Didn't the police give you the word?"

"They said something about a cute variation of the badger game."

"It was very cute. They couldn't convict. And it was very dishonest, Tal. But it wasn't a case of fleecing the innocent. It was pulled on some citizens who were trying to make a dishonest buck. Like this. I tell them my boy friend is on one of the wheels at the Aztec. I tell the sucker the wheel is gimmicked. My boy friend is sore at the house. The sucker has to have two or three thousand he wants trebled. I say I can't go in with him. I give him a password to tell the boy friend. So they let him win six or seven thousand. He comes here with the money. The boy friend is to show up later. But when the boy friend shows up he is with a very evil-looking citizen who holds a gun on him. Gun has silencer. Evil type shoots boy friend. With a blank. Boy friend groans and dies. Evil type turns gun on sucker. Takes the house money back, plus his two or three, and one time twelve, thousand. Sucker begs for his life. Reluctantly granted. Told to leave town fast. He does. He doesn't want to be mixed up in any murder. House money goes back to house. I get a cut of the take. I love acting. You should see me tremble and faint."

"Suppose he doesn't come back here with the money?"

"They always have. They like to win the money and the girl too. They think it's like the movies. Now will you trust me out of your sight?"

"I'll have to, won't I?"

"I guess that's it. You'll have to." She smiled lazily.

"I have some errands. You can wait here. I'm going places where you can't go. You can wait here or you can meet me here. It's going to take three or four hours. By then it's going to be too late to get to the money today. We can go after it tomorrow morning."

"How are we going to divide it up?"

"Shouldn't we count it first?"

"But after we count it?"

She came toward me and put her hands on my shoulders. "Maybe we won't divide it up, Tal. Maybe we won't squirrel it away. It's free money. Maybe we'll just put it in the pot and spend it as we need it until it's all gone. Maybe we'll see how far we can distribute it. We could spread it from Acapulco to Paris. Then maybe we won't be restless any more. It would buy some drinks to Timmy. In some nice places."

I felt uneasy. I said, "I'm not that attractive to you."

"I know you're not. I like meaner-looking men." She took her hands away. "Maybe to you I'm like they used to say in the old-fashioned books. Damaged goods."

"Not visibly."

She shook her head. "You kill me. It was just an idea. You seem nice and quiet. Not demanding. Let's say restful. You said you don't know what you'll do with the money."

"I said maybe I'll know when I get it."

"And if you don't?"

"Then we'll talk some more."

"You'll wait here?"

"I'll meet you here."

"At five-thirty."

She said she had to change. I left. I wondered if I was being a fool. I had lunch. I didn't have much appetite. I went to a movie. I couldn't follow the movie. I was worrying too much. I began to be convinced I had been a fool. She wasn't the sort of woman to trust. I wondered by what magic she had hypnotized me into trusting her. I could imagine her digging up the money. Once she had it there was nothing I could do. I wondered if my trust had been based on some inner unwillingness to actually take the money. Maybe subconsciously I wanted the moral problem off my hands.

She wasn't back at five-thirty. I waited in the lobby. I was sweating. She came in at quarter to six. She looked pale and upset. We rode up in the elevator together. She gave me the key to open her door. Her fingers were cold. She kept biting her lip. Once we were inside she began to pace.

"What's the matter?"

"Shut up and let me think. Go make some drinks. That thing there is a bar. Scotch on the rocks for me."

I made the drinks. After hers was gone she seemed a little quieter, more thoughtful.

"Sorry for being bitchy, Tal. I'm upset. My errands didn't work out the way I expected. Some people seem to have the idea that just because I was in on the festivities, I belong to the house. You don't need details. I have some funds around here and there. I got to the bank in time. That was fine. But it wasn't so good on the funds that are in, shall we say, safekeeping. I got some of them. Not all that's coming to me. Not by a hell of a lot. I'm not supposed to be able to take off. I made the mistake of saying I was thinking about it. They gave me some strong arguments. I made like changing my mind. Still I was tailed back. How do you like that? The hell with them. They might even be thinking of a hijack job. Now I know I've got to get out of here. I think I've got it worked out. Will you help?"

"I guess so."

"I'm leaving for good. I can't make it tomorrow. Maybe tomorrow I can pick up a little more of what's due me. You drive over here Thursday morning. There's a back way out of here, through the cellar. I can grease the superintendent. Park on the parallel street back of here. Be there at ten sharp, ten in the morning. I'll come out the back way and away we'll go. But, damn it, I hate to leave so much stuff behind. A whole wardrobe."

"Is it dangerous?"

"I don't know how rough they might get. I just don't like the sound of it. I don't like being patted on the shoulder and being given a big toothy grin and being told 'There, there, little Toni, you don't want to leave town. We all love you too much.'"

I said, "I could stay until after dark and you could pack things and I could take them out maybe. A couple of suitcases."

"You sure you want to?"

"I'm willing to. If somebody followed you, they don't know I'm here now. You could leave before I do. They'd follow you. Then I can take the stuff out to my car."

"That should work all right. Gosh, it would really help. I've put a lot of money in clothes. I think it would be better than trying to get the stuff out in the morning, even with your help. I want it to move fast and smoothly. Stay away from the windows."

She spent a lot of time packing. It was dark when she finished. She filled two big suitcases. They bulged and they were heavy.

"Leave them wherever you're staying when you come back for me."

"It's a motel."

"Get me a room, too. Please."

She seemed to relax then. "I think it's going to work out, Tal. They sort of—scared me. I know a lot. I don't plan to do any talking. That's what worries them, I think. You don't know how much I appreciate this. I'll—make it up to you."

She wanted to be kissed and I kissed her. There was an eagerness and warmth and sensuality about her that made it a shock to touch her and hold her. We rocked off balance as we kissed, caught ourselves, smiled a little sheepishly.

"For now," she said.

I took the suitcases into the hall. She went on down. I waited there for fifteen minutes and then I went down. The clerk was very dubious about my leaving with suitcases. He seemed about to speak, but didn't quite know what to say. I was gone before he had phrased the objection. I put the suitcases in the back seat and drove to Hillston. I ate at a drive-in on the edge of town. I took the suitcases back to my motel room. They were an alien presence there, almost as vivid as if she were there with me. I stowed them in the closet.

CHAPTER NINE

Wednesday was a gray day. I had hidden Grassman's body on Monday. It seemed longer ago than Monday. The memory was very vivid, but it seemed to be something that had happened a long time ago. I saw the suitcases when I opened my closet to get at my own clothes. I was curious about what she had packed. I felt guilty about opening them. Then I decided that I had earned the right to look.

I put the larger one on the bed and tried the latches. It wasn't locked. It popped open. There were furs on top, silky and lustrous. She had packed neatly. Underneath the furs were suits, dresses, skirts, blouses. The bottom layer was underclothing, slips, panties with frothy lace and intricate embroidery in shades from purest white through all of the spectrum to black.

The other suitcase was much the same. The clothing was fresh and fragrant with perfume. It was perfume that was not musky. It had a clean flower scent. I could understand how this was important to her. I remembered her speaking of the charity gifts of clothing, of the dirt in which she had grown up. She would want clothing, a great deal of it, and all fresh and clean. I found the black leather box in the bottom of the second suitcase. I opened it. Jewelry lay against a black velvet partition. Bracelets, rings, clips. I could not tell if the white and green and red stones were real. They were lustrous. They caught fire in the light. But I could not tell. I lifted the partition. There was money under it. Money in fifties and twenties and hundreds, a sizable stack of bills. I counted it. There was six thousand and forty dollars. When I replaced the partition the stones looked more real.

After the suitcases were back in the closet, I wondered what her thinking had been when she had packed the money in there. Perhaps she assumed I wouldn't search the bags. I hadn't intended to. Maybe she thought that even if I did search them and did find the money it would be safer with me than it would in the apartment. She could have been right. It was safe with me. Even had I been the sort of person to take it and leave, that sort of person would have waited for the chance of acquiring much more—a chance only Antoinette could provide.

I found the bird woman cleaning one of the rooms. I paid her another two nights in advance for myself and asked her to save the room next to mine for a friend who would check in on Thursday. I gave her one night rental on the second room.

As I drove toward town I found myself wondering if what Antoinette had proposed might be the best solution for me. It was tempting. I thought of the ripeness of her, the pungency of her personality, the very startling impact of her lips. There would be no illusions between us. She would make it easy to forget a lot of things. We would have no claims on each other—and would be wedded only by the money, and divorced when it was gone.

After I ate I went to the hardware store. I parked a half block from it. I wanted to talk to George again. I wanted to see if I could steer the conversation toward Eloise and Mr. Fulton. I wanted to see if he would say anything that would make more sense out of the Grassman death. Obviously Fitz hadn't contacted Antoinette. And she seemed confident that no one else could find the money. So it began to appear less logical that Grassman's death had anything to do with the sixty thousand. Then why had Grassman been killed? He could have gotten into some kind of argument with Fitz. We had seen Grassman at the lake on Saturday. Somehow I had spoiled things with Ruth and so I had gotten drunk on Saturday and again on Sunday. Fitz could have killed him on Sunday, not meaning to do so. He could have loaded the body in his car and gone looking for some place to put it, and spotted my car. The California plates would be easy to spot. But by putting the body in my car, he would be eliminating any chance of my leading him to the money Timmy had buried.

But maybe Fitz was convinced that with the clue in his possession, with the name Cindy, he could accomplish as much or more than I could. He was a man of great confidence in himself. And not, I had begun to believe, entirely sane.

If Grassman had contacted Fitz, perhaps George could provide me with some meaningful clue as to why.

But there was a sign on the door. The store was closed. The sign gave no additional information. It was crudely printed on paper Scotch-taped to the inside of the door: *Closed.* I cupped my hands on the glass and looked inside. The stock did not seem to be disturbed. It could not mean closed for good.

It took me several minutes to remember where George lived. I couldn't remember who had told me. White's Hotel. I found it three blocks away. It was a frame building. It was seedy looking, depressing. It had once been painted yellow and white. I went into the lobby. Old men sat in scuffed leather chairs and smoked and read the papers. Two pimpled boys stood by the desk making intense work out of selecting the right holes to punch on a punchboard while the desk man watched them, his eyes bored, his heavy face slack, smoke curling up from the cigarette between his lips.

"I want to see George Warden."

"Second floor. The stairs are over there. A girl just went on up to see him a minute ago." I hesitated and he said "Go ahead on up. Room two-oh-three. She takes care of him when he gets in rough shape. It's okay. George got taken drunk the last couple of days. She tried to phone him and he wouldn't answer the room phone so she came on down. Just now got here."

I guessed it was Ruth. I wanted to see her. I didn't know how she'd react to me. I didn't want to talk to George with her there, though. I went up the stairs slowly.

When my eyes were above the level of the second floor, I saw Ruth running down the gloomy hall toward me. I reached the top of the stairs just as she got there. Her eyes were wide and unfocused. Her mouth was working. Her face was like wet paper.

I called her name and she focused on me, hesitated, and then came into my arms. She was trembling all over. She ground her forehead against my chin, rocking her head from side to side, making an odd chattering, moaning sound. After a few moments she regained enough control to speak.

"It's George. In the room. On the bed."

"Wait right here."

"N—No. I've got to telephone. Police."

Her high heels chattered down the wooden stairs. I went back to room 203. The door was open. George lay across the bed, naked. There was a rifle on the floor. A towel was loosely wrapped around the muzzle. It was scorched where the slug had gone through it. I moved uneasily around to where I could see his head. The back of his head was blown off. I knew that before I saw his head because I had seen the smeared wall. In the instant of death all body functions had shared the smeared explosion. The room stank. His body had a gray, withered look. I moved backward to the door. I backed through it into the hall. I mopped my forehead. It was a hell of a thing for Ruth to have walked in on. They could just as well move the sign to this door, to this life. Closed. Closed for good.

I stood there in the hall and heard the sirens. The desk clerk came lumbering down the hall. Old men from the lobby followed him. They crowded by me and filled the doorway and stared in.

"Good Christ!" the desk clerk said.

"My oh my oh my," said one of the old men.

Some of the faces were familiar. I knew Hillis and I knew Brubaker and I knew Prine. Prine was not on top this time. He was taking orders from a Captain Marion. Captain Marion was a mild, sandy man who wanted everything cozy and neighborly. He had a wide face full of smile wrinkles, and a soft, buzzing voice, and little blue eyes sunk back beyond the thick crisp blond curl of his eyebrows.

Rather than individual questioning, he made it a seminar. I could tell from Prine's bleak look that he did not approve at all.

They got us all down into a room in police headquarters. There was a stenotype operator present. Captain Marion apologized for inconveniencing anybody. He apologized several times. He shifted papers and cleared his throat and coughed.

"Well now, as I finish with you people I'll tell you whether you can take off or not. Nothing particularly official about this. It's a sort of investigation. Get the facts in front of us. Let's see what we got here. First let me say a couple of words about George. I knew his daddy well and I knew George well, and I knew Timmy. George could have been a big man in this town. He was on his way in that direction, but he lost his grip. Lots of men never seem to get back on the ball after bad wife trouble. But I had hopes George would pull out of it. Seems to me like he didn't. And that's too bad. It's quite a waste. George was a bright man." I saw Prine shift his weight restlessly.

"I got it right here on this paper that the body was discovered at twenty minutes after ten this morning by Ruth Stamm. Now Ruthie, what in the wide world were you doing down there at that White's Hotel?"

"Henr—I mean Captain Marion, George didn't have anybody to look after him. Every once in a while I'd sort of—help him get straightened out."

"You used to go with Timmy, didn't you?"

"Yes, I did. I was trying to help George."

"Did Buck approve of that?"

"I don't think so. I mean I know he didn't."

"I see. Ruthie, what took you down there this morning?"

"I went by the store yesterday afternoon and there was a closed sign on it. It worried me. After I got home I phoned White's Hotel. Herman Watkins was on the desk. He told me George was drinking. This morning I phoned the store and there was no answer. Then I tried the hotel. George wouldn't answer the room phone. He does that sometimes. I mean he used to do that. I have a key. So I drove down and went up to the room. The door wasn't even locked. I opened it and—I saw him."

"What were you planning to do?"

"Get him some coffee. Get him cleaned up. Give him a good talking to, I guess. As I've done before."

"Ruthie, you can stay or go, just as you please. Now then, I've got this other name here. Talbert Howard. You came along right after Ruthie. What were you doing there?"

I saw Ruth Stamm start to get up and then sit back down. "I wanted to talk to George. I saw that the store was closed, so I went to the hotel."

"What did you want to talk about?"

Prine answered for me. "We had this man in last week, Captain. We thought he was another one of those people Rose

Fulton keeps sending down here. This man claims he's writing a book about men who died in the prison camp where Timmy Warden died. This man claims he was there, too. He's never written a book. He's unemployed, has no permanent address, and has a record of one conviction."

"For what?"

I answered for myself. "For taking part in a student riot when I was in school. Disturbing the peace and resisting an officer. The officer broke my collarbone with a nightstick. That was called resisting an officer."

Captain Marion looked at Prine. "Steve, you make everything sound so damn serious. Maybe this boy wants to write a book. Maybe he's trying."

"I happen to doubt it, Captain," Prine said.

"What did you want to talk to George about, son?"

"I wanted more information about Timmy." I glanced at Ruth. She was looking at me with contempt. She looked away.

"What happened when you got there?"

"The desk clerk told me a girl had just gone up. I met Miss Stamm when I got to the head of the stairs. She was too upset to talk."

"I got a look in that room myself. Hardly blame her. Terrible looking sight. All right, son. You can go if you want to."

"I'd prefer him to stay, if you don't mind, Captain."

Marion sighed. "All right, Steve. Stick around, Mr. Howard. Now, Herman, we'll get to you. The doc says he can fix the time of death about midnight last night. He may be able to get it a little closer but he says that's a pretty good guess. Did you see George come in?"

"No, sir. I didn't see him. It was a pretty noisy night last night. There were a lot of people coming and going. I heard George was doing his drinking at Stump's, until Stump wouldn't serve him any more. He left there about ten. Frankly, Captain, I was playing a little poker in the room behind where the desk is. I can't see the desk from there, but I can hear the bell on the desk and hear the switchboard if any calls come in. That's why I brought Mr. Caswell along with me."

"I'm Caswell," a little old man said. He had a thin, high voice and an excited manner. "Bartholomew Boris Caswell, retired eleven years ago. I was a conductor on the Erie and Western Railroad. I'm not what you call a drinking man and I see George Warden come in. I was behind him, maybe half a block. I just happened to look at my watch because I wondered what time I was getting in. Watch said eleven twenty-seven. Doesn't lose a minute a month. See it? One of the best ever made. Right now it's eleven minutes of two and that clock on the wall over your head, Captain, is running two minutes slow."

"Are you sure it was George?"

"Sure as I know my own name. Man alive, he was drunk. Wagging his arms, staggering all over. If it wasn't for his friend he'd never have made it home."

"Who was his friend?"

"Don't know him and didn't get a look at him. Stiff-legged man, though. Stiff in one leg. Like a limp. He horsepowered George right into the hotel. Time I came in, they were gone upstairs. The lobby was empty. I could hear some of the boys hooting and hollering and carrying on up on the second floor. So I went there. They were back in Lester's room. He had himself two gallons of red wine. At least he started with two gallons. I had myself a little out of my own glass that I got from my room. It didn't set so good on what I had been drinking. Didn't set good at all. It like to come up on me. So I went on down to bed. Got into my room at three after midnight. Right then I heard a funny noise. Just when I was closing my door. It sounded a little like somebody dropped a book or maybe tipped over in a chair and thumped his head. I listened and I didn't hear anything else so I went right to bed. It turns out that must have been when George shot himself."

"That would fit what the doctor says. Herman, could you find anybody else who heard anything?"

"I couldn't find anybody else at all."

"You don't need anybody else," Caswell said. "I've told you all you've got to know, haven't I?"

"Thanks, Mr. Caswell. You can go along if you want to."

"I'll stay and see what happens, thank you."

Captain Marion studied the papers in front of him and then muttered to himself for a while. At last he looked up. "It's not up to me to make any decision. That'll be up to the inquest. But I think we can figure that George was pretty beat down. Lost his wife. Lost his brother. Lost most of his business. Drinking heavy. It certainly looks to me that if any man had reasons for suicide, George did. Steve, you look uneasy. What's on your mind?"

"Captain, I don't think it's that easy. I've seen some suicides. I've read up on them. A towel was used as a crude silencer. I've never heard of that being used. A suicide doesn't care about the noise. He wants people to come running. He wants it to be dramatic. The towel-wrapped muzzle of the gun was in his mouth when it went off. The gun was new. A three-oh-three bolt-action rifle, right out of stock, with the tag still wired to the trigger guard. There were nice clean prints on the side of the action. Too clean. They were George's, of course. There were no prints on the inside doorknob. It wasn't wiped, but it had been smeared. That could have been accidental or purposeful. Many suicides are naked. More than half. That fits. Buttons had been ripped off his shirt. Maybe he was in a hurry. Maybe somebody undressed him in a hurry. There was a bottle on the floor, under the bed. Half full of liquor. George left very clear prints on that. I'm interested in the stiff-legged man."

"What do you mean, Steve?"

"I think somebody met George after he left Stump's. I talked to Stump. George was nearly helpless. He carried a key to the store. I think somebody went to the store with him and took a rifle out of stock. I think he slid it down his pant leg. That gave him a stiff-legged walk. He took George up to his room. He fed him more liquor. When he passed out he undressed him, sat him on the edge of the bed, wrapped the muzzle, opened his mouth, put it between his teeth, and pulled the trigger. He put prints on the gun and bottle, smeared the knob, and left."

"Steve, dammit, you always make things harder."

"Strange things are going on. I got a report from the county sheriff's office today. A man named Grassman left his stuff in a cabin and didn't come back for it. That was last Sunday. He'd been staying there a couple of weeks. Milton Grassman from Chicago. The county police found stuff in the cabin to indicate he worked for a Chicago firm of investigators, and was down here on that Fulton thing. He stayed twenty miles north of town, on the Redding road. Yesterday a car was towed in. Over-time parking. A routine deal. Blue sedan, late model, Illinois plates. Just before I came here I found out the registration on the steering post is to this Grassman. All right now. Grassman has disappeared, leaving his clothes and his car. George Warden dies all of a sudden. Grassman was down here looking into the disappearance of a Mr. Fulton who took off with George Warden's wife. It ties up, somehow. I want to know how. If we can tie it up, we can find out for sure if it was suicide or murder. I vote for murder. It was a bold way to do it, and a dangerous way to do it. The man who did it took chances. But I think he did it. Was it Grassman? Was it that man over there who claims to be writing a book? Who was it? And why was it done?"

Marion sighed heavily. "Steve, I could never get it through my head why you take off so ugly on those men who came down to poke around. That poor Fulton woman, if she wants to spend her money, why don't you let her? It's no skin off us."

"I don't want my judgment or the result of any investigation of mine questioned. We're the law and order here. I don't want amateur competition."

"Sometimes those fellas can help, Steve."

"I have yet to see the day."

"What did those Chicago people say? Did you get in touch?"

"No."

"Well, you phone them, Steve. Or teletype Chicago and let them handle it with the agency. Those fellows may want to send somebody else down."

"Why, for God's sake?" demanded Prine, losing control.

"Why, to look for Grassman!" Marion said mildly. "Missing, isn't he?"

I managed to walk out beside Ruth. She was cool, almost to the point of complete indifference. "Ruth, I want to be able to explain some time."

"I don't think it's worth bothering about, really."

The day had begun to clear and we stood in frail sunlight.

"I don't know why I should worry so much about your good opinion," I said, trying to strike a light note.

"If I were you, I wouldn't even think about it. I'm usually frank with people. Too frank, as you will remember. I expect others to be the same. I usually expect too much. I'm usually disappointed. I'm getting used to it."

I found myself becoming annoyed at her attitude. "It would be nice for you to get used to it. It would make it easier to be the only perfect person—surrounded by all the rest of us."

"What do you think you—"

"I think you sounded pretty stuffy. That's all. You make a lot of virtuous noise. And you condemn me without knowing the score."

"You don't seem exactly eager to tell me the score."

We stood glaring at each other. It suddenly tickled her sense of the ridiculous. I saw her struggle to keep from smiling. Just then a man came up to us. He was young, with a thin face and heavy horn-rimmed glasses.

"Hello, Allan," Ruth said. "Allan, this is Tal Howard, Allan Peary."

We shook hands and he said, "Ruthie, I just heard they're going to appoint me to straighten out George's estate. What there is left of it. Do you happen to know what happened to the household effects when he sold to Syler?"

"He sold everything, Allan."

Allan Peary shook his head. "I don't know where the money went. I've been in touch with the bank. There's only three accounts open. The lumberyard and the store and his personal account. And damn little money in any of them. You're about the only one of his old friends who saw much of him, Ruth. Where did it all go? He liquidated an awful lot of stuff in the past year. What the hell was he doing? Playing the market? Gambling? Women? Drugs?"

"He was drinking it up, I guess."

"Oh, sure," Allan said. "I know what Syler paid for the house. I know what he got when he sold the lease on Delaware Street. I know what he got for the cement trucks. If he didn't touch anything but Napoleon brandy at twenty-five bucks a bottle, he'd have to drink a thousand bucks a week worth to go through that money."

"Maybe it's in some other account, Allan."

"I doubt it." He looked at me uneasily and said, "I don't want to talk out of school, but he had a big tab at Stump's. He was behind on the room at the hotel. And I heard last week that Sid Forrester had a sixty-day exclusive listing on the lumberyard and had an interested customer lined up. That was the only thing George had left that was making any money."

"Maybe when you go over his accounts you can find what he wrote checks for, Allan."

"That isn't going to work, either. He wrote checks for cash and cashed them at the bank. Amounts ranging from five hundred to two thousand."

Ruth frowned. "He didn't seem worried about money."

"I've tried to talk to him a few times. He didn't seem worried about anything. He didn't seem to give a damn about anything. He almost seemed to be enjoying some big joke—on himself."

And right at that moment something became very clear to me. Something I should have seen before. I wondered why I had been so dense. Once you made the proper assumption, a lot of things fell into their proper place.

CHAPTER TEN

I realized they were still talking, but I was no longer listening to what they said. Then I realized that Ruth had spoken to me.

"I beg your pardon?"

"I said I have to be running along."

"Wait a minute. Please. Can we talk for a minute? You too, Mr. Peary." I saw that she was holding her shoulders as if she were chilled. The sun had gone under again and a raw April wind was blowing. "We could sit in my car a minute. I want to— make a guess as to what George was doing with the money."

They looked at me oddly. Peary shrugged and said, "Sure."

We crossed the street and got into my car, Ruth in the middle.

"It's just a guess. You know that Rose Fulton has never been satisfied with her husband's disappearance. Prine investigated and he's satisfied. George was out of town when Eloise ran off with Fulton. A neighbor saw Eloise carry a bag out to the car. Now suppose that Eloise wasn't running away permanently. Imagine that she was just going to stay the night with Fulton. She didn't want to stay at the house in case George should come home. And there were the neighbors to consider. She wouldn't want to go to a motel or hotel in the area. She was too well known. So she planned to go up to the lake with Fulton. She took just the things she'd need for overnight. Was it the time of year when there wouldn't be people up at the lake?"

"It was this time of year," Ruth said.

"Now suppose George came home and found she wasn't home. He started hunting for her. And went to the lake. Or imagine that for some reason, driving back from his trip out of town, he stopped at the lake and found them there together. What would he have done?"

"I see where this is heading," Ruth said. "It gives me a strange feeling. George loved Eloise and trusted her. I guess he was the only one who couldn't see what she was. If George walked in on the two of them, I think he would have gone temporarily insane. I think he would have killed them. He used to be a powerful man, Tal."

"So he killed them up there at the lake. He got rid of the bodies. He could have wired weights to the bodies and sunk them in the lake, but I'm more inclined to think he buried them. Maybe he buried them on his own land there. He was lucky in that she had been seen at the Inn with Fulton and she was seen leaving with Fulton. He had no way to know it would work out so well. He killed them in anger, and buried the bodies in panic. For a long time he was safe. He tried to go on as though nothing had happened. He played the part of the abandoned husband. And then somebody found the bodies. They didn't report it to the police. They went to George."

Peary said eagerly, "And put the bite on him. They demanded money and kept demanding money. He had to start selling things. When nearly everything was gone, he killed himself. He couldn't face exposure and trial and conviction. So we have to look for somebody who has gotten rich all of a sudden."

"Or somebody smart enough to just put it away and not attract attention by spending it," I said.

"He seemed so strange sometimes," Ruth said softly. "He said queer things I didn't understand. He was like—one of those bad movies where people laugh at the wrong places."

"It would be quite a thing to have on your mind," Peary said. "The more I think about it, the more logical it seems, Mr. Howard. I think you've hit it right on the head. The next step is to prove it. And that means looking for the bodies. I—I'd like to hear what Mrs. Fulton has to say, though. She's been annoying Prine by sending people here. I'd like to know why she's so convinced that she's willing to spend money."

"We could phone her," I said. "If you could get her address."

He got out of the car. "I think I can get it. I'll be back in a minute."

We placed the call from Peary's office. Peary talked to her from the inner office. Ruth and I listened on the extension, her ear close to mine.

The woman had a harsh voice. "How do you come into this?"

"I don't, really. Mr. George Warden committed suicide last night. It gives us a lead to what might have happened to your husband."

"He was killed and he was killed down there. Maybe that woman did it. I don't know. Now I hear that man Grassman is missing. I talked to him before he went down there. When are you people going to wake up down there? What kind of a place is that, anyhow?"

"What makes you think your husband is dead?"

"Henry was no damn good. He'd chase anything in a skirt. I knew it. That was the way he was. He'd always come crawling back. He even liked crawling, I think. This business with that Warden woman was more of the same. It wouldn't last any two years. He had fourteen hundred dollars in his personal checking account. That's all tied up. He's never drawn on it. He owed payments on the car. The finance company has never been able to find the car. We've got two kids in high school. I'll say this for him, he loved the kids. He couldn't go two years without seeing them. Not Henry. Personally, believe me, I'm convinced I'll never see him again and I don't care. But he had a couple of big insurance policies. I insisted on that to protect me and the kids. What protection have I got? The companies won't pay off. It has to be six years from the time he dropped off the face of the earth. Four more years I have to get along. What about college for the kids? I tell you, you people better wake up down there and find out what happened to Henry."

There was more, but she merely repeated herself. The conversation ended. I hung up and looked at Ruth. Her smile was wan and she shivered a little.

"That was pretty convincing, Tal," she said.

"Very."

Peary came into the outer office. He looked thoughtful. "Suppose I was the blackmailer. I find the bodies. I came across them by accident. Or maybe I was smart enough to look for them. Okay. What do I do? I make damn well certain that nobody else finds them and spoils the game. I want to do a better job of hiding them than George did. But I don't want to completely dispose of the bodies. I want them where they can be a threat. I want them where they can be dug up."

Ruth said, "That man Grassman. We saw him out at the lake, Tal and I did. And now he's disappeared. That could mean that he found the bodies."

"And found the blackmailer, too," Peary said.

I found myself remembering the odd conversation with George. When he had said he couldn't give me a job. And had offered me a gun out of stock. He had known I had come from Fitz. He had thought I was a friend of Fitz, cutting myself in on the take. It was obvious that Fitz was the blackmailer. I remembered the expensive look of the suit he was wearing when I had seen him at the Inn. He had come to Hillston with the idea of finding the money Timmy had hidden. He had stayed in the cabin out at the lake. He made a point of telling me that the money wasn't hidden out at the lake. He had looked there. And found something profitable and horrible.

But what was most convincing was Fitz telling me that he was certain Eloise hadn't taken the money with her. He must have appreciated his own joke. Eloise had never meant to leave permanently. She would have been a fool to leave as long as there was a chance of Timmy coming back. She knew about the money. Yet Timmy had been shrewd enough not to trust her with information about the hiding place.

I thought of that first conversation that must have taken place between Fitz and George after Fitz found the bodies.

"What should we do?" Ruth asked. "Should we talk to Captain Marion?"

At four-thirty that gray Wednesday I stood on the lake shore with Ruth and Allan Peary, Sergeant Brubaker and Lieutenant Prine. We were in front of the place that had belonged to George Warden before he had sold it. The narrow dock had been hauled out onto the shore for the winter and hadn't been replaced. The wind had died and the lake was like a gray steel plate. Voices had an odd resonance in the stillness. Captain Marion came out of the cabin with a husky young patrolman. The patrolman had changed to swimming trunks. He wore an aqualung with the face mask shoved up onto his forehead. He walked gingerly on the rough path in his bare feet. He looked serious, self-important, and chilled.

Captain Marion said, "Try to stay on this line right here. The water looks kind of murky. How's the light?"

The patrolman clicked the watertight flashlight on. "It looks bright enough."

Prine said in a low voice so Captain Marion couldn't overhear, "This is nonsense."

No one answered him. Brubaker moved away from us. I glanced down at Ruth's face. Her lips were compressed. She watched the patrolman wade out into the water. It shelved off abruptly. He thrashed and caught his balance, the water up to his chest. He adjusted the face mask, bit down on the mouthpiece. He glanced toward us, then moved forward and was gone, leaving a swirl of turbulence on the surface. The ripples spread out, died away.

Prine lit a cigarette, threw the match aside with a quick, impatient gesture. He had looked tall when I had seen him behind his desk. Standing beside me he was not tall at all. His trunk was very long, but his legs were short and heavy.

The long minutes passed. We made idle talk, but we kept our voices low. The pines on far hills looked black.

The man came abruptly to the surface about forty feet off shore. He swam to the shore and waded out of the water, dripping. He pushed the face mask up onto his forehead. He was shivering.

"Man, it's cold down there," he said.

We moved toward him. "Well?" Marion demanded.

"Here, sir." He handed Marion something. We looked at it as it lay on Marion's hand. It was the dash lighter out of an automobile, corroded and stained. "I came right up from where it is. It's in about fifty feet of water, half on its side. Gray Studebaker. Illinois plates. The number is CT5851. Empty. Rock bottom. It's on a pretty steep slope. I think it can be hauled out all right."

"That number checks out," Prine said in a reluctant voice. "Damn it, how can you figure a thing like that?"

"Steve," Marion said, "I guess maybe we goofed on this one. I guess maybe that Rose Fulton was right."

Ruth had gone back to town with Peary in his car. She had seemed subdued, thoughtful. As Peary had credited me with making the guess that led to the discovery of the car, I was in Marion's good graces. I had not told them the second installment of the guess—no longer a guess, actually—that Fitzmartin was the blackmailer.

The tow truck had arrived. It stood heading away from the water, brakes locked and wheels blocked. The taut cable stretched down into the water. At dusk they had turned on the big spotlights on the tow truck. About twenty people watched from a place just down the lake shore. Captain Marion had herded them down there out of the way. More men had come out from town. They had been searching the area, prodding into the soft earth with long steel rods.

The tired patrolman surfaced again and came to shore. "It ought to do it this time," he said. "I got the hook around the rear axle and fastened back on the cable." He stood in the light. He had scratched his arm on a rock. There was a sheen of water-diluted blood on his forearm.

"Try her again," Marion called.

The winch began to whine again. The cable tightened visibly. I watched the drum. The cable began to come in a few feet at a time. The progress was uneven. At last, like some surfacing sea monster, the gray back of the car emerged from the water. The car was resting on its wheels. It came backward out of the water, streaming. Bright metal showed where it had been dragged against rocks. The big truck moved forward until the car was entirely on dry land. Water ran out of the car, runneling back into the lake. There was a smell of dampness and weed.

"Get yourself dried off, Ben," Marion said quietly. "George, open up that back end with a pry bar."

The cold, weary underwater swimmer went up to the cabin. A stocky man in uniform opened the trunk expertly. The county police who had arrived moved closer. I could hear the spectators talking excitedly to each other. The floodlights illuminated the interior of the trunk compartment brightly. There was drenched luggage in there, sodden clothing. Water was still running out of the trunk.

Marion said, "Well, that's one place they ain't. Didn't expect them to be. Tight fit for two of them. But you can see how it was. Those shirts and socks. That stuff wouldn't jump out of the suitcase. He found them. After he killed them he just dumped their stuff in the back end, loose like. Then he aimed the car at the slope and started it up. It would be night and he wouldn't have the car lights on because that would attract attention. She got going pretty good. He knew it was deep right off here. Hitting the water probably slowed it a lot, but once on the bottom it would keep right on going down the underwater slope until it wedged in those rocks where Ben found it."

I could see a woman's red plastic purse in the back end. The red had stayed bright. It looked new enough to have been carried by Eloise yesterday. Captain Marion reached in and took it out.

He unsnapped it and poured the water out of it. A corroded lipstick fell to the ground. Marion grunted as he bent over and picked it up. There was a wallet in the purse. He took it out and shook the water off it, and opened it. He studied the soaked cards.

"Mrs. Warden's, all right. Al, can you tow the car on into town all right?"

"Sure, Captain."

"Well, when you get there, spread all this stuff out in the back end of the garage where it'll get a chance to dry off." In ten minutes the car had been lashed securely and towed off. I heard the tow truck motor labor as it went up the hill toward the road.

"Captain," Prine said, "shall I have the men keep looking? It's getting too dark to do much good. They haven't had any luck."

"Might as well save it until morning. Tom, can you detail some of your boys to help out in the morning?"

"I can send a couple around."

The spectators had gone, most of them. A wiry little man came over to where we stood. The swimmer, back in uniform, had come down from the cabin. I could smell a strong reek of liquor on his breath. Somebody had evidently found a cold preventative for him.

Prine said to the elderly little man, "I told you people to stay back there."

"Don't you bark and show your teeth at me, boy. I want to talk to you fellows. Maybe you might learn something."

"Get off the—"

"Hold it, Steve," Captain Marion said in a mild voice. "What's your name?"

"Finister. Bert Finister. Looking for bodies, somebody said. That's what you're doing. You could listen to me. I live off back there, other side of the road. I do chores around here. Most of the camps. Everybody knows me. Carpentry work, plumbing, masonry. Put the docks in. Take 'em out in the fall. I know these camps."

"So you know the camps. If you were hunting for bodies, Finister, where would you look?"

"I'm getting to that. I know the camps. I know the people that come stay in them. Knew George and Timmy Warden and their pa. Knew that Eloise, too. Knew when Timmy used to come up and swim all the way across to see Ruthie Stamm. Showing off, I guess. Then last year there was a fellow named Fitzmartin up here. Guess he rented this place from George. First time it was ever rented, and now it's been sold, but that's beside the point. You know there's all this do-it-yourself stuff these days. Takes the bread out of a man's mouth. Takes honest work away from him. People do things theirself, they botch it all up. Me, I take it like an insult. That Fitzmartin, he was digging around. Didn't know what he was doing. I figured whatever he was doing it was something he could hire me to do. Then by God, he trucks in cement and he knocks together some forms, and I be damned if he doesn't cement the garage floor. Pretty fair job for an amateur. But it was taking bread out of my mouth, so I remember it. He put that floor in last May. If I was looking for any bodies I'd look under that floor because that Fitzmartin, he's a mean-acting man. I come around to help and he chases me clean off the place. Walks me all the way up to the road with my arm twist up behind me and calls me a trespasser. Nobody ever called me that before. Folks are friendly up here. That man he just didn't fit in at all. And I'm glad he wasn't the one who bought it. The folks who bought it, people from Redding, they seem nice. Got two little kids. I let them know when they want anything done, they get hold of Bert Finister."

We stood in the glow of car lights. Captain Marion looked at Prine. "Fitzmartin?"

"Runs the lumberyard for George. Shall I go get him?"

"We better look first, Steve."

"That cement floor fooled me. I went over it carefully. It hadn't been dug up and patched. It never occurred to me that the whole floor had been—"

"I saw a pickax in the shed," Captain Marion said. "Maybe you better swing it yourself, Steve. Maybe you need the workout."

"Yes, sir," said a subdued Lieutenant Prine.

They parked the cars so that the headlights made the inside of the garage as bright as a stage. Prine swung and grunted and sweated until Captain Marion decided the punishment was enough. Finister came back out of the darkness with another pick and a massive crowbar. The work began to go faster. A big slab was loosened. They pried it up, heaved it over out of the way, exposing black dirt. The men worked silently. For a long time it didn't appear that they would get anywhere. I was out in the darkness having a cigarette when I heard someone say sharply, "Hold it!"

I started toward the garage and then thought of what they might find and stopped where I was. The one called Ben came out into the night. He bent forward from the waist and gagged dryly. He stood up and coughed.

"Find them?" I asked.

"They found them. Prine says it's her. He remembers the color of her hair."

I rode back in with Captain Marion. Prine had gone on ahead to pick up Fitzmartin. Captain Marion felt talkative.

"It isn't going to be too easy with this Fitzmartin. What can we prove that will stand up? Blackmail? We'd have to have the money and George's testimony. Concealing The evidence of a crime? He can say George told him to put a cement floor in the garage. He can say he didn't have any idea what was under it. No, it isn't going to be as easy as Steve thinks it is. Sometimes Steve worries me. He gets so damn set in his mind. He isn't flexible enough."

"But you think it was Fitzmartin."

"It has to be. He milked George clean dry. George didn't have much choice, I guess. Pay up or be exposed. If he was exposed, my guess is he would have gotten life. A good defense attorney could have brought out some things about Eloise that wouldn't sound very pretty to a jury. George could have figured that when he ran out of money, Fitzmartin might—probably would—take off without saying a word. That would leave him free to walk around broke. Better than not walking around at all. What I can't figure is how Fitzmartin got it in his head to look for those bodies. He wasn't in this town when George killed the pair of them. I understand he was in prison camp with Timmy. But how would Timmy have any idea about a thing like that. There's some angles to this we won't know unless that Fitzmartin wants to talk."

I could sense the way his mind was turning. He glanced at me a couple of times.

"You gave us some help, Howard. I grant that. But I don't feel right about the way you fit in, either."

"What do you mean, Captain?"

"Aren't you just a little too damn convenient? You hit town and everything starts to pop open. Why is that?"

"Coincidence, I guess."

"You knew Timmy and you know Fitzmartin. Maybe before you came here you knew Fitzmartin was milking George. Maybe that's why you came here, Howard."

"I didn't know anything about it."

"I'm not through with you, son. Don't take yourself any notion to disappear. I want you where we can talk some more. You're just too damn convenient in this whole thing."

At that moment, about a mile from the Hillston city limits, a call came over the radio. Marion answered it. I could barely decipher Prine's Donald Duck voice over the small speaker.

"He's gone, Captain. Fitzmartin is gone. I've put out a description of him and his car. He was living in a shed at the rear of the lumberyard. All his personal stuff is gone. I felt the space heater. There was a little warmth left. He didn't leave too long ago. How about road blocks?"

"Damn it, Steve, I've told you before. Road blocks aren't worth a damn around here. There's too many roads. There just aren't enough men and vehicles in this area to close all those roads. That stove could have been turned off three hours ago. You'd have to have your blocks set up right now this minute on every road within a hundred miles at least."

"What do you suggest, sir?" Prine said more humbly.

"Wait and see if somebody picks him up."

Marion broke the connection. "Okay, Howard. You seem to know Fitzmartin pretty well. Where does he come from?"

"Originally from Texas, I think."

"What's his line of work?"

"I think he worked in oil fields."

"Ever say anything about his relatives?"

"He never talked very much."

"That's not much help, I guess. Where can we drop you off?"

"My car's parked across the street from Peary's office."

"Want to tell you that I appreciate you making a pretty good guess about this whole thing, Howard. I can't help telling you I wonder just how much of it was guessing. And I wonder why you came here. I'd like it if you'd play the cards face up."

I had thought him amiable, mild, ineffectual. Hour by hour I had revised my opinion. I had thought Prine was the dangerous one. Prine was the fool. Captain Marion was something else entirely.

"I'm not hiding anything, Captain."

"We've got George dead, and that Grassman missing, and we've got those two bodies, and now Fitzmartin on the run. It has to get tied together a little better before I feel right about it."

"I'm sorry I can't help you."

"I'm sorry you won't help, son. Good night."

They drove away. It was after ten and I was famished. In twelve hours I would be picking Antoinette up. With luck, in twenty-four hours I would be gone. Either with her or alone. I didn't know which it would be. Call it a form of monomania. I had thought about the money for too long. I had aimed toward it for too long. Tomorrow I would have it. Once I had it, maybe I could begin to think clearly again.

I found a place to eat. I was just finishing when Brubaker came in. He sat beside me at the counter and gloomily flipped the menu open. "A hell of a long day," he said.

"It has been."

"And not over yet. At least they're giving me time to eat. And then back on the job. Until God knows when. Nobody will get any sleep tonight."

"I thought Captain Marion said he'd just wait and hope Fitzmartin gets picked up."

"That's right. I mean about the girl."

I suddenly felt very cold. "What girl?"

"I thought you knew about that. The Stamm girl. Peary brought her back to town. He left her off at her car. They found her car parked on North Delaware. And nobody's seen her since. Her old man is fit to be tied. Everybody is running around in circles."

I couldn't finish the little bit of food that was left I couldn't drink the rest of my coffee. It was as though my throat had closed. I wondered how soon they'd add two and two. Ruth had been subdued and thoughtful when she left the lake. She would remember that Fitzmartin had acted strangely. She was the sort of person to do her own investigating. She was the sort of person who would go and talk to Fitzmartin. She would have no way of knowing that he was a killer. She would underestimate his cleverness. It wouldn't take him long to learn that the car had been found, to learn that they were searching the area of the lake cabin. It was time to go. The string was running out. I could guess how it had happened with Grassman. Grassman, as a result of his quiet investigation, had made some sound guesses as to what had happened. He had paid a call on Fitzmartin. Maybe Grassman had wanted to cut himself in. Maybe he had made a search of the place where Fitzmartin lived while he was out. He could have found the large sum of money Fitz had extorted from George Warden. Fitz could have found him there and killed him, driven the body into town, and put it in my car.

From the violence of the blow that had killed Grassman, it could be assumed that it was an unpremeditated killing. In the moment he killed Grassman, Fitz became more deeply involved. He waited, expecting me to be jailed for the Grassman murder. When I wasn't, he would know that I had successfully gotten rid of the body. No one had spotted it in my car. Thus, when it was found, it could as readily be traced back to him as to me.

Assuming he could be questioned about Grassman, then George became the weak link. George, by talking, could disclose Fitz's motive for the Grassman murder. And so George had to die. Fitz had killed him boldly, taking his risk and getting away with it. Prine had been right about the towel.

Just when he thinks everything has been taken care of, Ruth Stamm arrives. He can't leave without her immediately spreading the alarm. He needs a grace period, time enough to get far away before someone else makes the same guess she has made. That left him with a choice. He could tie her up and leave her there. But that would be too clear an admission of guilt. He could take her with him. That would be awkward and risky. Or he could kill her. One more death wouldn't make any difference in the final penalty.

"You're doing a lot of sweating," Brubaker said. "It isn't that hot in here."

I managed a feeble smile. I said I would see him around. I paid and left. It was too easy to visualize her dead, with raw new lumber stacked over her body, her dark red hair against the damp ground in the coolness of the night. What shocked me was the stunning sense of loss. It taught me that I had underestimated what she meant to me. I could not understand how she had come to mean so much, in so short a time. More than Charlotte had ever meant.

CHAPTER ELEVEN

I went directly to police headquarters. I demanded to see Captain Marion. After fifteen minutes they let me see him.

I told him that I thought Ruth's disappearance had something to do with Fitzmartin. He looked older and tireder. He nodded without surprise.

He said, "She knew George pretty well. Maybe she remembered something George said about Fitzmartin. So she tried to check it out herself. Maybe he'd think she was the only one who'd guess. I've thought of that, Howard. I don't like it. I've got a crew out there searching the yard. I thought of something else, too. Maybe Grassman guessed. Maybe that's why something happened to him. Thanks for coming in, Howard. I added it up about a half hour ago. I don't like the total."

"Can I help in any way?"

"You look like hell. You better try to get some sleep."

"I don't think I'll be able to sleep."

I drove back out to the motel. It no longer seemed important about meeting Antoinette in the morning. It didn't matter any more. I had come here to Hillston to find treasure. I had thought I would find it buried in the ground. I had found it walking around, with dark red hair, with gray eyes, with a look of pride. And I hadn't recognized it. I had acted like a fool. I had tried to play the role of thief. But it didn't fit. It never would fit. The money meant nothing. Ruth meant everything. I had had a chance and I had lost it. They don't give you two chances.

I parked in front of my motel room. The office was dark, the *No Vacancy* sign lighted. Cars sat in the light of an uneasy moon, and the travelers slept.

I unlocked the door with my key and stepped inside, reaching for the light switch. Something came out of the darkness and slammed against my jaw. Pain blossomed red behind my eyes, a skyrocket roaring was in my ears and I felt myself fall into nothingness.

I came to in a brightly lighted place. I opened my eyes and saw nothing but the white glare and closed them quickly. The white glare hurt. My hands were behind me, fastened there somehow. I was in an awkward position. Something soft filled my mouth, holding it open.

I opened my eyes again, squinting. I saw that I was in the small tile bathroom of the motel. The door was closed. I lay on my side on the floor. Earl Fitzmartin sat on the side of the tub. He wore khakis. He looked at me with those eyes like smoke. His pale colorless hair was tousled. I could sense at once that he had gone beyond the vague borderline of sanity. It was like being in a cage with an animal.

He stood up, closed the lid on the toilet, bent over me, picked me up with disconcerting ease, and sat me on the closed lid, holding me for a moment until he was certain I wouldn't topple over. He sat on the rim of the tub again, facing me.

"We aren't going to talk over a whisper, Tal. We aren't going to make any sudden noises. If we make any sudden noises I'm going to snap your neck with my hands. It wouldn't be hard to do. Nod your head if you're going to be quiet."

I nodded. He took a knife out of his pocket, opened the blade, and leaned toward me. He put the cold steel against my cheek, holding it there, smiling in an odd way, then yanked it toward him, cutting the strip of sheeting that held the dry washcloth in my mouth. I pushed the washcloth out with my tongue and it fell to the floor at my feet.

"Where's Ruth?"

"That was just a little bit too loud. Not much too loud. Just a little bit. So soften it up, Tal. Ruth is all right."

"Thank God."

"Not God. Me. I had the idea, not God. She was on the ground. On her face. Out like a light. I took hold of that wonderful hair in my left hand and I pulled her head up. I held this little knife against her throat. It's sharp enough to shave with. I was about to pull it through her throat when I suddenly began to wonder if she might be worth something. So I didn't do it. She's all right. Don't thank God. Thank Earl Fitzmartin. She isn't comfortable. She isn't happy. But she's still alive, Tal."

"Where is she?"

"Not over a half mile from here. But you don't know what direction. It's across country. I was trained to fight at night. I move well at night, Tal. I'm good at night. You know how I used to get around the camp. You remember that. She's well tied, Tal. She can't even wiggle. She can't make a sound. You're really worried about her, aren't you? She came to the yard. For a little heart-to-heart talk. Did they find the bodies, Tal?"

"They tore up the garage floor."

"Now they can ask George all about it. But George won't have a word to say. George isn't talking. George didn't have much more left. Just a little equity in the lumberyard. A little stock in the store. Not enough left to stay around for. He was good for forty-seven thousand, seven hundred dollars. It should have been more. He didn't have to give up. He could have gotten on the ball and started making more. He could have tried to fatten up the kitty. But he was selfish. He would have lived longer."

"You killed him."

"That was a shade too loud, Tal. Just a bit too loud. How are you coming with Cindy, Tal. Find her?"

"You took an awful chance killing George."

He smiled again. "You won't believe this, but I didn't kill him. He started to come to while I was stripping him, but I poured more liquor into him. I read that people drown themselves and shoot themselves and cut their wrists naked. Did you know that? Very interesting. I got him propped on the side of the bed. I got the muzzle with the towel around it between his teeth. The gun was about the only thing holding him up. I wanted the angle to be right and I wanted to do it when there was a lot of noise on the floor. But I wanted to do it, Tal. You know, you plan a thing, and work it out just right, you want to do it. But he opened his eyes. He looked right at me. He looked ridiculous, with the gun in his mouth. He looked right at me and put his big toe against the trigger before I could stop him. I don't know if it was an accident. What do you think?"

"I think he did it on purpose."

"So do I. So do I. It makes me feel a little strange. He maybe did it like a joke. He did that well. He didn't do much else well. He didn't do well marrying that woman or burying her, either. I thought I'd hit the sixty thousand when I dug under the pines. But it turned out to be the woman and the salesman. It disappointed me, Tal. But it turned out to be just like finding money, didn't it?"

"They're all after you now."

"Do you think that worries me? Now hear this. It doesn't worry me a bit. Maybe you ought to be worried. Where is Grassman? I didn't think you could get out of that. You surprised me a little, Tal. I thought it would give you the jumps. What did you do with it?"

"I hid the body in a barn, an abandoned barn."

"And I bet you did some sweating. Grassman was smart. He was in my league, Tal. Not yours. He added things up. He was a pro. He added things, up and came after the money. He knew I had to have it around somewhere. He knew I was too smart to spend it. I caught him looking for it. We had a little talk. He got rough. I got mad and hit him too hard. That made it awkward. I put him in the back end of my car. I didn't know where to dump him. I was thinking of an alley, so they'd think he'd been mugged. But I found your car by accident. It saved me a lot of time. After I killed Grassman, I knew I had to get George out of the way. He was the only one who could tie me to Grassman. It took some planning, and some luck. I won't have time to work on the Cindy angle. How are you coming?"

I could see the shape of it. George could tie him to Grassman and George was dead. I could tie him to both of them. It was only through his greed that I could buy time, buy my life. "I found her."

He waited ten seconds. He said, "A hundred and seven thousand sounds better than forty-seven. I think I better have that much before I take off, Tal."

"They're going to get you."

"I don't think so. I don't figure it that way. They might have got me if I'd cut her throat. I wanted to. But I didn't let myself. They would have hunted me too hard. Now you can trade information for her, Tal. If she doesn't mean anything to you, too bad. I can kill you right here and go and kill her and be on my way and be careful and take my chances. I couldn't leave you here telling them about George and Grassman and then finding my sixty thousand. I'd rather nobody found it."

"Somebody is going to find it, anyway. The girl is going to find it. She knows where it is."

"Where is it, Tal?"

"She wouldn't tell me. I told her too much. I couldn't find out any other way. She's—more in your league, Fitz. I'm picking her up tomorrow morning in Redding. At ten o'clock. She's going to go with me to where the money is hidden."

He smiled in that wild, unpleasant way. "You're kidding the troops, boy. You're stalling. I scared you and you're making things up. You're just smart enough to know that if you are going to get it tomorrow, and yet you don't know where it is, I've got to leave you alive. You're that smart, and that's why you made it up."

"It's the truth."

"I don't think it's the truth at all. I think maybe you haven't gotten any place. I think I've stalled around here too long. I think I'd like to hear your neck snap. I can do it so quick you'll hardly know it happened. Maybe you won't know it at all."

"Wait a minute. Look in the closet in the bedroom. Her luggage is there."

For the first time he looked uncertain. He turned out the bathroom light and went into the next room. He came back with the two suitcases. He shut the door, turned the light on again. He opened them and looked at the clothing.

"This is pretty good stuff. This belongs to her? What's it doing here?"

"We were going to get the money and go off together."

I could see him appraise that, and half accept it. "But I don't like the idea of letting you go and get it. I can't keep an eye on you."

"Fitz, listen to me. I don't give a damn about the money. You can have every cent of it after I get it. I'll trade all of it for Ruth Stamm. Then see how it will be. You'll have the hundred and seven thousand. They think George was a suicide. Maybe they'll never find Grassman. I covered the body with hay. The barn is about to fall down. Nobody ever goes in there. They won't look as hard for you. You'll be a lot safer."

"You're lying. This is a stall."

"It's not. I'll prove we were going to go away together when we got the money. Look for the small black box in the bottom of the smaller suitcase. Under all the clothes. Yes, that's it. Look under the partition."

He took the money out. He riffled through it. He folded it once and put it in his shirt pocket. He looked at me for long moments, his eyes dubious.

I do not like to think about the next half hour. He put the gag back in my mouth. He had his strong hands, and he had the small sharp knife, and he had a sadistic knowledge of the nerve ends. From time to time he would stop and wait until I quieted down, then loosen the gag and question me. The pain and humiliation made me weep like a child. Once I fainted. Finally he was satisfied. He had learned how much I thought of Ruth.

He had learned that I knew that we had to go where the money was hidden by boat. He knew that I had guessed we would start from the Rasi house north of town. And he knew that I knew no more than that.

After that he cut my hands loose. He was perfectly safe in so doing. I was too enfeebled by pain to be any threat to him.

"You'll get the money. You'll dig it up. You'll come back here with it."

"No."

He took a quick half step toward me. I couldn't help flinching. Memory of what he could do was too clear.

"What do you mean?"

"I mean I don't trust you to do what you promise, Fitz. I've got to know Ruth will be all right. I've got to know she'll be safe. Or you don't get the money."

"I broke you this far. You want to be broken the rest of the way?"

"I don't think you can do it."

After a long time he gave a shrug of disgust. "Maybe not. How do you want it worked?"

"I want to see her. I want to see that she's alive before I give you the money. It could be by the river. Then if you try to cross me, I'll throw the money in the river. I swear I'll do that."

"You would, wouldn't you? You're making it rough. I can't risk being seen."

"I'll see that we start off by boat at one o'clock. I don't know how far we have to go or how long it will take. You could bring her to the Rasi house at two."

"It's a risk."

"It's isolated. There's no phone there. At least I don't think they have a phone. I'll give you the money and I'll see that you get a fair start. That's the most I can do. I won't try to make it any safer for you."

"But you promise a fair start?"

"I promise that."

He snapped out the bathroom light. I heard the door open, and then heard the outer door open and close. I walked unsteadily through the dark room to the front door. I opened it.

The moon was gone. A wind sighed across the flats on the far side of the road. There was no sign that Fitzmartin had ever been there. The night was still. He was very good in the night. I remembered that.

There was a first-aid kit in the trunk compartment of my car. I got it. The small cuts had not bled very much. I cleaned myself up and bandaged the cuts. I ached all over. I felt sick and weak, as though I were recovering from a long illness. I kept seeing his eyes. His powerful hands had punished nerves and muscles. Even my bones felt bruised and tender.

I went to bed. I was certain that Ruth was still alive. I hoped his greed would be stronger than his wish to kill. I hoped his greed would last through the night. But there was something erratic about his thought patterns. There was an incoherency about the way he had talked, jumping from one subject to the next. He had a vast confidence in his own powers.

I wondered where he had Ruth. A half mile away. Across country. Maybe she was in his car, and it was parked well off a secondary road. Maybe he had found a deserted shed.

As I lay awake, trying to find some position in which I could be comfortable, I heard it begin to rain. The rain was light at first, a mere whisper of rain. And then it began to come down. It thundered on the roof. It made a drench of the world, bouncing off the painted metal of the cars, coming down as though all the gates of the skies had been opened.

CHAPTER TWELVE

I awoke at dawn. It was still raining. It seemed to be raining harder than before. I was surprised that I had been able to go to sleep. I took a hot shower to work the stiffness out of my muscles. The small cuts stung. My face in the mirror looked like the face of a stranger, with sunken eyes and flat, taut cheeks.

I prayed that Ruth was still alive. I prayed that she had lived through the night. I knew what would have happened the previous night had I not found Cindy. I would be lying dead on the tile floor. They would find me there.

I shaved and dressed and left the motel. I got uncomfortably wet in the ten feet from the motel door to the car door. I drove slowly into town, the lights on, peering ahead through the heavy rain curtain. I drove through town and found a gas station open on the far side. I had the car gassed up. Farther along I found an all-night bean wagon. A disc jockey in Redding was giving the seven-o'clock news. The plastic radio was behind the counter.

"…as yet on the disappearance of Ruth Stamm, only daughter of Doctor Buxton Stamm of Hillston. It is believed that the young woman was abducted by a man named Earl Fitzmartin, Marine veteran and ex-prisoner of war. Fitzmartin had been employed for the past year by George Warden, Hillston businessman. Fitzmartin was a newcomer to Hillston. George Warden committed suicide this week. But certain peculiarities about the circumstances of Warden's suicide have led Hillston police to believe that it may have been murder. Yesterday the Hillston police, assisted by Gordon County police officers, searched a summer cottage once owned by George Warden and found, under a cement garage floor, the bodies of Eloise Warden, wife of George Warden, and Henry Fulton, of Chicago. At the time of the Warden woman's disappearance two years ago, it was believed she had run off with Fulton. Discovery of the bodies and of the Fulton car, which had been driven into the lake into deep water, has led police to believe that George Warden killed both of them after finding them together at the summer cottage.

"An intensive search is being made for Fitzmartin and Miss Stamm. Full details of the case have not yet been released, but it is believed that there is some connection between Fitzmartin and the bodies discovered yesterday at the summer cottage. It is expected that federal authorities will be called in on the case today. Miss Ruth Stamm is twenty-six years old, five feet eight inches tall, and weighs about a hundred and twenty-eight pounds. She has dark red hair and gray eyes and was last seen wearing a dark green skirt and a white cardigan sweater. Fitzmartin is about thirty years old, six feet tall, weighs about a hundred and eighty pounds. He has very blond, almost white hair, pale gray eyes. He may be driving a black Ford, license BB67063. Anyone seeing persons of this description should contact the police at once. Listen again at eight o'clock to WRED for complete local news."

The disc jockey stopped and whistled softly. "How about that, folks? They give me this stuff to read and sometimes I read it and don't even listen. But that's a hot one. That one can grab you. Bodies under concrete. Cars in lakes. Suicides that aren't suicides. A red-headed gal and an ex-Marine. Man, that's a crazy mixed-up deal they've got down there in Hillston. That's got all the makings of a national type crime. Well, back to the mines. Got to spin some of this stuff. But before I do, let me tell you a little something you ought to know, you good folks out there, about the Atlas Laundry and Dry Cleaning people right here in Redding, over on Downey Street. If you've got clothes you're really proud of, and I guess we all got one set of those good threads at least, then you—"

The fat young girl behind the counter turned off the radio. "That character," she said amiably to me. "Ten minutes of commercials between every number. Drive you nuts. I just turn him on for the news. If you want, I can turn him back on or find something else."

"No thanks."

"How about that Stamm girl? I met her once. We had this dog, see. Got him when he was a puppy. But this highway, it's bad to try to have a dog when you live on the highway. He got himself hit and we took him to Stamm's. The girl was real nice. Pretty sort of girl. But Blackie was too far gone. Busted his back, so they had to give him a shot. Honest, I cried. And you know what I think? I think it's a big deal for those two. I think she maybe ran off with that Marine. You can figure she wasn't getting any younger. She'll hear about all the mess she's causing and she'll get in touch. That's just what will happen."

"Could be," I said.

"Of course it could be. You want more coffee, maybe? Sometimes I think I'd run off with anybody asked me just to get out of this rat race. That's on my bad days. Isn't this day a stinker, though? It keeps coming down like this, every creek in the county will be flooded. It gives me the creeps to think about those two buried under a garage floor all that time. I never knew her, but my sister knew her. She was in the high school with her, before my time. My sister says she did a lot of running around. The way I see it, mister, if a husband catches his wife and another man, he's got a right to kill the two of them. It's like what they say the unwritten law. When I get married, I'm not going to do any cheating. I guess it isn't so bad if a man does a little cheating. They're all alike, beg your pardon. But no woman with a home and husband and everything has any right to jump the fence. Don't you think so? He made his big mistake burying the two of them like he did. He should have just got on the phone and said to the police, 'You boys come out here and see what I did and why.' Then it would have been just what they say formalities. The way I look at it—"

I was saved by two truck drivers who came in from the big red combo that had just parked in front of the place. After she served them she came back, but I had finished.

As she gave me my change she said, "You remember what I told you, now. That girl and that Marine ran off some place. Drive carefully."

I drove on through the rain. The cars I met were proceeding with great care. It should have been full daylight, but it hadn't gotten appreciably lighter since first dawn. It was almost nine o'clock before I got to Redding. I parked near a drugstore and phoned her number from a booth in the back of the store.

She answered the phone at once. "Hello?"

"This is Tal."

"I'm sorry. I'm afraid you have the wrong number."

"I'll be there at ten like you said."

"That's perfectly all right." She hung up. Her last comment had been the tip-off. Somebody was there with her. She had answered as though I had apologized. I wondered if it would be all set for ten. I wondered if I dared try again. I went to the drugstore counter and had coffee. The counter was emptying rapidly as people went to work. I bought a Redding paper. The discovery of the bodies had been given a big play. The article filled in a little more background than the radio item, but essentially it was the same.

At nine-thirty I tried again. She answered on the second ring. "Hello?"

"This is Tal again."

"Yes?"

"Is this deal off or on. What goes on? Should I be there at ten?"

"This coming Saturday? No, I'm very sorry. I have a date."

"I'm at a pay phone. The number is 4-6040. I'll wait right here until you can call me back."

"No, I'm so sorry. Maybe some other time. Give me a ring."

"Phone as soon as you can."

"Thank you. Good-by."

I took a booth near the phone booths. I went and got my paper and ordered more coffee. I waited. Two people used the booth. At five minutes to ten the call came.

"Hello?"

"Is that you, Tal? I couldn't talk before. I'm glad you phoned. Make it ten-fifteen. What does your watch say?"

"Exactly four minutes of."

"Don't park out back. Park a block away. Start up at exactly ten-fifteen and go slow. When you see me coming, unlatch the door. Don't waste time getting away from there."

I began to be more nervous. I had no way of knowing what she was mixed up in. I knew her playmates would be hard people. I didn't know how closely they would be watching her.

The rain had begun to let up a little. I parked a block away from her apartment house. I could see it. I kept the motor running. I kept an eye on my watch. At exactly ten fifteen I started up. I drove slowly. I saw a man in a trench coat across the street from the apartment house, leaning against a phone pole.

As I drew even with the apartment house, slowing down, she came running. I swung the door open. I didn't stop. She piled into the car. She wore a dark coat, a black hat with a veil, and carried a brown case like a dispatch case.

"Hurry!" she ordered. Her voice was shrill, frightened.

I speeded up. She was looking back. I heard a hoarse shout.

"Keep going!" she ordered. "He's running for his car. It's headed the wrong way. They posted a man out in back. I didn't know it until yesterday afternoon."

A light ahead turned red. There was cross traffic. I ran the light. Tires yelped and horns blatted with indignation. I barely made the next light. She kept watching back over her shoulder. It took fifteen minutes to get to the southbound highway, the road to Hillston.

Once we were out on the highway and I was able to open it up a little, she turned around. I glanced at her. Her left eye was badly puffed and discolored. Her left cheek was bruised. I remembered the story of the small girl who had stayed home from school because her brother had blacked her eye.

"What happened to your face?"

"I got bounced around a little. People got annoyed at me."

"What the hell have you been mixed up in?"

"Don't worry about it."

"I'd like to know how much chance I was taking."

"You weren't taking it. I was taking it. They didn't want me to leave. Anybody leaves they get the idea there's a subpoena in the background. And a committee and an investigation. They were careless. I learned too much. So they had a problem. Do they kill me or watch me. They watched me. I'm stupid, I guess. I was having a big time. I thought I could pull out any time. I didn't know they played so rough. If I'd guessed it could be that rough, I wouldn't have gotten that far in."

"You can't go back, then."

"I can't ever go back. Don't make jokes. Just drive as fast as you can."

She had changed in the short time since I'd seen her. There had been a lot of arrogance about her. Confidence and arrogance, and a flavor of enjoyment. That was gone. She was bitter and half-frightened and sullen.

I drove. The rain finally stopped. The sky had a yellow look. Tires made a wet sound on the road. The ditches were full. We went through a village. Children romped in the schoolyard under the yellow sky.

I did not like what I was going to have to do to her. She had given me a certain measure of trust. She had no way of knowing that the stakes had changed. She could not know I was willing to betray her—that I had to betray her. I knew I could not risk taking her to the motel. She would want her luggage first of all. She would want to check on the money. It was gone. She would want an explanation. And there was no explanation I could give her.

I would betray her, but it was the money balanced against Ruth's life. It seemed fantastic that I could have seriously considered going away with this woman who sat so silently beside me, fists clenched nervously against the dark fabric of her skirt. It seemed fantastic that I could have gotten wound up in the whole thing. Charlotte was several lifetimes in the past. When I had come home I had felt half alive. Now I was entirely alive. I knew what I wanted, and why, and knew that I would go to any lengths to get what I wanted.

"Are you serious in thinking they would kill you?" I asked.

She laughed. A single short, flat sound. "I know where the body is buried. Ever hear that expression? It was a party I didn't want to go on in the first place. I knew it would be a brawl. It was. A man got himself killed. He got too excited. Not a bad guy. Young guy. Rich family. Got a big whomp out of running around with the rougher element. You know. Liked to know people by their first name, the ones who had been in jail. Liked to be able to get his parking tickets fixed. He got suddenly taken dead. Sort of an accident. A very important fellow shot him in the head. I was the only outsider. I know where they put him. The family has spent a fortune in the last five years, looking for their kid. They're still looking. It could be very bad. It was very bad at the time. I'd never seen anything like that before."

"They would kill you?"

"If they think I'll talk. If they were sure of it and had a chance. There wouldn't be much heat over me. Not over this pair of round heels. The kid they killed is real heat. The man with the gun was drunk. I was with the man with the gun. The kid thought he was too drunk to know or care. He had his arms around me when he was shot in the head. When the bullet hit his head, he grabbed onto me so hard I couldn't breathe for a week without it hurting. Then he let go and fell down and tried to get up and went down for good. It was at a farm. They put him in an old cistern and filled it with big rocks. They had his car repainted and sold through channels. If nothing happens in six months or so, they'll stop worrying about me, and maybe they'll stop looking. But I know what I'm going to do. Blond dye job. Maybe glasses. I'll feel better if I don't look like myself."

I was wondering how I could keep her away from the motel and still stall long enough to get to the Rasi place at one.

She helped out by saying, suddenly, "What's been going on down in Hillston, anyhow? Eloise and her boy friend under the cement. That Stamm girl missing. George knocking himself off. Sounds like it has been pretty wild down there."

"I want to talk to you about that."

I sensed a new wariness about her. "Just what do you mean?"

"I'm new in town. There's been a lot going on. I haven't had anything to do with it. I mean I've been in on it as a bystander, but that's all. But the police like to keep busy. I think it would be better if we didn't go on back through town to the motel. I think it would be better if we went after the money first."

"You could be picked up?"

"I might be."

"But what for? I don't like this. If they pick you up they pick me up. And word would get back to Redding too damn fast."

"I'm sorry, but that's the way it is."

"I don't like it."

"I can't help that. I think we ought to go after the money. When we get it, we can circle around town and get to the motel from the south. Then we can pick up our luggage and be on our way."

"Then that means spending too much time in the area with the money on us. Why don't we circle around and get the baggage first? Then when we get the money, we're on our way."

"They know where I'm staying. Suppose they're waiting there to pick us up."

"Damn it, how did you manage to mess this up, Tal Howard?"

"I didn't mess it up. It isn't a big city. I'm a stranger. They're after a man named Fitzmartin."

"I remember that name. You said he knows about the money, too."

"He doesn't know where it is. You're the only one who knows where it is."

"Why are they after him? On account of the girl? They think he took her?"

"And they think he was blackmailing George because he found out about Eloise and her boy friend being dead. And they think he killed George, and maybe a private detective named Grassman."

"Busy little man, isn't he?"

"That puts me in the picture because the three of us, Fitz, Timmy, and I, were in the same prison camp."

"I knew this was going to be a mess. I knew it."

"Don't be such a pessimist."

"Why the hell didn't you bring all the stuff along right in the car? Why didn't you check out?"

"If I checked out, they'd be looking already."

"I suppose so. But you could have brought my stuff, anyway."

"I didn't think of that."

"You don't seem to think of much of anything, do you?"

"Don't get nasty. It isn't going to help."

"Everything gets messed up. I was all right. Now I'm out on a limb. I should be laughing?"

"I think we ought to get the money first."

"I can't go like this. I don't want to ruin these clothes."

"Ruin your clothes? Where are we going?"

"Never mind that."

"You haven't got anything but good clothes in—" I stopped too suddenly.

"So you had to poke around," she said, vibrating with anger. "Did you have a good time? Did you like what you saw?"

"It's nice stuff."

"I know it's nice. Sometimes it wasn't so nice earning it, but I know it's nice. I have good taste. Did you count the money? Attractive color, don't you think? Green."

"I counted it."

"It better all be there. And the jewelry better all be there. Every damn stone. The jewelry more than the money. A lot of people thought it was junk jewelry. It isn't. It's worth three or four times the money."

"It's all there. It's safe."

"It better be. I can't go in these clothes. We'll have to go somewhere where I can pick up some jeans. I thought I could buy them in Hillston. Now you can't go into Hillston. So where do we go?"

"You know the area better than I do."

"Let me think a minute."

She told me where to turn. We made a left, heading east, twenty miles north of Hillston. It was a narrow, busy road. Ten miles from the turn was the town of Westonville, a small, grubby town with a narrow main street. I circled a block until I found an empty meter. I watched her walk away from the car. Men turned to look at her. Men would always turn to look at that walk. I went into a drugstore and came back with cigarettes. She was back in about ten minutes with a brown parcel.

"All right," she said. "Let's go. I've got what I need."

We headed back toward the Redding road. She said, "Find a place where you can get off the road. I want to change into this stuff. How about ahead there, on the left, that little road."

I turned up the little road she pointed out. We passed two dreary farmhouses. The road entered a patch of woods. I turned onto an old lumber road. The clay was greasy under the wheels. After we went around a bend, I stopped.

She opened the door on her side and got out. She bent over the seat and undid the parcel. She took out a pair of burnt-orange slacks, some cheap sneakers, and a wooly yellow sweat shirt. She took the black suit jacket off and folded it and put it on the back seat. The odd light of the yellow sky came down through the trees. The leaves dripped. She undid her skirt at the side and stepped out of it carefully. There was no coyness about her, not the slightest flavor of modesty. She did not care whether I stared at her or averted my eyes. She folded the skirt and put it with the jacket. She took her blouse off and put it carefully on the back seat. She stood there in the woodland in black hat with veil, black shoes, skimpy oyster-white bra and panties, looking both provocative and ridiculous. The hat was last.

She gave me a wry look and said, "Strip tease alfresco. Aren't you supposed to stamp your feet or something?"

"Aren't you cold?"

"I'm a warm-blooded thing." She put the wooly, baggy sweat shirt on, then stepped into the slacks and pulled them up around her full hips and fastened them with zipper and buttons. She sat on the car seat and took off her black shoes and put them in back and put on the sneakers and laced them up.

"Good God, I haven't had clothes like this in years. How do I look, Tal?"

I couldn't tell her how she looked. It wasn't a return to the girl who had gone on the bike trips with Timmy. I would have guessed it would have made her look younger and fresher. But it didn't. Her body was too ripe, her eyes and mouth too knowing. The years had taken her beyond the point where she could wear such clothes and look young.

She read the look in my eyes. "Not so good, I guess. Not good at all. You don't have to say it."

"You look fine."

"Don't be a damned fool. Wait a minute while I use the facilities, and then we'll get out of here." She went off into the woods out of sight of the car. She was back in a few minutes. I backed out. I looked at my watch. The time problem had been nearly solved. It was a little past twelve-fifteen.

I pulled into the yard of the Doyle place, the Rasi place where she had been born. I saw that the boy had finished painting the boat.

"It looks even worse than I remember," she said. She got out of the car and went toward the porch. The chickens were under the porch. The dog lay on the porch. He thumped his tail. Antoinette leaned over and scratched him behind the ear. He thudded the tail with more energy.

Her sister came to the doorway, dirty towel in her hand.

"Hello, Anita," Antoinette said calmly.

"What are you doing here? Doyle don't want you coming around here. You know that."

"—Doyle," Antoinette said.

"Don't use that kind of language with kids in the house. I'm warning you." The girl who had cried came up behind her mother and stared at us.

"You're so damn cautious about the kids," Antoinette said with contempt. "Hi there, Sandy."

"Hi," the girl said in a muted voice.

"You give the kids such a nice home and all, Anita."

"I do what I can do. I do the best I can."

"Look at the way she's dressed. I sent money. Why don't you spend some of it on clothes. Or does Doyle drink it?"

"There's no reason for her to wear her good stuff around the house. What do you want here, anyway? What did you come around here for?" She gestured toward me with her head. "He was here asking about you. I told him where to look. I guess he found you there, all right."

"In the big sinful city. Good God, Anita. Come off it. It eats on you that you never figured it out right. You never worked it so you got up there. Now you've got Doyle and look at you. You're fat and you're ugly and you're dirty."

The child began to cry again. Anita turned and slapped her across the face and sent her back into the house. She turned back to Antoinette, her face pale. "You can't come in my house."

"I wouldn't put my foot in that shack, Anita. Are the oars in the shed?"

"What do you want with oars?"

"I'm taking that boat. There's something I want to show my friend."

"What do you mean? You can't use any of the boats."

"Maybe you want to try and stop me? I'm using a boat. I'm taking a boat."

"You go out on the river today you'll drown yourself. Look at it. Take a good look at it."

We turned and looked at the river. The gray water raced by. It had a soapy look. The boil of the current looked vicious.

"I've been out in worse than that and you know it. Is the shed locked?"

"No," Anita said sullenly.

"Come on, Tal," Antoinette said. I followed her to the shed. She selected a pair of oars, measured them to make certain she had mates. We went to the overturned boat. We righted it. It was heavy. She tried the oars in the locks to be certain they would fit.

She got on one side and I got on the other and we slid the boat stern first down the muddy bank to the water. We put it half in the water. The current caught at it, boiling around the stern.

Antoinette straightened up and looked at the river. Anita was watching us from the porch. The pale face of the little girl watched us from a cracked window.

"It's pretty damn rough," Antoinette said. "We won't have much trouble getting down to the island."

"Island?"

"Right down there. See it? That's where we're going."

The island was about three hundred yards downstream. It was perhaps three hundred feet long and half as wide. It was rocky and wooded. It split the river into two narrow areas of roaring turbulence.

"I don't think we can make it back to here. We can walk the boat down the shore and land further down when we leave. Then walk back up to the car and tell them where the boat is. They can get it when the river quiets down. The worst part is going to be right at the start. Let's get it parallel to the shore, Tal."

We struggled with the boat. She slipped on the muddy bank and sat down hard and cursed. I held the stern. The bow was pointed downstream.

"Shall I row?" I asked, over the sound of the water.

"I'm used to it. Wait until I get set. When I say go, you get into the stern."

She got in and put the oars in the locks, held them poised. She nodded to me. I got in. The current caught us. It threatened to spin the boat but she got it quickly under control. It wasn't necessary to row. She watched over her shoulder and guided us by fast alternate dips of the oars. She was quick and competent. As we neared the island the fast current split. She dipped both oars and gave a single hard pull that sent us directly at the island.

The boat ran ashore, the bow wedging in the branches and rubble that had caught there on the shelving shore, brought downriver by the hard rains.

She was out quickly, and pulled the boat up farther. I jumped out onto the shore and stood beside her. Her eyes were wide and sad and thoughtful. "We used to come here a lot. Come on."

I followed her. We pushed through thickets and came to a steep path. They had come to the island often. And so had a lot of other people, leaving behind them empty rusting beer cans, broken bottles, sodden paper plates, waxed paper, tinfoil, empty cigarette packs.

The path climbed between rocks. She walked quickly. She stopped at a high point. I came up beside her. It was the highest point of the rocky island, perhaps sixty feet above the level of the river. We stood behind a natural wall of rock. It came to waist level. I could see the shack, see Anita, in the distance, walking heavily across the littered yard, see the gleam of my car through the leaves.

"Look!" Antoinette said sharply. I looked where she pointed. A flat-bottomed boat was coming down the river. It was caught in the current and it spun. The man, kneeling in the stern, using a single oar as a rudder, brought it under control. A dingy red boat under a yellow sky on a soapy gray river. And the man in the boat had pale hair. He came closer and I saw his face. He looked up and saw us. To him we were outlined against the yellow sky. Then the dwarf trees screened him.

"He landed on the island," Antoinette said.

I knew he had landed. I knew he had watched us. I guessed that he had gotten hold of a boat and waited on the opposite shore. Fitzmartin would not take the chance of trusting me. Maybe he couldn't. Maybe Ruth was dead.

"That's Fitzmartin," I said.

She stared at me. Her eyes were hard. "You arranged this?"

"No. Honestly. I didn't arrange it."

"What does he know? Why did he follow us?"

"I think he's guessed we're after the money."

She leaned calmly against the rock and folded her arms. "All right, Tal. This is the end of it. You and your friend can hunt for it. Have fun. I'll be damned if I'll tell you where it is."

I took her by the shoulders and shook her. "Don't be a damn fool. That man is insane. I mean that. He's killed two people. Maybe three. You can't just wait for him and say you won't tell him. Do you think he'll just ask you, politely? After he gets his hands on you, you'll tell him."

She pushed my hands away. I saw the doubt in her expression. I tried to explain what Fitzmartin was. She looked down the path the way we had come. She bit her lip. "Come on, then," she said.

"Can we circle around and get to the boat?"

"This is better," she said.

I followed her.

CHAPTER THIRTEEN

I thought I heard him call, the sound mingling with the noise of the river. I followed Antoinette. She led the way down a curving path toward the south end of the island. The path dipped into a flat place. Rock walls were high on either side of us. It was a hollow where people had built fires.

She paused uncertainly. "It's so overgrown," she said.

"What are you looking for?"

She moved to one side and looked at the sloping wall. She nodded to herself, and went up, nimble as a cat, using the tough vines to pull herself up. She stopped and spread the vines. She was above a ledge. She turned and motioned to me. My leather soles gave me trouble. I slipped and scrambled, but I made it to the ledge beside her. She pushed tough weeds and vines aside.

She sat down and put her feet in the dark hole and wormed her way forward. When she was in up to her hips she lay back and, using her hands on the upper edge of the small slit in the rocks, pulled herself in the rest of the way.

I made hard work of it. It was narrow. She pulled at my ankles. Finally I was inside. She leaned across me, her weight on me, and pulled the weeds and vines back to cover the hole. At first I could not see, and then my eyes became used to the light. Daylight came weakly through the hole. The hole itself, the slit in the rocks, was not over thirty inches long and fourteen inches high at its widest point. Inside it widened out to about five feet, and the ceiling was about three feet high. It was perhaps seven feet deep.

She said, in a low voice, "Timmy found it. He was climbing on the rocks one day and he found it. It's always dry and clean in here. See, the sand is dry, and feel how fine it is. It became our place. It became my favorite place in the whole world. I used to come here alone, too. When things got too—rugged. We used to keep things here. A box with candles and cigarettes and things. Nobody in the world could ever find us here. We kept blankets here and pillows. We called it our house. Kid stuff, I guess. But it was nice. I never thought I'd come back here."

"Then this is the place he meant."

"Let's look."

It was easy to dig in the sand. She found the first one. She gave a little gasp of pleasure when she found it. She dug it out of the soft sand. We held it close to the weak daylight and opened it. The wire clamp slid off easily. The rubber ring was stuck to the glass. I pulled the top off. The bills were tightly packed. I pulled some of them out, two tens and a twenty.

We both dug in the place where she had found it. We found three more jars. That was all. We lined them up against the wall. I could see the money through the glass. I looked at the money. I remembered how I had thought it would be. I had thought it would be an answer. But I had found the answer before I found the money. Now it meant only that perhaps it could still be traded for a life.

"Now he's coming this way," she whispered.

I heard him when he called again. "Howard! Tal Howard!" We lay prone, propped up on our elbows, our heads near the small entrance, her cheek inches from mine.

"Tal Howard!" he called, alarmingly close. He was passing just below us, his head about six or seven feet below the ledge.

He called again at a greater distance, and then all we could hear was the sound of the river.

"What will we do?" she whispered.

"All we can do is outwait him. We can't deal with him. He won't make any deals. He's way beyond that. We'll have to wait until night. I don't think he'll leave. We'll have to try to get to the water at night. Can you swim?"

"Of course."

"We can make it to shore then, with the money."

There was no point in telling her the deal I had planned. There was no chance of making the deal. I was certain that if he found us, he'd kill both of us. When he had talked to me, I had sensed the pleasure he took in killing. The way he had talked of George, and the way he had talked about holding the knife at Ruth's throat. That can happen to a man. There are men who hunt who do not take their greatest pleasure in the skill of the hunt, but rather in the moment of seeing the deer stumble and fall, or the ragged bird come rocketing down. From animal to man is a difference in degree, not in kind. The lust to kill is in some men. It has sexual overtones. I had sensed that in Fitzmartin. I could even sense it in the tone of his voice as he had called to me when he had passed the cave. A warm, almost jocular tone. He knew we were on the island. He knew he would find us. He felt warm toward us because we would give him pleasure. *Come out and be killed, Tal Howard.* A warm and confident voice. It was not so much as though he had stepped beyond sanity, but as though he had stepped outside the race, had become another creature. It was the same way we all might one day be hunted down by the alien creatures of some far planet. When the day comes, how do we bargain for life? What can the rabbit say to the barrel of a gun?

I lay on my side. She lay facing me. I saw the sheen of her eyes and the whiteness of her teeth in the half light of the cave. I could sense the soft tempo of her breathing.

"So we wait," she said.

"And we'll have to be very careful. He likes the night."

"We'll be careful. It's worth being careful. You know, Tal, I thought all along this would get messed up. Now I don't think so any more. Isn't that strange? Now that it is as bad as it can get, I think we're going to make it."

"I hope so."

She rolled onto her back. Her voice was soft. "We're going to make it. We'll get to the car. There's enough money here. It isn't worth the risk of going back after my things. We'll drive through the night, Tal. We'll drive all night. We'll take turns. I'm a good driver. I know just how it's going to be. We'll go to New Orleans. We can be there late tomorrow. I know a man there. He'll help us. We'll sell the car there. We'll catch our plane there. We'll have everything new. All new clothes. Mexico City first, I think. Then over to Havana. I was in Havana once. With—a friend. No, not Havana. Where will we go from there, Tal?"

"Rio, Buenos Aires. Then Paris."

"Paris, of course. It's funny. I've always been looking. Like that game where you come into the room and they've named something but you don't know what it is and you have to find out. I've been looking for something I don't know the name of. Ever feel like that?"

"Yes."

"You don't know what it is, but you want it. You look in a lot of places for it. You try a lot of things, but they aren't it. This time I know I'm going to find it."

We were quiet for a long time. She turned toward me again. I put my hand on the curve of her waist, let it rest there, and felt the quickening tempo of her breathing.

I do not try to excuse it. Until then she had had no special appeal to me. I can try to explain it. It is an urgency that comes at times of danger. It is something deep in the blood, that urgency. It is a message from the blood. You may die. Live this once more, this last time. Or it may be more complicated. There may be defiance in it. Your answer to the blackness that wants to swallow you. To leave this one thing behind you. To perform this act which may leave a life behind you, the only possible guarantee of immortality in any form.

When catastrophe strikes cities, people learn of this basal urge. Men and women in war know it. It is present in great intensity in many kinds of sickness. Men and women are triggered by danger, and they lie together in a hungry quickness in the cellars of bombed houses, behind the brush of mountain trails, in lifeboats, on forgotten beaches, on the grounds of sanitariums.

By the time it happened I knew that I was hopelessly in love with Ruth Stamm. And I knew this woman in the cave with me was hard as stone. But she was there. I took from her the stubborn slacks and the bulky sweat shirt and the satin white bra. Her flesh gleamed dusky in the cave light. We did not speak. It was very complete for us.

It was enough that she was woman. But with her first words she turned back into Antoinette Rasi, and destroyed any possible emotional overtones. "Well, aren't we the ones," she said, her voice a bit nasal.

She bumped her head on the roof as she was getting her shirt back on, and commented on it with a very basic vocabulary. I turned so that I did not have to look at her. I lay and looked out the entrance, through the gaps between the vines and leaves. I could see the rock wall on the other side of the hollow, thirty feet away. By lowering my head and looking up, I could see a wedge of yellow sky above the rock.

As I watched I saw Fitzmartin's head and then his shoulders above the rock wall. Behind me Antoinette started to say something in a complaining voice. I reached back quickly and caught her arm and grasped it warningly. She stopped talking immediately. She moved forward and leaned her warm weight against the back of my left shoulder so that she too could see. It was instinctive to want to pull back into the cave, but I knew he could not see my face or hers behind the dense screen.

He stood on the rock against the sky, feet spread, balancing easily. He held a gun in his hand. His big hand masked the gun, but it looked like a Luger. The strange sky made a dull glint on the barrel. When he moved his head he moved it quickly, as an animal does. His mouth was slack, lips parted. His khaki pants were soaked to the knees. He studied the rock wall where the cave was, foot by foot. I flinched involuntarily when his gaze moved across the cave mouth. He turned and moved out of sight.

She put her lips close to my ear. "My God, I can see what you mean. Dear Jesus, I'm glad I didn't wait to have a chat with *that*! He's a damn monster. How come he was running around loose?"

"He looked all right before. It was on the inside. Now it's showing."

"Frankly, he scares the hell out of me. I tell you they ought to shoot him on sight, like a crazy dog."

"He's getting worse."

"You can't get any worse than that. What was he looking over here for?"

"I think he's eliminating places where we could be, one by one. He's got a lot of daylight. I hope he eliminated this place."

"You can't see much from over there. Just a sort of shadow. And the hole looks too little, even if it didn't have the stuff in front of it."

"I hope you're right."

"He gives me the creeps."

I kept a careful watch. The next time I saw him, he was climbing down the wall on the far side. Antoinette saw him, too. Her hand tightened on my shoulder. Her breath was warm against my ear.

"What's he doing down there?" she whispered.

"I think he's trying to track us. I don't know how good he is at it. If he's good, he'll find that our tracks end somewhere in the hollow."

"The ground was soft," she whispered. "Dear God, I hope he doesn't know how."

He was out of sight. We heard one rock clatter against another, audible above the soft roar of the river. We moved as far back in the little cave as we could get. Nothing happened for a long time. We gradually relaxed again, moved up to where we could watch.

It must have been a full half hour later when I saw him on the far side, clambering up. He sat on the rim at the top. He aimed carefully, somewhere off to our right, and pulled the trigger. The sound was flat, torn away by the wind. He aimed and fired again, this time closer.

I realized too late what he was doing. I tried to scramble back. He fired again. Antoinette gave a great raw scream of agony. Blood burst from her face. The slug had furrowed down her face, smashed her teeth and her jaw, striking at an angle just under her cheekbone. She screamed again, the ruined mouth hanging open. I saw the next shot take her just above the left collarbone, angling down through her body. She dug her fingers down into the sand, arched her body, then settled into death as the next bullet slapped damply into her flesh. I was pressed hard against the rocks at the side. He shot twice more into her body and then there was silence. I tried to compress myself into the smallest possible target.

When he fired again, it was from a different angle. The slug hammered off rock, ricocheting inside the small cave, hitting two walls so quickly the sound was almost simultaneous before it buried itself in the sand. The next one ricocheted and from the sharp pain in my face I thought it had hit me. But it had filled my right cheek with sharp rock fragments. I could move no farther to the side. If he found the proper angle he would hit me directly. If he did not, a ricochet could kill me. I grasped her body and pulled it over me. He fired several more shots. One broke one of the jars. Another hit her body. My hands were sticky with her blood. I shielded my head against her heavy breast, my legs pulled up. I tried to adjust the body so it would give me maximum cover. A ricocheting slug rapped the heel of my shoe with such force that it numbed my foot.

I gave a harsh, loud cry of pain. The shooting stopped. After a few minutes he spoke in an almost conversational tone. He was close under the cave.

"Howard! Howard! Come on out of there."

I did not answer. He had thought of caves, had fired into the shadowy places, had hit the right one. I hoped he would believe us both dead. It was my only chance, that he should believe us both dead. I wormed my way out from under her body. There was no loose stone in the cave. There were only the jars of money.

I took one jar and crouched off to the left of the entrance. I heard the rattle of the rocks and knew he was climbing. I saw the vines tremble. I was poised and ready to hurl the jar at his face. But his face did not appear. His strong hand appeared, moving slowly into the cave, inviting me to try to grasp it. It was a clever move. I knew that he was probably braced there, gun in the other hand, waiting for such a try. More of his arm came into the cave. I could see his shoulder, blocking off the light. But I could not see his head.

His brown hand crept across the sand. It touched Antoinette's dark hair, paused for a moment, felt its way to her face, touched lightly her dead eyes. She lay curled where I had pushed the body in crawling out from under it. The hand moved across the sand again. It came to her flexed knee, touched the knee, felt the material of the jeans. In that moment I realized that he thought it was my knee. He had only seen her from the waist up when he had approached the island in the boat. She was curled in such a way he did not relate the knee to the face he had touched. His powerful fingers bit through the blue jean material, caught the flesh underneath and twisted it cruelly.

I heard his soft grunt of satisfaction. I readied myself. He put both arms in, and wormed his way in head first. I knew he would not be able to see immediately. The gun was in his hand. As soon as his head appeared in the opening, inside the vines, I smashed the glass jar full into his face.

The jar smashed, cutting my hand. I tried to snatch at the gun, but I was too slow. He was gone. I heard the thud as he fell. I knew that I could not afford to give him time to recover. I scraped myself badly as I slid through the entrance. I grasped the vines and stood up, teetering on the ledge. I saw him below me. He was on his hands and knees, gun still in his hand, shaking his head in a slow, heavy way. It was a twelve foot drop, perhaps a little more. I dropped onto him. I landed on the small of his back, heels together, legs stiff.

My weight smashed him to the ground. The fall jolted me. I rolled to my feet with agonizing slowness and turned to face the expected shot. He lay quite still. His finger tips touched the gun.

I picked it up and moved back away from him and watched him. By watching closely I could see the movement of his back as he breathed. I aimed at his head. But I could not make myself fire. Then I saw that the breathing had stopped. I wondered if it was a trick. I picked up a stone and threw it at him. It hit his back and bounded away.

Finally I approached him and rolled him over. And I knew that he was dead. He died in a curious way. He had fallen back off the narrow ledge, fallen with the broken pieces of the heavy glass jar. Stunned, he had gotten to his hands and knees. He was trying to clear his head. When I had smashed him back to the ground, a large piece of the broken jar had been under his throat. As I had watched him his blood had soaked into the sandy soil. His blood had soaked a thick wad of the money that had been in the jar. A wind blew through the hollow. There were some loose bills. The wind swirled them around. One blew toward me. I picked it up and looked at it stupidly. It was a ten-dollar bill.

I went up to the cave again. I think I had the idea of carrying her down. I knew I could not make it. I looked at her. Paris was out. It was done. I looked at her and wondered if this, after all, had been what she was looking for. It could have been. It could have been the nameless thing she sought. But I guessed that had she been given her choice, she would have wanted it in a different form. Not so ugly. Not with ruined face and cheap clothes.

I climbed back down. I was exhausted. A few feet from the bottom I slipped and fell again. I gathered up all the money. I put it in the cave with her. They could come and find it there when I told them where it was. I went back to where we had left the boat. The river seemed a little quieter. I took the line and walked the boat down to the south end of the island. The current tugged at it. Below the island the river was quieter. I got into the boat. Just as I started to row toward the shore, it began to rain again, rain that fell out of a yellow sky. The rain whispered on the gray river. It diluted the blood on my hands. The rain was on my face like tears.

The banks were high. I found a place to beach the boat about a thousand yards below the Rasi place. I walked through wet grass to the road. I walked to the Rasi place.

Anita came out. I asked if she had a phone I could use.

"We've got no phone. Where's the boat? What did you do with the boat? Where's Antoinette? What's all the blood on your clothes? What's happened?"

She was still screaming questions at me when I fitted the key into the ignition, started the car, and drove away.

Heavy clouds had darkened the afternoon. I had never seen it rain as hard. Traffic crept through the charcoal streets of Hillston, their lights yellow and feeble in the rain.

I turned through the arch and parked beside the police cars in the courtyard of the station. A man yelled at me from a doorway, telling me I couldn't park there. I paid no attention to him. I found Prine. Captain Marion wasn't in. He'd gone home to sleep.

Prine stared at me in a funny way. He took my arm when he led me to a chair. "Are you drunk?"

"No. I'm not drunk."

"What's the matter with you?"

"I know where to look for the girl, for Ruth. North of town. Near the river. If she's alive. If she's dead I don't know where to look. She wouldn't be far from where he got the boat."

"What boat?"

"Will you have people look for her? Right now?"

"What boat, damn it?"

"I'll tell you the whole thing after you look. I want to come, too. I want to come with you."

They sent cars out. They called Captain Marion and the Chief of Police. They sent people out to look in the rain. Scores of people searched. I rode with Prine. In the end it was a contingent of Boy Scouts who found her. They found the black coupé. The trunk compartment was open a half inch. We sped through the rain when word came over the radio. But the ambulance got there first. They were loading her onto the ambulance when we arrived. They closed the doors and drove away before I could get to the ambulance.

The car was parked behind a roadside sign. It had been covered with roofing paper. Some of the paper had shifted in the wind. One of the Scouts had seen the gleam of metal.

Two policemen in black rain-wet rubber capes were there.

"What shape was she in?" Prine demanded.

One of the men spat. "I don't think she'll make it. I think she was about gone. She looked about gone to me. You know, the way they all look. Just about breathing. Color of putty. Pretty banged up."

Prine whirled toward me. "All right. We've got her now. How about Fitzmartin? Start talking."

"He's dead."

"How do you know he's dead?"

"I killed him. I'll tell you the rest later. I want to go to the hospital."

CHAPTER FOURTEEN

I sat on a bench in a waiting-room in the hospital. Water from my sodden clothing dripped onto the floor. Captain Marion sat beside me. Prine leaned against the wall. A man I didn't know sat on the other side of me. I looked at the pattern of the tiles in the floor as I talked. From time to time they would ask questions in a quiet voice.

I told the complete truth. I lied about one thing only. I told them that Fitzmartin had told me that he had hidden Grassman's body in a barn eight or ten miles south of the city, on a side road. In a ruined barn near a burned house. Marion nodded to Prine. He went out to send men out to hunt for the barn. He had gone out once before, to send men to the island. I had told how to find the cave, and told them what they would find in the cave. I told them they would find the gun in my car. I lied about Grassman, and I left out what I knew about Antoinette.

It would do them no good to know about her. They would learn enough from the Redding police. They did not have to know more than that.

I told them all the rest. Why I had come to Hillston. Everything I had seen and guessed. Everything Fitzmartin had said. Timmy's dying statements. All of it. The whole stinking mess. It felt good to tell about it.

"Let me get this straight, Howard," Marion said. "You made a deal with Fitzmartin. You were going to have the girl find the money. Then you were going to turn it over to Fitzmartin in return for Ruth's safety. You made that deal yourself. You thought you could handle it better than we could. Is that it?"

"I thought that was the only way it could be handled. But he crossed me up. He followed us."

"We could have grabbed him when he got to the river. We'd have gotten to Ruth earlier. If she dies, you're going to be responsible."

I looked at him for the first time in over an hour. "I don't see it that way."

"Did he say how he killed Grassman? You told us why he did it."

"He hit him on the head with a piece of pipe."

"What do you think the Rasi girl was going to do when you turned the money over to Fitzmartin? Assuming that it went the way you thought it would go."

"I guess she wouldn't have liked it."

"Why didn't she come and get the money herself, once she knew where it probably was?"

"I haven't any idea. I think she felt she needed help. I think she decided I could help her. I think she planned to get away with all of it somehow after we were both well away from here. When I was sleeping. Something like that. I think she thought she could handle me pretty easily."

"How many shots did he fire into the cave?"

"I wasn't counting. Maybe twenty."

A doctor came into the room. Marion stood up. "What's the score, Dan?"

The doctor looked at us disapprovingly. It was as though we were responsible for what had happened to Ruth.

"I think I can say that physically she'll be all right She's young and she has a good body. She might mend quite rapidly. It's hard to say. It will depend on her mental condition. I can't answer for that. I've seldom seen anyone handled more brutally. I can give you a list. Dislocated thumb. Broken shoulder. Two cracked ribs. A cracked pelvis. She was criminally attacked. Two broken toes. We nearly missed those. She was beaten about the face. That wouldn't have killed her. It was the shock and exposure that nearly did it, came awfully close to doing it. She's been treated for shock.

She's out of her head. She doesn't know where she is. We just put her to sleep. I say, I can't estimate mental damage."

I stood up. "Where is she?"

The doctor stared at me. "I can't let you see her. There's no point in seeing her."

I moved closer to him. "I want to see her."

He stared at me and then took my wrist, put his finger tips on my pulse. He took a pencil flashlight out of his pocket and shone it directly into my eye from a few inches away.

He turned to the captain. "This man should be in bed."

Marion sighed. "Have you got a bed?"

"Yes."

"Okay. I'll have to put a guard on the door. This man is under arrest. But look. Just let him look in the door at Ruth. Maybe he earned that much. I don't know."

They let me look. She was in a private room. Her father sat near the bed. He didn't look toward the doorway. He watched her face. She was no one I would have ever recognized. She was puffy, discolored. She breathed heavily through her open mouth. There was an odor of sickness in the room. I looked at her and I thought of the movie heroines. They go through terror and capture and violence, yet four minutes after rescue they melt, with glossy hair and limpid eyes and gown by Dior, into the arms of Lancaster, or Gable, or Brando. This was reality. The pain and ugliness and sickness of reality.

They took me away.

The formalities were complicated. I had to appear and be questioned at the joint inquest. I told all I knew of the deaths of Antoinette Christina Rasi and Earl David Fitzmartin. I signed six copies of my detailed statement. The final verdict was justifiable homicide. I had killed in defense of my life.

Both the money found in Fitzmartin's car and the money in the cave became a part of George Warden's estate. A second cousin and his wife flew in from Houston to protect their claim to the money and whatever else there was. They arrived on Sunday.

George and Eloise were buried in the Warden family plot. Fulton, identified through his dental work, was sent to Chicago for his third burial. No relative of Fitzmartin could be found. The county buried him. Grassman's body was found. His brother flew down from Chicago and took the body back on the train.

I had told them about Antoinette's clothes and jewelry and the money, the precise amount, that Fitzmartin had taken. The court appointed an executor for Antoinette Rasi's estate, and directed that the clothing and furs and jewels be sold, and made an informal suggestion to the executor that the funds be used for the Doyle children.

When something is dropped and broken, the pieces have to be picked up. The mess has to be cleaned up.

They were through with me on Tuesday. Captain Marion walked down the steps of the courthouse with me. We stood on the sidewalk in the sunshine.

"You're through here, Howard. We're through with you. There are some charges we could have made stick. But we didn't. You can be damn glad. We don't want you here. We don't want to see you back here."

"I'm not leaving."

He stared at me. His eyes were cold. "I don't think that's very bright."

"I'm going to stay."

"I think I know what's on your mind. But it won't work. You've spent all the time you could with her. It hasn't worked, has it? It won't work for you. Not with her."

"I want to stay and try. I've made my peace with her father. He understands. I can't say he approves. But he understands enough so he isn't trying to drive me off."

"You're beating your head against a wall."

"Maybe."

"Prine wants to run you out of town."

"Do you? Actually?"

His face flushed. "Stay then, dammit. Stay! It will do you no good."

I went back to the hospital. Because of her private room, visiting hours were less restricted. I waited while the nurse went to her. The nurse came back. Each time I was afraid the nurse would say I couldn't see her.

"She'll see you in five minutes, Mr. Howard."

"Thank you."

I waited. They told me when it was time. I went to her room as before and pulled the chair up to the bed. Her face was not as swollen, but it was still badly discolored. As before, she turned her face toward the wall. She had looked at me for a moment without expression before turning away. She had not yet spoken to me. But I had spoken to her. I had talked to her for hours. I had told her everything. I had told her what she meant to me, and had received no response at all. It was like talking to a wall. The only encouragement was her letting me see her at all. The doctor had told me she would recover more quickly if she could recover from her listlessness, her depression.

As on other days, I talked. I could not tell if she was listening. I had told her all there was to tell about the things that had happened. There was no point in repeating it, no point in begging for understanding or forgiveness.

So I talked of other things, and other days. Places I had been. I told her about Tokyo, about Pusan, about the hospital. I told her about the work I used to do. I conjectured out loud about what I could find to do in Hillston. I still had seven hundred dollars left. I was careful not to ask questions. I did not want it to seem to her as though I were angling for a response.

She lay with her face turned toward the wall. For all I knew she could be asleep. And then suddenly, surprisingly, her hand came timidly from the cover of the hospital blanket. It reached blindly toward me and I took her hand in both of mine. She squeezed my hand hard once and then let her hand lie in mine.

That was the sign. That was enough. The rest of it would come. Now it was just a matter of time. There would be a day when there would be laughter, when she would walk again in that proud way of hers. All this would fade and it would be right for her and for me. We both had a lot of forgetting to do, and we could do it better together. This was the woman I wanted. I could never be driven away.

This was treasure.

THE END

Made in the USA
Las Vegas, NV
20 March 2021